BENNETT

LIGHTHOUSE SECURITY INVESTIGATIONS WEST COAST

MARYANN JORDAN

Bennett (Lighthouse Security Investigations West Coast) Copyright 2023

All rights reserved. No part of this book may be reproduced or transmitted in any form or by any means, electronic or mechanical, including photocopying, recording, or by any information storage and retrieval system without the written permission of the author, except where permitted by law.

If you are reading this book and did not purchase it, then you are reading an illegal pirated copy. If you would be concerned about working for no pay, then please respect the author's work! Make sure that you are only reading a copy that has been officially released by the author.

This book is a work of fiction. Names, characters, places, and incidents are either products of the author's imagination or are used fictitiously. Any resemblance to actual persons, living or dead, events, or locales is entirely coincidental.

Cover: Graphics by Stacy

ISBN ebook: 978-1-956588-40-8

ISBN print: 978-1-956588-41-5

❦ Created with Vellum

Author's Note

Please remember that this is a work of fiction. I have lived in numerous states as well as overseas, but for the last thirty years have called Virginia my home. I often choose to use fictional city names with some geographical accuracies.

These fictionally named cities allow me to use my creativity and not feel constricted by attempting to accurately portray the areas.

It is my hope that my readers will allow me this creative license and understand my fictional world.

I also do quite a bit of research on my books and try to write on subjects with accuracy. There will always be points where creative license will be used in order to create scenes or plots.

1

Inhale. Exhale. Inhale. Exhale.

Consistency. Steady. Positively identify target. In front of target. Behind target. Check cosine indicators. Adjust power. Check scope shadow. Assess. Evaluate. Focus. Breathe.

Staff Sergeant Terrance Bennett lay prone on the ground with the M2010 enhanced sniper rifle tucked against his shoulder. Staring through the scope, he followed the mental process the Army had trained him to use. His tailored weapon accommodated his preferences and was as much a part of him as his arms.

As an Army Ranger sniper, he and his spotter, Sergeant Michael Pascal, had advanced ahead of their team. The others would arrive the next day to take the village, rendering it unusable for the Afghans. Intelligence had also indicated the possibility of the arrival of a terrorist leader, and if so, Bennett's mission included taking him out.

He and Pascal had located the position that would give him the best chance of providing coverage for the team. When they arrived, they completed a hasty search, near-to-far, looking for any immediate threats and dead space, breaking down their sectors and identifying reference points.

Once finished, they checked their equipment and settled into position. The team would approach from the west, and he and Pascal needed to know the area intimately to provide the required support.

Like much of the Afghanistan terrain, the brown and tan landscape blended with its surrounding village. The same dirt and mud formed the buildings, creating a beige panoramic view. The village appeared empty without the usual hubbub of activity with women, children, and families around. No laundry hung on lines. No women gathered near the wells. No children played with a ball in the streets.

Instead, the sight gave every evidence of being used for small enclaves of enemy soldiers. Exactly what Bennett expected.

They'd now been in position for twenty-four hours, and during these moments, the past could slide into his thoughts. He'd become an expert at blanking his mind when needed. Still, something about staying in one position for hours allowed even the most disciplined soldier to enable ruminations to creep forward, slithering on their belly to surprise and annihilate.

"Get me another beer, you dumb fuck kid."

A slap usually accompanied those words, or when Bennett got older, a direct punch or even a kick. It generally depended on how many beers his dad had already consumed.

"You ain't good for nuthin', you know that? Your ugly ass

ran your momma off. She couldn't even stand the sight of you."

His mom had left when he was four, and the only reason he'd been given was the blame his dad laid squarely at Bennett's feet every day.

"She was fine till you came along. Then, Jesus, you fucked up my life good."

Growing up, he'd tried to do what his dad wanted. Kept his room neat. Did his homework. Cleaned the house and washed the clothes. He even cooked as soon as he learned how to work the microwave. He figured if it was his fault that his mom left, the least he could do was help take care of things. But it was never enough to make Sheldon Bennett happy. Nothing made his dad happy except being handed his next drink and lashing out at Terrance.

Made fun of and called names by other kids because of his worn-out, ill-fitting clothes, he'd found solace in his books. But, of course, as soon as his dad discovered his cache of library books, he'd thrown them out, calling him a worthless idiot for wasting time reading when he could be cleaning or mowing the grass.

Once he was old enough, he worked out, determined not to stay the weakling his dad always said he was. By the time he was sixteen, he could have landed a punch to take out his dad. But he never did. What purpose would it have served?

The coaches wanted him to play ball, but he preferred his own company. After all, the guys who wanted him on their team now were the same ones who'd made fun of him when he was younger. And talking to girls just made him nervous—they must be desperate if they showed any interest in him.

"Team is approaching."

Pascal's eye was pinned on his scope, calling out the visual coordinates while Bennett's focus snapped back to the mission. He stared through the extended-range rifle scope with the targeting reticle, verifying his spotter.

"Three alpha. Four men entering."

"Contact."

"Four beta. No activity."

"Contact."

"Two alpha. Gathering. Shadows behind."

"Contact."

The two Rangers had worked together for two tours and operated as a single unit. Pascal radioed the captain leading the team, letting them know they were in position and ready.

Bennett had remained focused since he and Pascal had arrived, but now his attention never wavered as he stared through his scope. If it was a simple take-out mission, he would wait on his spotter's command, but giving his team sniper support meant he had to be ready at a millisecond's notice to keep the other Rangers safe.

The first of his team came over the hill to the east, blending in with the landscape as they made the early dawn attack. Soon, gunfire sounded out, but nothing detracted Bennett from keeping his cool as he and Pascal scanned the area.

"Four alpha," Pascal called out at the same time Bennett observed three of his team race around the corner of a building, unable to see the armed insurgent coming from the other direction. In a split second, he fired, dropping the enemy into the dirt with a single shot, saving the life of at least one of his team members.

"Three beta," Pascal called, and Bennett immediately spotted the man slipping out the back of one building, hustling to one of the vehicles. Several others surrounded their target as they tried to escape. Pascal identified the target, and Bennett confirmed. Pascal checked the winds as Bennett began the firing sequence.

Inhale. Exhale. Inhale. Exhale.

Consistency. Steady. Positively identify target. In front of target. Behind target. Check cosine indicators. Adjust power. Check scope shadow. Assess. Evaluate. Focus. Breathe.

"Left four," Pascal commanded at Bennett's natural respiratory pause.

Bennett squeezed the trigger. The target dropped, and the men scattered, quickly descended upon by the other Rangers.

There was no time for congratulations or celebrations as the two packed their gear and hauled ass to the rendezvous point. Hustling over the rough terrain, they met with the others as the helicopter descended. Once aboard, the team grinned widely as they leaned back, the successful mission felt by each one.

Bennett offered chin lifts, but his mind was on the just-completed mission, analyzing each part. Never satisfied, he wanted to learn from every instance that could have been smoother, faster, and more accurate.

"Lay it to rest, bro," Pascal said, shaking his head.

Bennett snorted. His spotter knew he was mired in evaluation. He cast his gaze around at the others, all good men, including the support team they had back on base. Once there, he took extra time to break down his weapon, cleaning it with the same precision he completed each task. Once their equipment was squared away, their captain walked through, calling for the debriefing, and each followed him into the cramped space used for an office.

By the time they finished, Bennett was ready to crash. He and Pascal stepped outside and walked along the dirt road between the tents to the DFAC. A hot meal, coffee, and the indulgence of a piece of pie not only served to fill his stomach but made his eyes heavy. It didn't take long for them to walk a little farther before entering their tent, the four beds in each corner anchoring the space along with their lockers.

One more month on their deployment, and his team would head back home. He grabbed clean clothes and hit the showers before the others had a chance to use all the hot water. Letting the stream of water wash away the dirt, dust, sweat, and smell, he reveled in the few minutes of bliss. Ten minutes later, he was back in his tent and fell onto his bunk, throwing his forearm over his eyes. He heard Pascal moving around and his other two tent mates entering, but that was the last thing he remembered before falling asleep.

Bennett stretched his legs as the transport plane touched down in the States. As soon as they finished their duties on base and were dismissed, many of his teammates headed out to the local bar to celebrate.

He always accompanied them for the one celebratory drink he allowed himself to have at the end of each successful tour or mission. With an alcoholic father, he never overindulged. The last thing he wanted was to become like his old man.

Soon, though, he offered a chin lift as the others continued to drink or began the process of picking up a woman for the night. Those with wives or girlfriends stayed for a few more drinks before heading home. But Bennett craved the consistency of his routine.

Once in his apartment, he walked into the kitchen. He pulled out a loaf of homemade bread from the freezer, noting he needed to make more soon since this was his last loaf. While he hated to take the shortcut of using the microwave, he thawed the loaf just enough to cut a thick slice. Once toasted, he slathered it with extra creamy, salted butter. He poured a couple of fingers of whiskey into a tumbler before heading into the bedroom. Placing both on the nightstand, he walked into the bathroom, stripped, then took a shower even though he'd already taken one on the base. Again, his routine eased the tension built during the mission.

Unlike a few snipers he knew, he never kept a running count of his kills. He didn't celebrate the death of anyone, nor did he wallow in guilt. His job was necessary. Wars had been fought since the beginning of time, and he was proud of his service. But standing under the showerhead as the hot water sluiced over his body, he wondered how many years he had left in him. At one time, he'd assumed he would be a career soldier.

Twenty-plus years in. Then maybe teach at the Ranger or Army Sniper School in Fort Benning.

Stepping out of the shower, he briskly rubbed the towel over his body before pulling on clean boxers. With his hands gripping the counter's edge, he stared into the mirror. A sprinkling of gray hair was now discernible in his trimmed beard. He scrubbed his hand over his shorn head, preferring to keep it short to stay out of his face when lining up a kill shot.

His nose had been broken twice, but no entertaining bar fight story existed to explain why. His dad had caused that damage—once when he was only eleven and again when he was fourteen. He had a puckered scar on his back where his dad burned him with a cigarette when he was trying to help the old drunk to bed. A few scars were from previous missions, but those could be considered badges of honor.

Standing straight, he heard his back crack as each vertebra slid into place with protestation. Lying prone on the hard ground for up to seventy hours caused pains he never used to feel.

And with each mission, he wondered if he wasn't beginning to lose a little more of himself. Grimacing at the path his thoughts had ventured down, he flipped off the light and walked back into the bedroom. He slid under the covers and sat with his back against the headboard, cushioned by a pillow. He sipped his whiskey and ate the aromatic bread. Once finished, he sighed in contentment while reading the latest fiction mystery from one of his favorite authors.

Tonight, his thoughts wandered down the path of a

time in the future when he wasn't a sniper. A part of him longed for that, while the other part of him was more scared of not having a Ranger identity. Sighing heavily, he tossed back the last of the peaty beverage while placing the book on the nightstand.

It takes a hard man to be a sniper. Almost anyone can shoot. Many can aim well in an active fight. But pulling the trigger when the crosshairs are centered on a human from a distance after you had spent time studying them? That was only for a few. He knew a couple of married snipers, but many stayed single or were now divorced.

He closed his eyes, wondering what future a man like him could have when his soldiering days were at an end. All he could imagine was a life alone.

2

FOUR YEARS LATER

Bennett, deep in the workroom of Lighthouse Security Investigations West Coast, leaned back in his seat. He cast his gaze around the familiar room, and while he didn't need to analyze the location of each piece of equipment, ingrained habits rarely died.

Carson Dyer, the founder of LSIWC, shared a soldier's background with Bennett. He'd served with the Army Special Forces before leaving the military and starting a Los Angeles security bodyguard business. If Carson had stayed that course, Bennett wouldn't be sitting where he was right now. Keeping his eye on overindulged starlets, drunk rock stars, or actors who worked on their bodies in pristine gyms with personal trainers, all with egos fatter than their bank accounts, was not a job Bennett would have considered.

But thankfully, Carson quickly realized that his idea of security didn't align with LA's bright lights. He'd partnered with another former Special Forces soldier with a vision of true security. Mace Hanover created the original Lighthouse Security Investigations in Maine. When Carson opened the West Coast branch in a remote area of California, he followed Mace's initiative, inviting only those he considered a good fit. Those hired were known as Keepers, after the lighthouse keeper heroes of old.

By the time Carson had his business up and running, Bennett was ready to leave the Rangers, met Carson, and knew he'd found his next career. Bennett respected and liked each of the men and women Carson hired to become LSIWC Keepers. They'd all come from various military or intelligence backgrounds, each bringing their strengths to the group.

Former SEALs included Chris Andrews, Rick Rankin, Frederick Poole, and Jeb Torres. Frank Hopkins, known as Hop, had served with the Air Force Special Ops as a pilot, flying planes and helicopters. Rick's fiancée, Abbie, former Army, was recruited from the CIA Special Ops. Lionel Parker, known as Leo, had served with Carson with the Army Deltas, and his wife, Natalie, had been part of Leo's Delta support team. Rounding out their active Keepers were fellow Army Rangers Jonathan Dolby and Adam Calvin, another pilot. Bennett hadn't served with Calvin, but he'd known Dolby through another Ranger team.

Bennett couldn't imagine a stronger team for providing private security and conducting investigations, often at the behest of the US government.

His musings were jerked back to the tasks at hand when Rachel Moore, the administrative assistant, hurried into the room with several forms for Carson to sign. She smiled at the Keepers in the room before turning to leave. Rachel was another priceless gem Carson had snapped up. Retired from the Navy and widowed, she was the epitome of efficiency and no-nonsense dedication. She also had a soft spot for all the LSIWC employees.

"Okay, let's get the staff meeting over with," Carson called out. "Jeannie has a party planned."

Bennett covered his snort as he turned to the tablet before him. Carson had met his wife, Jeannie, on a mission in Mexico. He'd watched as the beautiful nurse turned his boss inside out until Carson finally admitted he was in love. Now, he couldn't imagine Carson without his wife in his life. She'd integrated perfectly with LSI and brought all his fellow Keepers' wives and girlfriends into her circle.

But not me. Bennett wasn't looking for a relationship. Not that his friends had been looking either when they found love, but he knew it wasn't in the cards for him. His parents hardly qualified as a resounding matrimonial advertisement. He'd never seen his mother after she'd left and hadn't seen his dad since the day he'd stepped onto the bus to head to boot camp. Bennett liked to think that history wouldn't repeat itself but wasn't willing to take that chance.

The assignments were distributed, and Bennett waited patiently to see what was coming his way. He never cared what mission Carson gave him. Simple or complicated. Overseas or Stateside. Investigation or security. Now that he thought about it, none of the Keepers ever balked at Carson's decisions.

"Okay, Bennett," Carson said, focusing his attention on him. "You're needed for personal security for a scientist attending a conference. There's no overt threat against her, but the company has security concerns. The conference location is Las Vegas."

Several of the other Keepers grinned while Hop called out, "Damn! Sin City!"

Leo shook his head. "Fuckin' nightmare of a city for security if you ask me."

Bennett was inclined to agree with Leo but kept his expression neutral. He looked down at his tablet, but no information on his mission appeared. Glancing toward Carson, he lifted a brow in silent question.

"Dr. Diana Olson," Carson continued. "Chemistry background and explosives expert. She works for Olson GeoTech—"

Several Keepers murmured in recognition. Bennett's attention stayed on Carson as he asked, "That's one of the leading explosive companies in the US, right?"

"That's right. Her father, James, started the company with his brother, Jerry. James died four years ago, but Jerry still runs the company. Diana has worked for them ever since she graduated from college."

"Is there a particular reason she needs security, boss?" Bennett asked.

"Technology from the explosive companies is a high commodity on the black market. Her uncle fears she'll be in an unfamiliar location with hundreds of others who might look for a way to obtain information from her. The Koreans may have some of the technology, but the CIA isn't sure where they obtained it. Obviously, the Russians are a concern."

"Does he think she's selling the technology?"

"No." Carson shook his head. "She's vulnerable, though. She was injured two years ago in an industrial accident."

Not one to take things at face value, Bennett's brows lifted. "Just an accident?" he asked, his voice hard.

"All indications are that it was a laboratory experiment that went wrong. She lost partial sight. Her uncle says she is independent, but her world is mostly work and home. She's attending the conference because a posthumous award is being given to her father, and she'll accept it for the company. But getting around Las Vegas will be a challenge, and her uncle would like someone with her to keep anyone from getting to her."

"Wouldn't an assistant or guide be better? Someone she's used to. Someone who helps her get around?"

"According to Jerry, she maneuvers independently with her limited vision but is used to her familiar surroundings at home and work. At the conference, with so many people, both part of the organization and just visitors, she's more at risk. She may be seen as a weak link for obtaining information with industrial espionage."

Bennett leaned forward, his forearms on the table in front of him. His peripheral vision gave evidence that the other Keepers had leaned forward as well, but his focus was on Carson.

"While Jerry is the business backbone of the company, he readily admits his brother, Diana's father, was the chemical genius who made the industrial discoveries that took Olson GeoTech to the top of their field. With him now gone, Diana has stepped into her father's shoes. But there's competition in the business, other countries are interested, and other companies want their research. He would feel safer if she traveled with security."

"She's a mark? Does she have security on a regular basis?"

Carson grimaced, shaking his head. "He says there's never been a threat directly to her, but she has lived a quiet life since the accident. She works at the facility she's familiar with. She's conducted classes and lectures, but since the accident, only at those hosted by their company. He's just afraid of the possibility of a problem in an unfamiliar area."

"Like I said… fuckin' nightmare of a city," Leo added again.

"She's willing to go to Las Vegas just to accept the award?" Bennett asked.

"She used to present at this conference before the accident, and they're doing a tribute to her father. She's there to accept an industry award for Olson GeoTech."

Bennett nodded slowly, shifting backward in his seat. He had more questions but kept them to himself for the time being. Looking down at his tablet again, he opened the file on Diana Olson. Thirty-two years old. Chemistry degree from California Institute of Technology. Doctorate degree from Stanford. Employed with Olson GeoTech for the past six years. Her employee photograph showed a smiling woman with blond hair pulled back and glasses that did nothing to hide the blue eyes peering at the camera.

Damn. She's pretty. He wasn't sure why that fact surprised him, although, upon reflection, he had expected someone older. And if honest, someone more nerdish and less attractive.

Shoving his thoughts away from her looks, he began reading about her background and GeoTech. While not familiar with some of the technical material, he'd had enough experience with military explosives to appreciate the company's innovations. Diana and her father were behind GeoTech's trademarked Contrasting Explosive Energy.

Another hour passed while Bennett continued his research on the mission, including the conference and the location. He offered chin lifts to the others as they finished their work and left, but he stayed, wanting to become familiar with every aspect of Diana Olson.

After poring over her professional circumstances, he moved to the health information provided. Flash blindness. A small explosion in one of the labs where Diana worked produced a bright flash of light that caused partial loss of sight. If she had been looking directly at the light, she would probably be completely blind. While her vision was blurry, she only had total vision loss on the left side.

He read the reports from the explosion but discerned no alarm from the investigators as to what happened. His eyes narrowed as his suspicious mind ran down several possibilities.

Next, he reviewed her family and close associates.

Two years after her dad died, just before her accident, her mother remarried Phillip Markham, an employee of the company. He had a son, Alex, who had just graduated from a small college and was now also employed with the company, serving as Diana's assistant.

Jeb forwarded a company organizational chart to his tablet. Her uncle was the CEO, and Bennett was not surprised to see that Diana was the head of the chemical division. *Impressive for someone in her early thirties.*

"Are you going to stay here all night?"

He jerked his head around, seeing Carson nearby with his arms crossed over his chest. Bennett chuckled. "I just wanted to ensure I knew everything I could about Dr. Olson."

"You'll have a chance to meet her before the conference starts this weekend," Carson said. "Her uncle thought it would be a good idea if the two of you met beforehand so that you would understand how she moves around."

Bennett's chin jerked downward in surprise. "At GeoTech?"

"No," Carson said with a grin. "It seems she's invited you to dinner. Tomorrow night." Walking to the door, he called over his shoulder, "Don't be late."

Bennett groaned. This type of mission was more suited to Hop or Rick. Hell, even Adam or Poole. Most of the other Keepers were adept at small talk, something he hated. Sighing heavily, he stood and walked to his truck. Rachel stood by her vehicle with Teddy. Theodore Bearski was also a former sniper and was now LSIWC's weapons and equipment manager. And from the looks of the laughter coming from him and Rachel as their heads leaned close together, Bennett wondered if the two had more going on than just work.

"Enjoy dinner tomorrow night," Rachel called out with a smile.

His mouth tightened into a thin line as he threw his hand into the air and heard Teddy chuckle. Bennett was a firm believer that successful missions required complete focus. Pretty women couldn't be a distraction.

I can do this, he vowed, already dreading the next evening's dinner plans.

3

Bennett parked outside the four-story condo building and looked up. He'd only driven an hour east to get to her residence. It was close to Olson GeoTech's main company building, but the testing quarries extended into Eastern California.

He'd had no idea what to wear and glanced down at his typical black jeans and boots. He'd decided on a long-sleeved navy shirt with the sleeves rolled up his forearms. Walking inside the lobby, he barely managed to hide his eye roll at the concierge security... or lack thereof. The young man sitting behind the desk chatted with another woman who'd stepped off the elevator with a small dog in her arms. When Bennett approached, the man turned, and his eyes bugged as soon as his gaze landed on him.

He'd seen that expression many times before. Wariness. Bennett was a big man—he knew it and didn't hide it. He didn't intend to intimidate needlessly. He did not want to engage in a dick-measuring contest with a man who felt he had something to prove. He also had no problem using his size to make his point.

"I'm here for Dr. Olson," Bennett said, his gaze staying on the concierge.

"Uh... yeah. She said... uh, someone was coming." His gaze dropped to the computer screen, his Adam's apple moving up and down.

"Hello," the woman said, turning so that her tiny dog was now held tighter to her chest as though to ward off the threat of him.

He kept his gaze on the man who was stammering again.

"Um... are you Mr. Bennett?"

"Yes."

"Okay, you can go. Go on up, I mean. Third floor. The elevator is—"

"Got it," Bennett said, turning away. Walking toward the elevator, he pinched his lips together.

"What an asshole!" the woman grumbled behind his back.

He entered the elevator and turned, his gaze boring straight toward the pair. The man blushed as he immediately dropped his gaze back to the computer screen. The woman narrowed her eyes and tossed her hair over her shoulder as she flounced toward the front door.

Stepping out of the elevator, he walked straight to the door. He'd already familiarized himself with her building. Four floors. Four condos on each floor. Hers was at the front, with windows facing north and west.

He lifted his finger to ring the bell when the door opened. His gaze dropped to the woman in front of him, and his breath snagged on its way out of his lungs at the sight.

He'd stared at her photographs enough in the past twenty-four hours to know it was her. Like with any mission, he'd studied her sparse social media profile and pictures and even watched a brief presentation she'd given with her father at a conference before the accident. Accustomed to analyzing a mission's every nuance, he wasn't prepared for the beauty standing before him.

Her straight blond hair was loose around her shoulders, the ends curling. It was parted on the side and tucked behind her ears. Her blue eyes moved over him, but he didn't know how much she could discern. The left eye was clear, and if he didn't know she had vision limitations, he wouldn't have been able to tell.

A pale-pink sweater hung below her hips with black leggings covering her legs. Black slippers were on her feet. He knew her height was only five feet, four inches, but seeing the top of her head being able to tuck next to his chest, she appeared more petite. Her porcelain skin with a touch of pink blush was almost luminescent. And her lips were slicked with a pale pink gloss, drawing and holding his attention. The scent of vanilla wafted from her, and he was struck with the sweet essence that seemed to fit her appearance.

"Mr. Bennett?"

He jerked. Her voice was soft, more delicate than he'd imagined. The video clip of her speech with her father showcased her confidence, but she spoke his name on her lips with hesitation.

Hating he'd caused any uncertainty, he rushed, "Yes, Dr. Olson. I'm Terrance Bennett."

Her shoulders relaxed as soon as he spoke, and her lips curved into a beautiful smile. "Oh, good. Bobby called up to let me know you were on your way."

"Bobby?"

"Yes, the young man who works downstairs." She stepped back, one hand on the door as she made room for him to enter.

Bennett grunted as he walked past her. "He didn't ask for identification." As soon as he stepped inside, he was hit with the aroma of garlic and warm bread fresh from the oven.

His gaze swept around the room, instantly clocking the space. Living room with comfortable furniture around the edges and no coffee table to trip over. The dining room with a four-seater table set for two. A counter separated the kitchen, and from the looks of it, she had been preparing the dinner. That surprised him, having assumed she might have ordered delivery. He was struck by how much he didn't know about her visual abilities or limitations, and now understood why their meeting where she was comfortable made sense.

She shut the door behind him, turned, and tilted her head slightly. "I'm sorry?"

It took a second for him to remember what he'd said to her before he began analyzing her space. "Identification. If he's supposed to limit who can come into the building, he should check ID."

Her mouth opened, then closed. Hesitating, she shook her head. "But I had given him your name."

Bennett faced her, trying to ease the irritation in his voice. "I understand, Dr. Olson. Yet he didn't ask for my name or an ID. So I could have been anyone who now has access to your home."

Whatever responses he expected, her laughter wasn't one of them. But damn, how her face lit when she was amused had him continue to stare.

"I realize you're in the security business, Mr. Bennett, and I'm used to such scrutiny when at work. But I assure you that I'm in no danger here. Although, I do take your point. He really should have verified your identity."

"Why aren't you in danger here, Dr. Olson?" he pushed. "You're in your condo with a strange man who you assume is from a security company. But you really don't know who you let in, do you?"

Her smile faltered as her brows lowered. "Are you deliberately trying to scare me?"

Sighing, he stepped back and lifted his hands to the side. So far, their meeting wasn't getting off to a good start. "Dr. Olson, I don't want to make you uncomfortable other than to remind you—hell, any woman living alone—that you should take your personal safety very seriously."

She remained statue still, and he wasn't sure if she would kick him out. And truthfully, he probably deserved to be kicked out. *Shit... this isn't how I wanted things to go.*

Just when he opened his mouth to offer the services of another Keeper, one who wouldn't scare the hell out of the client, her lips curved again.

"Point well taken, Mr. Bennett," she said, inclining her head. She reached her hand out toward him. "And please, call me Diana."

He started to accept her handshake, then hesitated. Her fingers were long and slender, in stark contrast to his much larger and rougher hands. Firing a weapon over and over for years had created calluses, and more than a few fights had caused scarring. Once again, he spied the uncertainty on her face and hated that he had been the one to cause it.

Wrapping his hand around hers, he initially wanted to maintain the hold for two seconds. As far as he was concerned, that time defined the appropriate number of seconds for shaking a woman's hand. But the instant her palm connected with his, and her fingers curled to grip his hand, warmth moved from their connection up his arm and settled in his chest. Before he had a chance to wonder if she felt it too, her brows dipped together as she looked down toward their hands.

The sensation didn't stop after two seconds, and he couldn't force his fingers to relax and let go of the grip. Instead, they stood in her living room for several long seconds as the warmth built between them.

Finally, as though both shocked, they jerked apart, and her gaze shot back up to his face.

"Well, Mr. Bennett," she began, then cleared her throat. "Dinner is ready." She turned and glided her hand lightly along the counter as she moved into the kitchen. "What would you like to drink? I have wine, beer, soda, and water."

While she was a perfect hostess, gentle and inviting,

Bennett once again felt ill at ease. Shooting a glance toward the table setting, he couldn't gain any visual cues about what to drink since no glassware was already set out.

She opened the refrigerator and pulled out a beer in one hand and a soda in the other. Turning back, she smiled. "I'm not sure if either of these is a brand you like. I also have white wine."

He'd normally go for a beer but wanted his wits about him while he got to know her and didn't want to give the impression he drank on the job. "Soda is fine."

She nodded and placed the beer back into the refrigerator. He wondered how she knew which was which but didn't ask. He hoped that by observing her during the evening, he'd discover her level of vision.

She moved to the stove, and he sucked in a quick gasp as her hand moved toward the pot. She looked at him and smiled again. "I'm sure you're wondering how much I can see, right?"

He lifted his arm and squeezed the back of his neck. "Yes, ma'am, I am. I need to know the specifics to provide the appropriate level of security."

"Please," she reminded. "Call me Diana. Do you go by Terrance?"

"Yes… um… well, most people call me Bennett."

She kept her gaze on him. He usually hated to be the object of someone staring but found that he didn't mind that she was, understanding she had to search more for visual cues that most people take for granted.

"I'd like to call you whatever makes you the most comfortable," she said.

His call sign with the Rangers had been something he'd laid to rest when he separated, and since he'd been employed with LSIWC, he'd gone by Bennett. When he was a kid, he'd asked his dad where Terrance came from. His dad shrugged and said it was just a name they picked out of a baby book. With his parents, it seemed that everything was an afterthought to them, even him. But hearing his name come from Diana's lips, he had to admit he liked the sound of it. "Terrance is fine."

"Lovely." Gifted with another one of her smiles, he felt as though he'd answered a test question correctly and couldn't help but smile in return.

She turned back to the stove. "It's easier if I serve our plates from here. You can certainly get seconds and thirds, but it makes less of a mess if I don't put the food out on the table."

She forked strained noodles onto the plates and then covered them with a thick, homemade marinara sauce filled with tomatoes, garlic, and chopped zucchini. He'd noticed the cutting board, knives, and the cheese grater next to the bowl of cheese that she liberally topped the meal with. The bread was buttered and toasted, and she laid thick slices on each plate. Another bowl held a salad, and she used tongs to place the veggies on the side. Turning, she handed one of the plates to him.

His mouth watered at the scents wafting through the air. He cooked out of necessity, but other than baking bread, he didn't spend much time on it. Food was for nourishment, but with the bounty she'd plated, it was also for pleasure.

Jeannie and Carson threw cookouts and get-togethers, but not like what Diana was serving. Staring down at the full plate of food, he hesitated. This was more like a... gift.

"Is it okay, Terrance? I should have ascertained to see if you had any preferences first."

He lifted his gaze from the delectable food to her face, now marred with a questioning expression. "It's fine. It's... just... yeah... fine." He could tell by the way her smile no longer beamed that he was fucking everything up. "No, really. It's great. It smells good, and I can't wait to dig in."

Her shoulders relaxed again. "Good. Then let's eat."

He waited until she walked to the table and set her plate down before following. He reached to pull her chair out for her, then stopped, once again uncertain what the protocol should be with someone with a visual impairment.

She pulled her chair out and sat, placing her napkin in her lap. He followed her example, and they began eating, conversation not being necessary while they devoured dinner. She ate heartily, for which he was glad, considering he was trying not to shovel the food down. He usually ate alone or with friends but hadn't shared a meal with a woman in a long time.

The flavors exploded in his mouth, and he groaned. "This is excellent, ma'am... Diana."

She turned her face toward him and grinned. "Thanks. Cooking isn't a lot of fun when it's just me. So when my uncle suggested I meet my security detail before the trip, I jumped on the excuse to fix dinner."

Unable to keep his gaze off her gorgeous face, made

even more beautiful with her eager smile, a tight ache hit his chest again. Her sweater was modest, yet the way it hung showcased her curves. *Shit... this could be a fuckin' disaster. Only one fuckin' meal, and I'm already losing focus. And losing focus gets team members killed.* Keeping his expression neutral, he offered a curt nod as he shoved his chair backward. Standing, he leaned over and snagged her now-empty plate. Taking them to the sink, he groused, his tone intentionally hard. "I'll clean up, Dr. Olson. Then we can talk about the particulars of the trip and the necessary security precautions."

4

Diana blinked at the sudden about-face in Terrance's demeanor. In a flash, she'd gone from Diana to Dr. Olson. Pressing her lips together, she wondered what instigated the change.

When her uncle suggested she attend the conference in Las Vegas to accept the award for their company, she'd balked. Before the accident, she'd loved to travel. It was one thing to become accustomed to her vision limitation at home, work, and in her daily life, but traveling to a crowded city full of tourists, bright lights, and the noise was not her idea of a good time. Even with her stepbrother going as her assistant, she still hesitated.

"Uncle Jerry, you should go. You're the head of the company now."

He'd winced and sighed heavily. "Diana... I'm the financial backbone but not the real head. That was your dad's role and now yours."

She reached over and took his hand in hers. "Do you really think I should go?"

He nodded and squeezed her fingers. "Yes, but we need to talk about your safety while there."

She cocked her head to the side at his unexpected comment. "Safety? Won't Alex go with me?"

"Yes, yes," Jerry agreed. "But things are happening that I haven't talked about with you."

"You're scaring me, Jerry."

"Oh, Diana. I'm not trying to scare you. Well, maybe a little." He used his free hand to jerk at the knot in his tie, loosening it slightly. "There are rumblings in the industry about what's showing up on the black market."

"Okay," she replied. "That's not unusual. Governments and terrorists alike all buy explosives on the black market."

"Yes, but now that has expanded to ideas... research... prototypes. They've become more aggressive in their search for getting their hands on explosives technology."

"More aggressive?"

"More persistent, shall we say. The board and I are certain we are protected, and every employee is vetted and has a background check, but I'd feel better if you had security while in Vegas. I have no doubt that some of the ones looking for black-market gains are going to be there, and I'd prefer you not be hassled by anyone." He swiped his hand over his face. "Anyway, with someone in security accompanying you, I'd know you could go without worry."

So she'd agreed even though having a bodyguard felt like overkill. She'd imagined a former FBI agent dressed in a white shirt and black suit like in the movies. Hating to spend close time with a stranger, she'd insisted that they meet for dinner at her place so they could become acquainted before the trip. But when she'd opened the door, she stared in shock because his features were a little fuzzy, but his sheer size was impressive.

He had filled her doorway and was dressed in such dark clothing that to discern anything, in particular, was almost impossible. She couldn't tell if he was bald or had shorn his hair very close to the scalp. Because his shirtsleeves were rolled up, she could tell his skin was tanned, and his arms were muscular.

She spent most of her education and career with men, yet the man standing in her doorway didn't remind her of anyone she'd ever met. An air of intensity and hardness poured off him— certainly felt even if she couldn't see his expression. As he'd entered her condo, he'd had to walk right past her, and for the first time, she could focus on his face. The angles were sharp, and his features were hard. But his eyes... pale gray rimmed in a darker smoky gray. She had the feeling there was little those eyes missed.

After he'd grumbled about the lack of security in her building, she'd relaxed, assuming he was simply doing his job. She could appreciate his concern, considering she worked in a highly secure and guarded facility. But at home, she never worried about her safety.

As she finished the introductions, she'd reached her hand out and waited before he enclosed her fingers in his gentle grip. The spark was undeniable. For a second, she thought it was a shock from static electricity, but when the warmth continued, she realized it was just from their connection. His hand was rough, calloused— a working man's hand. It was so much larger than hers, and the strength in his hand and arm could have easily crushed hers. But he held her hand as though it was precious, and she didn't want to let go.

Her cheeks heated, and she stepped back and hurried into the kitchen to plate their meal. *Slow down... go slow.* Accidents in the kitchen can occur with anyone in a rush, but especially someone who has limited vision. Managing to plate their food, she was thrilled when he ate enthusiastically.

As the meal finished, his demeanor changed, and Mr. Gruff reappeared. As he cleaned their plates, she moved back into the kitchen and began to put away some of the leftovers.

"I can do that," he said.

His rough voice moved over her as they stood side by side. "I appreciate the offer of help, but I assure you that I'm used to taking care of things in my kitchen." He stepped back, and she immediately missed the warmth. *He's a big guy, and it's just body heat.* But even that thought didn't make the loss feel less intense.

With a shake of her head to dislodge the feeling, she carefully poured the extra into two smaller containers, pleased when she only dribbled a small amount. Snapping on the bright red lids, she placed them into the refrigerator. Wetting a cloth in the sink, she wiped the counters with efficiency. He had already placed the dishes in the dishwasher, so after laying the cloth on the edge of the counter to dry, she turned to face him, crossing her arms around her waist.

From several feet away, she could easily see him but was not able to discern his expression. Sadly, the idea of spending days with this mercurial man by her side didn't seem palatable. Sighing heavily, she clasped her hands together in front of her. "Look, Terrance, I'm not sure what happened, but there is no obligation here. I'll call my uncle and tell him that this isn't a good idea—"

"No," he all but shouted, causing her to jump. "Shit, I'm sorry, Diana." He scrubbed his hand over his head before his hands were planted on his hips. "I'm fucking this up."

She'd learned to cope with vision loss in her daily life, but not being able to see someone's expression clearly was one of the hardest losses. Licking her lips, she offered a small smile. "You're not fucking anything up. It's just that you don't seem comfortable with me, and that's okay."

"It's not that," he countered. He glanced to the side and then faced her again. "Can we sit down and talk? I don't want you to feel that I'm not able to provide proper security for you."

She hesitated, then nodded. "Sure. Lead the way."

He walked over to the sofa and sat on one end. She followed and sat on the other end, twisting to face him, tucking her legs underneath her bottom. "What can I do to make this assignment more comfortable?"

"Diana, that's not your job. It's not on you to make me comfortable. It's my job to analyze the situation and provide a safe environment for you."

"Okay..." She bit the edge of her bottom lip, still uncertain what he needed from her. "So... um..."

"I don't want to make you uncomfortable, but can you explain your vision abilities to me? What you can and can't see?"

She breathed a sigh of relief. This need from him made sense. "Of course. And it doesn't make me uncomfortable. The accident created a bright flash that was too close to me. Luckily, I wore eye protectors, so it kept me from losing sight completely. I have very little vision out of my left eye. I see light and dark and the barest hint of shapes. My right eye was much less affected. In practical terms, I can see you. I can tell that you're a tall man wearing dark pants and a dark shirt. I can see the contrast of skin against clothing. I can tell that your hair isn't long. But unless you're very close, I can't discern your expression. When talking to someone, I pick up on other things like tone and mannerisms such as body language."

"And here in your apartment? I confess that I was surprised you had cooked our meal."

"I use cues to help me."

"Cues?"

Nodding, she smiled. "I group my clothes by color and category in the closet and drawers. I have raised dots that I put on toiletries and items in the kitchen to help me discern what's in my hand. Even the TV remote has some of the dots."

She reached out to the end table next to her and grabbed the remote from the location she always left it. When she handed it to him, her fingers grazed his as he took the remote from her. Once again, the tingling felt like a static shock but lasted much longer. As he bent his head to look at it, she curled her fingers inward as though to hold on to the warmth.

"I see," he said, drawing her attention back to what they were talking about.

"Ye—" Clearing her throat, she began again. "Yes. They're just little sticky tabs that I put on certain items. It helps me keep the sugar and the salt in the correct containers. I've memorized where and how I use them, so it keeps me organized."

"And cooking?"

She heard the awe in his voice and chuckled. "Because I had my full sight for almost thirty years, I knew how to cook. Losing some of my sight just meant I have to be more careful and thoughtful about what I'm doing. When I turn on the oven or stove, I make sure to turn them off when finished. When I use knives... well, that takes extra care." Shrugging, she admitted, "It's not that hard once I got used to my new vision limitations."

"What about work? I can't imagine that you feel safe in the labs?"

A heavy sigh left her lips as her smile dropped. "No. That's the hardest. I was always used to being in the labs, running experiments and tests. For a while, I was lost. As though my whole reason for getting up in the morning was gone."

"I'm really sorry."

She cocked her head to the side, hearing the sympathy in his words. She'd learned to discern the differences in people's tones—the inflections, intonations, and added emphasis. This rugged man in front of her exuded strength, but his softly spoken words also displayed care. And she was struck with the idea that caring might be something unfamiliar to him.

Shrugging again, she nodded. "It was hard. But everyone at GeoTech was wonderful. I have specialty computers with large print keyboards. I have lots of visual aids to assist. And I teach at our academy instead of working in the field. But I still develop new explosive compounds, just more in theory, and leave the practical lab experiments to my team."

After a moment where he seemed to digest her information, he shifted on the sofa, and his body turned more toward her. "And in a crowd?"

Her lips pinched as she breathed through her nose. "I… I'm not as comfortable in unfamiliar surroundings. Or rather, not comfortable at all."

"Are you sure you want to make this trip to Las Vegas?" he pressed.

Snorting, she shook her head. "Honestly, Terrance? Not really. But the association is giving an award to GeoTech… to honor my late father's work, and my uncle thought I should be the one to accept it."

"And the reason for security?"

She narrowed her eyes. "I'm sure you've been briefed."

"I have," he agreed, his forearms resting on his thighs. "But I'd like to hear from you how you see Las Vegas going."

Sucking in a deep breath through her nose again, she let it out slowly as her shoulders slumped. "As far as the conference? I'm not presenting or lecturing. I know that for the trade show, I'd get little out of it, so Alex is going, along with a few other employees. Some of our engineers will be there, also. My presence is really for the dinner and awards."

"I would need to be with you," he said. "Not just in the back of the room. I would stand on the side, as close to you while still being able to see all around."

"Like in the movies?" She wondered if her feeble joke fell flat when he didn't laugh.

"Since it would be more difficult for you to find me in an emergency, I would need to be able to get to you. Not across the room from you."

"Terrance, I don't expect there to be a problem. I think my uncle is overreacting, but I'm more than willing to have you accompany me on the trip."

"That's what I hope, as well."

He must have read her quizzical expression because he continued, "I hope that there isn't a threat, as well. I'd like to ensure you have a safe trip, but I must be ready for anything."

Hearing his words and the memory of his curt change of demeanor at the end of dinner, she nodded her understanding. Before he'd walked through her door, she had hoped he would be someone she could chat with on the trip. Someone who wouldn't make her feel inadequate. And with the warmth she'd felt at his touch, she was sure that just might be a possibility.

But her visual limitations made his job harder. *He's here for security only. Not fun. Not relaxation. And not friendship.*

Funny, that last thought caused a small sigh to escape. Forcing her lips upward, she stood. "It's been a pleasure to meet you, Terrance. I suppose I'll see you in a few days when we leave."

If he was surprised at her hasty actions, she couldn't tell. It was one of the many things she hated about not being able to see anyone's expressions unless she was close. Sticking her hand out as he took to his feet, she tried to ignore the spark and warmth when his hand wrapped around her fingers again.

"I'll be in touch, Diana. Thank you for dinner."

She walked him to the door, opened it, and stepped to the side. After he departed, she closed it and flipped the locks. With her ear pressed against the wood, she heard his boot steps fade and then the elevator ding.

Her heart felt strangely heavy. She wished she had someone to talk to, but the reality was that she had few friends she could confide in. Her social world had never been extensive, and she was more isolated after the accident.

"Ugh!" she groaned, pushing away from the door and walking back into the kitchen. Opening the refrigerator, she spied the pie she'd baked for dessert. The dessert they'd never gotten to. "Fine. More for me." Pulling out the pie, she decided to forgo the knife and serving spatula. Instead, she set it on the counter and dug into the gooey goodness with her fork, shoveling it into her mouth directly from the pie plate.

Chewing, she closed her eyes and moaned at the silky chocolate flavor. Licking the fork, she grinned. "Too bad, Terrance. You totally missed out!"

5

"I'm so fucked. I've never felt so fucked before a mission before in my life." Bennett let the weight bar drop into the supports with a clink before sitting up. Leaning forward, he covered his face with his hands before swiping up along his scalp.

When he pulled his hand away, Dolby, Poole, and Rick stared at him. His mouth twisted in a grimace, hating the whiny-ass statement he'd just made and wished he could stuff it back into the depths of whatever-the-hell was wrong with him.

"Is it because of Vegas?" Dolby asked.

"I know it's not your scene," Poole added. "You'd be more at home in the desert than in a desert city."

"No, it's not that. I mean, Vegas has never been on my bucket list of places to vacation, but I've never worried about where the mission took me."

"Hell, it's probably the conference," Rick surmised, slowing the treadmill to a walk. "Although, a bunch of nerds talking about blowing shit up could be kinda interesting."

Shaking his head, Bennett replied, "No, that's not it, either. The mission is just about keeping Dr. Olson safe."

"Is it because she's blind?" Dolby asked.

Jerking his head up, he glared. "She's not fuckin' blind. She has vision limitations, but she can still see."

He didn't miss the looks being shared by the other three Keepers and once again wished he'd kept his mouth shut. Since he had no idea what it was about this mission making him twitchy, he couldn't begin explaining it to anyone else.

"Look," Rick said. "Carson always says that we can turn down any mission that we don't feel is right for us. If that's what you need to do—"

"No way. I've never turned down a mission, and I'm not about to start now." He didn't speak his next thought aloud but couldn't stand the idea of someone else providing the security for Diana. "No, thanks, I've got this."

As a few more of the Keepers came into the gym, he headed to the showers and then back into the work room. He'd spent most of the day with Jeb poring over the background information on Alex, Jerry, and the two employees going and the information on explosives bought on the black market. He'd even read up on her father's death, but his cursory search found nothing suspicious. Hating coincidences, he asked Jeb to keep looking.

He'd also worked with Abbie to review the

schematics of the hotel where the conference would be held and where he and Diana would be staying. He memorized the floor maps, the elevators and stairs, and the entrances and exits for the visitors and staff. When he determined that he had learned all he could for the day, he headed into the equipment room with Teddy.

Checking out the necessary equipment that he would travel with but hoped he wouldn't need to use, he secured his weapon and carried the body armor.

"I think you're ready," Teddy said with a dip of his chin, his blue eyes moving over the items in Bennett's hands. "But if you need anything else, let me know, and I can get it to you. Same day."

Bennett appreciated many things about LSIWC, and the employees were top of the list. Shaking Teddy's hand, he waved goodbye before seeking out Carson for the last briefing. Finding Dolby, Poole, Abbie, Rick, Leo, and Natalie still in the workroom, Carson assured him they would all be working security with him.

"I know Teddy has already said this, but if you need anything, let us know. You're the most focused employee I have and unparalleled at professional security. I know you'll provide exactly what Dr. Olson needs."

Properly equipped and ready, he offered a chin lift acknowledging that Carson's confidence in him would not be misplaced. *Professional security. Focus. Dr. Olson. Got it.*

He was picking her up at six o'clock the following morning to go to the airport. Her uncle had arranged for a company jet to fly them to Las Vegas. Her stepbrother wouldn't be accompanying them since he had already left for a few days of Vegas vacation before the conference. The other two employees were driving.

Walking outside, he was ready for the active mission to begin. He could handle being around her... just ignore the spark that seemed to move between them, keep her safe, and fulfill his duty. No problem.

The following morning, Bennett pulled his SUV up to the front of her building. Just as he climbed down, the front door opened, and she walked out. Her hair was pulled back in a no-frills, low ponytail. With her subtle makeup, dark jeans, blue sweater, and sneakers, she looked like she could be walking out of a college dorm as a freshman, not a woman in her thirties with a doctorate. *Shit. She's fuckin' beautiful.* Then she smiled. His heart jolted at the sight. *Drop-dead gorgeous, and I'm definitely fucked.* She spoke while he continued to stare like a teenager desperate for a breadcrumb from the head cheerleader.

"Hello!" she called out, facing him, her hand lifted in a little wave. "I was waiting in the lobby, and Bobby told me that you had arrived."

Bobby trailed her, lugging a small suitcase with a scowl on his face.

Bennett was used to processing changing information quickly, but something about Diana's smile muddled his mind. He'd managed to convince himself he was immune to her beauty... hell, he'd provided security for attractive women before. There was a fragility amid her strength that he couldn't define. Maybe that was why when Bobby's eyes dropped to her ass, and Bennett knew she wasn't able to see that reaction, his temper flared. Stalking over, he snagged the suitcase from the smaller man. "Got it."

He lifted it with ease and placed it in the back of his SUV. She packed light for a woman going to Vegas for a week. Glaring at Bobby, he sent the young man scurrying back inside. Opening the passenger door, he watched as she twisted her head toward the seat and tentatively lifted her foot. *"Almost no vision in the left eye."*

Her words from their previous meeting hit him, and he inwardly cursed his lack of foresight. "Here, let me assist you." He wrapped his hand around her arm and guided her up into the passenger seat and was struck with the delicate scent of vanilla and the tingle of a current running between them.

She looked toward him, her smile still in place. "Thank you."

He nodded, then hurried to offer a verbal reply, "No problem. Buckle up." He waited until she complied before carefully closing her door. Rounding the front of his vehicle, he climbed behind the wheel. "Ready?"

"Absolutely," she said, her face still lit with a smile. She shifted in her seat to face him more fully. "How about you?"

His chin jerked downward as his brows lifted. He couldn't remember a client asking about him before. "Me?"

A light chuckle slipped out. "Yes, you. Are *you* ready for Vegas?"

"I'm just here for you, Dr. Olson."

As he pulled onto the road, her blink didn't go unnoticed. Nor did the way her smile seemed to fall.

"What happened to calling me Diana?"

He expected surprise and maybe puzzlement, but her words held a tinge of hurt. Clearing his throat, he kept his eyes on the road, although with little traffic, he could have easily spared her a glance. "I think I'm more focused if I keep us on a strictly professional level. It makes my job easier."

There were a few seconds of silence, and his exceptional peripheral vision made it easy to see the wince that marred her previously smiling face. His jaw tightened, but she nodded before he could take back what he'd said.

"Of course. I should have realized that, Mr. Bennett. Thank you."

He grimaced at her polite tone. Hearing her call him Mr. Bennett instead of Terrance should have made him happy to know that she agreed with his need to keep things impersonal. Instead, it stole the warmth he'd felt as soon as he'd seen her walking toward him.

He remained quiet for most of the drive to the airport, unable to think of anything to say. He sucked at small talk and had already managed to hurt her feelings. Keeping quiet seemed the safest thing to do. It would have been uncomfortable if she had done the same, but Diana broke the silence with occasional comments about the trip. Soon, they parked at the airport and made their way to the private hangar.

The company's private jet was large enough for ten passengers to be seated in plush leather seats, but Bennett and Diana were the only ones aboard. She settled into a seat and smiled up at him. He didn't want to crowd her, so he moved to a seat on the other side of the plane and several seats behind her. She'd twisted around to look at him, a slight frown on her face, but he focused on stowing his bag and looking at his phone, pretending he didn't notice her furrowed brow.

The flight would only take an hour, but he wanted to go over their travel plans once they landed. With his tablet in hand, he tried to keep his mind on the mission but kept glancing toward her. Once the pilot began takeoff, Bennett observed her leaning toward the window, her face pressed near the glass.

A heavy sigh left her lips as she shifted in her seat and laid her head back.

He unbuckled and moved to the seat across the aisle from her. "Hey, are you okay?" he asked, leaning closer.

She nodded, but the jerky movement gave little evidence that her action met her emotion.

"Are you airsick? Or afraid of flying?"

Shaking her head, she smiled, but it was easy to see it wasn't real. "No, Mr. Bennett, I'm fine."

"I don't believe you, Dr. Olson. And I can only keep you safe if you're honest with me."

Her eyes narrowed as though readying to argue with him. Then her shoulders hefted in a small shrug. "I used to love to fly. Sometimes I might have to study or prepare for a presentation, but usually, I'd spend a lot of time looking out the window. But since my accident, flying isn't fun."

He nodded, thinking of all the ways her life would have changed in the past two years. "That's understandable."

"You would think that being unable to see out the window wouldn't make a difference. But I used to love looking out and seeing the cities, towns, mountains and plains. I especially loved the various colors of the farmland. But since I can't discern any of that anymore, fear takes over my enjoyment."

"Can I help?" The blurted words had erupted so quickly that he wasn't sure where they came from or how to take them back. But he hated to see her sad.

Her lips curved again, but this time her smile was genuine. "Are you sure you have time? You looked busy back there."

Now it was his turn to shrug. "I was just reviewing the details of our travel and the hotel. But I absolutely have time."

She inclined her head to the side and said, "Then come sit next to me and look out the window."

Her unexpected request surprised him, but he didn't argue. Unbuckling his seat belt, he stood again and stepped across the aisle. Passing her, he settled in the wide, comfortable seat next to her. "You want me to look out the window?"

"Tell me what you see."

He turned and looked out, and now it was his turn

to furrow his brow. "There's not much to see. Mostly desert."

Her hand came down on his arm in a pretend slap. "Mr. Bennett! I know you must have better descriptive skills than that!"

Her words struck straight through him. She had no idea he had been a sniper, yet she was right. He and his spotter spent countless hours scoping out areas, cataloging everything they saw, and using descriptors to make sure they were in sync.

Turning back to the window, he swept the view below. Keeping his words to those a civilian would understand, he said, "There are mountains to the north."

"Describe them."

"The colors are pale gray and green."

"Like your eyes."

He jerked his head around to stare at her. "What?"

An adorable blush formed at the top of her sweater and rose up her neck until her entire face was filled with a light-pink hue. "Oh, I'm sorry. It's just that I noticed your eyes the evening we met. They're so unusual. So pale gray with a touch of green. Then they're ringed with a smoky gray. Really quite lovely. Actually, they're very intriguing." She shook her head, her blush deepening. "I suppose calling your eyes lovely and intriguing sounds ridiculous to a man like you. You'll have to forgive me. I tend to over-describe things now that catch my attention."

He stared, feeling his face heat at hearing her description. He'd never had anyone in his life mention his eye color. Women noticed muscles, of which he had plenty. But eye color? Never. Yet a strange pleasure moved through him that she'd noticed and remarked on a feature he'd never noticed. He smiled but had no idea how to respond to her perusal.

"Please, continue," she encouraged.

Thankful she'd given him a task to turn to, he looked out the window again, filled with the desire to give back something to her. "From the east all the way to the west and south, there's farmland. Mostly tan with plow lines still visible. A few plots are dark brown, and the rest are green. From the west leading up to the mountains, are green hills. A few houses are dotted along the narrow roads winding among them." Looking upward, he continued, "The sky is blue, and at our altitude, the white cumulus clouds are above us."

She remained quiet, her hand still on his arm, and he twisted his neck to see her looking at him with a soft smile.

"That was perfect. Thank you." The tension in her body had eased, and the taut lines bracketing her mouth had disappeared. "Alex has been with me the few times I've flown since I lost my sight, but he wanted to go early to enjoy Vegas."

"As your assistant, shouldn't he be with you?"

"Not really. He's my lab assistant, but he deserves a break. He's also my stepbrother. Anyway, he never seemed to describe things quite the way you just did, so I'm glad for the change in a travel partner." She laughed, adding, "I'm not sure why I asked you to do so, but I appreciate that you did."

He breathed easier before his gaze darted down to

his arm. She jerked her hand off as though just realizing they were still connected. Instantly, cool air replaced her warm touch. He'd never had such a reaction to a woman before, and while part of him wanted to embrace the new feelings, the fact that he was there to protect her, not flirt with her, slammed into him. Inwardly scoffing, he knew some of his fellow Keepers would have acted on their interest—not to the detriment of a mission. They were all too professional to make such a blunder. But if they found someone whose touch seemed to connect them, he had no doubt they would pursue it. After all, that was how they met the special women in their lives.

But not for me. Women touched him for sex—that he understood. In a bar, a woman's hand would land on his shoulder, his arm, his thigh. It was the universal signal that they were up for a night. Or, in his case, just for the sex because he'd never found anyone he wanted to spend the whole night with. In truth, no one had ever seemed keen on spending the whole night with him either.

The daily spewing of words from his father's mouth about being ugly and unlovable had taken deep root. Basic Psych 101. Of course, his father had also called him worthless most days, but he'd learned that all he had to do was find a calling, and those words no longer fit. But with relationships? *I'd be a fool to think a warm touch would mean anything to her.*

He offered the barest hint of a chin lift before he stood and moved back to his seat. Her smile had faltered as he stepped away, but he shoved that observation down. He continued to stare at his tablet for the rest of the flight but barely looked at the schematics. His thoughts swirled with the beautiful woman sitting several feet away whose touch was a brand. And, in truth, he missed it.

6

Diana waited until the plane had taxied into the hangar and heard the seat belt click from Terrance before she unbuckled as well. *Mr. Bennett. I need to remember to call him Mr. Bennett.*

It had caught her off guard when he insisted on the formality, considering at GeoTech, her father had always encouraged the employees to use their first names. He felt that it fostered an all-for-one atmosphere, and she'd never minded not going by the moniker of doctor.

But he knows his business, and I need to follow what he thinks is best.

She startled when he suddenly appeared. "Sorry," she said, standing while looping her purse over her shoulder.

"No, I'm the one who should apologize. I shouldn't have approached you from behind on your left side."

She looked up, glad he stood close enough that she

could see the expression of contrition on his face. Not that she needed him to be apologetic, but that he was quickly learning her visual abilities. Approaching on her left side would catch her off guard, and standing this close allowed her to see him clearly. It took most people longer to acclimate to what worked best for her, and she still had some employees who forgot. She didn't expect people always to accommodate her but appreciated it when they could.

The pilots stepped from the cockpit, and she walked forward, extending her hand while thanking them. The door opened after an airport employee rolled the staircase to the plane, and she hesitated, waiting to see what Terrance wanted her to do. He stepped in front of her, stopped at the top of the stairs, and looked around. Turning, he gently took hold of her arm, escorted her down the steps, and then led her to a dark SUV parked nearby.

When the luggage was stowed in the back, she climbed into the passenger side. "I was prepared to taxi into town."

He wasn't close enough for her to see his expression, but the under-his-breath mutterings about safety indicated he didn't think much about her idea.

They pulled away from the airport and started down the road. The sun was bright in the sky, and she slipped on sunglasses to keep the glare from causing a headache. She didn't waste time looking out the side window, knowing the passing scenes would be too blurry to enjoy the view. Keeping her face forward, she stared out as the highway became more crowded when they neared Vegas.

"Palm trees line the side of the road. The land is pretty flat here, but mountains are in the background. With some clouds in the distance, it's hard to see them clearly, but they're a darker blue than the sky."

She whipped her head around so fast that her ponytail slapped the side of her face. Staring at him, she grinned, stunned that he was describing the scenery for her. "Thank you."

As they merged onto another highway, he said, "We can just start seeing some of the skyscrapers in the distance." Only a few more minutes passed, and he added, "The sports stadium is on the left. It might seem like just a massive, dark building to you."

"Yes, I can see it. And on the other side of the road?"

"That's one of the bigger hotels. Some of them have marquee signs listing the acts for their shows. There's a lot more to the city than just the casinos and the Strip. Of course, those are the main attractions, but not all of the skyscrapers belong to the casinos and hotels."

She leaned forward, swinging her head from side to side as she attempted to discern more of the view. It helped that Terrance gave her descriptions as they passed the various buildings.

"There's the Bellagio," he said. "From here, on the highway, there's really nothing important to see. It's just a big sign near their parking garage next to the highway."

"I can't wait to see the fountains. Have you ever been to Las Vegas?"

"I've only been through here once and didn't pay attention to the sights."

"Hmm." She pressed her lips together, wondering about his experiences in security. *Is it all work, looking for danger and never for enjoyment?*

She heard the blinker as he exited the highway, giving them a closer view of the Strip where the hotels lined both sides. Traffic crowded the multi-lane street, and pedestrians bustled on the sidewalks.

"A few palm trees line this road, too, but other than that, it's mostly just concrete and asphalt."

Now that they were going slower and stopping at traffic lights, she could see more clearly what he was pointing out. He called out the various hotels along the way. "There's the Venetian."

She leaned forward and looked up. It was blurry, but she had no trouble making out a massive building with a tall tower in the front.

"Shit," he muttered.

"What?" She jerked her head to where she could use her right eye to see what he was looking at.

"Oh, sorry. Just looking at the LINQ. It's got that huge-ass Ferris wheel. It has to be over five hundred feet tall."

"Whoa. That's so not for me, and it sounds like it's not for you either." She laughed.

"Fuck, no!"

They went through a few traffic lights, and the street became even more crowded. "Caesars Palace. And over there is Bally's and Paris."

She swung her head back to try to take in everything he pointed out. At the sound of the blinker again, she twisted to the left just as he called out, "And here's the front of the Bellagio."

"I can't believe the conference is being held here," she murmured.

"I was surprised, too, until I reviewed the information about who was represented. There's some money backing this conference."

She nodded and sighed. "It's like an alphabet soup. Its major contributor is the ISEE. The International Society of Explosive Engineers. That's why so many foreign companies will be represented. But there will be an ATF and an OSHA presence. My uncle really should be here also. He's the one who understands the political workings of the industry. I'm more like my father… the chemist behind the products."

He pulled up to the front. "Wait here."

As he alighted from the SUV, she leaned forward and looked up, spying the covered area that extended over multiple lanes of vehicles discharging. Light filtered from above, but she couldn't discern if it was an atrium or open to the sky above. "I guess an *open* covered area wouldn't make much sense," she muttered to herself. Turning around at the sound of the SUV's back door opening, she could make out Terrance pulling out their bags.

"Bags stay in our sight," he said to the doorman who'd called for a porter. "Valet for the vehicle."

"Yes, sir," came the hasty reply.

She pressed her lips together to keep from grinning. She'd always carried her own luggage, and while the security seemed to be overkill, she had to admit it was interesting watching Terrance in his element.

He came to her door, and he assisted her down with a gentle touch that seemed incongruent with the rugged man. They walked into the lobby, and her feet stuttered to a halt at the assault of bright lights and multitudes of people moving around. Terrance was behind her, and his body jerked as he barely managed to stop before running into her. She twisted her neck and looked up. He appeared to be searching before he dropped his chin, and his eyes landed on her face.

"Dr. Olson. Are you okay? What happened?"

"I'm sorry," she mumbled as her face heated. "It's just a bit overwhelming."

"Shit, you're right." He reached down and took her hand, placing it on his arm. "Stay with me, and we'll check in."

Nodding, she kept her eye on him as he maneuvered them through the crowds toward the reception counter.

"The colors and shapes above are glass sculptures," he whispered, leaning closer.

"I can see beautiful colors," she admitted, looking up at the ceiling, the swirls of reds, oranges, yellows, and blues creating a blurry rainbow. Continuing to hold him with a light touch, she allowed him to guide her to the long, marble-top counter. She was about to step forward when he squeezed her fingers.

As she lifted her chin to look at him, his attention was on the receptionist.

"Dr. Diana Olson. Suite."

"Yes, sir. Two keys?"

"Yes."

She blinked, and her fingers tightened against his involuntarily. When he dipped his chin to look at her, she whispered, "I don't have a suite."

"You do now."

Blinking again, she pinched her lips together. He released her hand to sign for the room, and she instinctively took a step back, needing a little space. She had no problem surviving in the academic world of science that was predominantly filled with men. And while she knew her family's business gave her a guaranteed job out of college, she had worked just as hard as anyone else at GeoTech to advance in her field. She was educated, hard-working, and confident and had no problem standing on her own. Until the accident. And overnight, thrust into a world of shapes and shadows in one eye and slight blurriness in the other, she often struggled with mundane tasks.

Driving wasn't possible, and she missed it. Not the traffic but the occasional long drives she'd take to unwind. Or when heading out to one of their testing site quarries, she loved driving on the backroads. Now? She relied on Alex to drive her around. Her stepdad had even set Alex up in a condo in her building so he would be more readily available. If she wondered how a twenty-six-year-old man liked being stuck with his stepsister so often, she supposed most twenty-six-year-old men didn't have a paid-for condo in an upscale building. She'd certainly never heard him complain.

At work? She managed very well, considering the other employees knew her before the accident and assisted her with whatever she needed help with. But she'd adapted her career, still providing a necessary function.

But out in the world? That was where she felt the sting of her limitations. Shopping took longer, and some cashiers or other shoppers grew impatient. Torn between fear at times and frustration, it was hard to force herself to get out into new situations. Thus, online grocery shopping and ordering had become the norm.

Lost in her deep breathing, she was surprised when Terrance shifted and placed his hand over hers. Stunned at how easily she accepted his help, she fell into step with him, noting he shortened his stride to walk at her pace.

"There's a large atrium over there with a ton of shops," he said, his mouth close to her ear as they followed the porter.

Reaching the elevator, she breathed easier when the doors closed, and the sounds of the lobby fell away. After several stops, he squeezed her hand. "We're here."

The carpeted hallway was quiet, and she let out a long sigh. When he halted outside a door, he reached into his pocket while turning to the porter. "Thanks. I have it from here."

The young man grinned and offered his thanks before walking back down the hall, his muted footsteps fading. Terrance unlocked the door with their key card and ushered her inside.

"Whoa!" She looked around as she stood in a living

room with a sofa, two chairs, a flat-screen TV, and a coffee table. It appeared there was a counter, and as she moved closer, she could see it contained a mini-refrigerator and bar. A bank of windows covered the far wall, the bright light causing her to squint. He walked over to the wall and pressed a button, automatically closing the sheers to defuse the light and make it easier for her to focus. She moved forward, but he jumped in front of her, his hands up to stop her progress.

"Hang on," he said, bending to pick up the coffee table.

Stunned, she watched him carry it to the side of the room and place it against the wall. "This should make it easier for you to maneuver around without tripping."

The breath left her lungs, and her lips curved at the gesture. It didn't matter why he did it... just that he'd thought about her safety. "Thank you."

He offered a curt nod, and she hid the sigh that threatened to slip out at his hasty dismissal of her appreciation. Turning, she moved toward one of the doors at the back of the room. "Oh, my," she said as she walked into the bedroom. Moving around the bed, she discovered the bathroom before returning to the living room. "Why did I need a suite? This is much larger than I need."

Not seeing him, she turned toward another open door and walked into a second bedroom, identical to the first. "Terrance—um... Mr. Bennett?"

He was setting his bag on the bed and turned toward her. "Is your room okay?"

"Okay? This is beautiful, but... it's... well, I didn't realize we'd be sharing a suite."

"It makes it easier for me to provide the highest level of security."

She sucked in a deep breath before saying, "I can't imagine how much this suite costs—"

"It's covered."

She blinked, her brow knitting. "Covered?"

"Yes. I'm sorry. I'm not being clear. It's covered by LSIWC."

She blinked again, having no doubt her expression was as blank as her mind.

He dropped his chin and sighed before looking up at her again. "The company I work for is Lighthouse Security Investigations West Coast. LSIWC. They split the cost of the upgraded suite with your company." Tilting his head to the side, he added, "Jerry Olson approved."

"Oh, right. I have no doubt he did as much as he worries about me." She loved her family but wished her uncle had discussed the arrangements with her first. *Terrance probably thinks I can't be trusted to make decisions for myself.*

She pressed her lips together, then turned away so he couldn't see her blush. There were so many things she'd lost along with her vision, but not being able to see people's expressions unless she was close was one of the most she missed.

"Dr. Olson?"

His voice came from just behind her, and she hadn't heard him approach. "Yes!" she replied in an overly bright manner. "I'll just go unpack." She hastened back into her bedroom. It only took a few minutes after she opened her suitcase to hang her conference outfits in the closet and place her other garments in the drawers. Carrying her toiletry case into the bathroom, she aligned her shampoo and conditioner in the shower and her makeup on the counter.

She leaned closer to the mirror and stared. The reflection was the same woman she'd always seen. Petite. Blond hair. She used to wear glasses but not since no correction was available for her new vision problems. Sighing, she wished that just being in Terrance's presence didn't throw her so much. But he was the most handsome man she'd been close to in a very long time. *And sharing a suite? Knowing he was sleeping in a room just across the hall from me?* Everyone saw her as Dr. Olson, the chemist, but the reflection staring back was just Diana, the woman.

Standing straight, she sucked in a deep breath and let it out slowly. "Okay, you got this, girl." As she walked out of the bathroom, she wasn't sure if she was referring to the conference or to being in such proximity to Terrance. Both were frightening. One would be over within a couple of days. The other had the potential to stay in her mind for a long time.

His bedroom door was open, and she stood in the doorway, not wanting to intrude but curious at the objects he'd placed on his bed. He turned and cocked his head to the side. "You can come in."

She stepped closer until she could see two guns lying

on the bedspread. Jerking slightly, she looked up, her brows lowered. "Guns?"

"Yeah."

"But... why?"

He stepped closer, and his face angled down toward her. His gaze never wavered as he stared at her. For a moment, she forgot what they were discussing as his features came into focus. His hair was almost shaved off, just the barest hint of darkness covering his scalp. She'd never spent much time around a younger man with a shaved head, but on him, it only added to the appeal. The same dark shadow covered his jaw, but she could see he shaved his beard—it was just trimmed closely. His features were hard and angular. But his eyes held her captive, making it difficult to look away even if she had wanted to.

"Dr. Olson."

Her name from his lips drew her attention to his mouth. Was there nothing about him that wasn't appealing? He was unlike any man she'd spent time with, yet just the sound of his voice drew her in. "Yes?" she whispered.

"You know why I'm here."

At the mention of his duty, ice water dropped over her as she was catapulted from her musings about his gorgeous, masculine face. "Yes. Yes." Her shoulders slumped. "I just can't help but think that all this security is over the top. I'm not in danger, Mr. Bennett. Yes, companies do compete for the same contracts. That occurs in any business or industry. But it's not like someone is after me." She dropped her chin and sighed.

"I just feel as though my uncle is using the pretense of danger as a way to have someone here to assist with my getting around." She lifted her gaze and stared at his face. "You are much more capable of a bodyguard than just leading me around to make sure I don't trip over a coffee table."

7

Bennett stood so close to Diana that the toes of his boots nearly touched the toes of her sneakers. Normally, he never stood this close to someone unless he meant to intimidate them. And that was the last thing he wanted to do to her.

He knew she needed the closeness to see his face. He almost snorted at that thought. He was nothing to look at, but when the world had become a blur to someone, being able to discern nuances must be as necessary as breathing. He'd vowed to tamp down his desire to keep a distance and stay close. Not like that was a difficulty in her case.

But he faltered when she turned her questioning and trusting face to him. "Dr. Olson, you know your uncle has concerns about this trip. And while I'm not trained in assisting someone who is visually impaired, I can certainly perform those duties and make sure you're not harassed, cornered, or taken advantage of in any way."

Her gaze dropped from his face to the bed, and the

lines on her forehead increased. He longed to smooth them out but kept his hands at his sides.

"But those guns…"

"I travel with weapons. It's a precautionary measure."

"It seems excessive."

He didn't mention that two more guns were in the hotel room safe or the three knives inside the nightstand drawer and one strapped to his ankle. "I want to be prepared."

"Prepared?"

He spoke cautiously, uncertain of her comfort level with guns. "Yes. Prepared."

A crinkle formed between her eyebrows. "For what? Armageddon?"

A bark of laughter erupted from deep inside, surprising him. He rarely laughed and usually only with friends, but sure as hell not on a mission. But if she only knew what weapons he used to carry around with him, and still did, depending on the mission, she would really think Armageddon was coming.

"No, Dr. Olson. Just in case something happens, I want to be ready. Better prepared than to be caught with my dick in my—um…sorry… um… to not be ready." His entire head burned at the slip of his tongue, and he had no doubt he was bright red. *And I sure as fuck don't need to think about my dick at the same time I'm talking to her.* Stepping back, he hated the loss of closeness but needed the separation to regain his composure. "It's all just to be cautious."

Her head moved up and down slowly before her lips twitched upward. "Okay. I'm sure you're right."

His body screamed to step closer again, but he forced his feet to remain glued to the carpet. Turning back to his bag, he reached inside and pulled out a small box. "I have something else for you." Taking out a lighthouse charm dangling on a chain, he held it up. "I need you to wear this at all times."

She squinted as she stepped closer and reached out her hand to touch the delicate necklace. "I don't understand."

"It contains a micro-tracer. If anything happens where we're separated, then I can find you."

Her fingers had closed around the charm, but she jerked at his explanation. "You're serious?"

She was so close it was easy to see her incredulous expression with a lowered brow forming a scowl.

"Of course, I'm serious."

Shaking her head slightly, she nonetheless lifted her hair and gave him her back. "It seems like overkill, but I know I need to trust you."

The charm dangled in front of her before resting at the top of her cleavage, with his fingers barely touching the back of her neck as he fastened the clasp. The feel of her skin sent tingles along his spine.

A knock sounded on the door, and she was grateful for the reprieve. "Hey, Diana! Are you there?"

His eyes narrowed as she turned and started toward the living room. His long stride caught up and surpassed her with ease. "I'll get it." Looking through the peephole, he spied Alex Markham, her stepbrother.

Throwing it open, he filled the doorway as he stared down at the younger man.

Alex blinked and looked up, an expression of surprise quickly followed by a loud huff. "Who are you? Where's Diana?"

Alex was close to six feet tall and had a lean runner's body, but Bennett towered over him at six feet, six inches and outweighed him by fifty pounds of pure muscle. Not inclined to step back, he remained in place, a glower firmly etched in his features.

"Diana? Are you okay?" Alex attempted to lean around Bennett, but until Diana indicated she wanted Alex in the room, Bennett wasn't budging.

He was impressed, considering the kid thought he might be able to get past him.

"Hey, man, do you mind?" Alex stepped closer, but Bennett still didn't move.

A soft hand landed on his back, and he steeled his expression not to show the tingle that he felt. Shifting to the side, he gave Diana room to see her stepbrother.

Alex's face broke into a grin as he stepped forward and hugged Diana. Bennett grimaced but had to admit that the young man seemed genuinely glad to see her. *But I wish it was my arms around her.* Tightening his jaw at the unbidden thought, he tamped down the useless emotion and grunted, "Come in so I can close the door."

"Alex, this is Terrance Bennett. Uncle Jerry hired his company for security."

Alex shook his hand but immediately dismissed him as he focused on his stepsister. She led Alex over to the sofa, her face soft with affection. "We just got here. What have you been doing for the past couple of days?"

"Oh man, Diana, you wouldn't believe everything. Hell, there are rides, shows, and casinos. I went on the Ferris wheel, where they have a bartender right there. You should go even though I know you wouldn't be able to really see anything from there. But you could drink and just talk to people."

"You mentioned shows. Any performers I might know?"

Bennett's fingers clenched as he noticed how Diana subtly changed the topic when Alex mentioned her lack of sight.

"I hit a couple of shows but not the big acts. They were the late shows. You know… um… exotic. Anyway, you could go to those as well. They've got them with male strippers, too. You could try to get seats up front so you could see."

Diana smiled as Alex prattled on, but Bennett perceived it wasn't from enthusiasm. He hesitated, the desire to kick her stepbrother out of the room mixed with not overstepping his bounds.

"I thought I might like to visit the art museum downstairs," she said. "Maybe we could do that together."

"Sure, sure." Alex nodded, then chuckled. "Although, it's not really my scene."

"Right. Yes, of course, you're right."

Done. Fuckin' done. "We need to eat," Bennett interrupted. "We can go out or order in."

Alex blinked, his head jerking back slightly. "Oh, I guess she needs to order in—"

"I'd like to go out," Diana interjected.

Bennett grinned as he leaned closer and offered his hand, cutting off Alex and forcing the younger man to shift backward. "Then that's what we'll do. And we can look at the art gallery afterward."

She smiled widely as she took his hand, and it was easy to see it was real with the way her face lit.

Alex's expression scrunched slightly. "I met some guys that I was going to have lunch with. They're here for the conference, too. I thought you might like to join us."

"Oh." Diana hesitated, but Bennett still held her hand and squeezed her fingers slightly. She stared at the connection, and her lips remained curved upward. "Alex, I'll have the next few days with convention goers. I'd rather dine in peace today. But maybe I can join you for drinks later this evening. Before you hit the *exotic* shows."

"That'd be great, Diana," he enthused, offering her another hug, made awkward considering Bennett didn't release her hand.

Alex walked out, and Bennett reluctantly released her to secure the door. Turning, he said, "We can have lunch whenever and wherever you like."

"I think perhaps we should stay in the hotel for this meal?"

"Sure thing. Let me know when you're ready."

She nodded and moved into her bedroom, and he heard the bathroom door close. He'd already scoped out the Bellagio and knew it had numerous restaurants, many with dress codes. He'd come prepared and was about to head into his room to change into slacks, but Diana's reappearance in her travel clothes of jeans and sneakers halted his progress.

"I thought we'd eat simple for lunch," she offered. "I'm not in the mood to dress up, and while I don't want to assume, I really don't want you to have to do so either."

Chuckling, he planted his hands on his waist and nodded. "Yep. You read me right."

"Oh, good! I saw where there was some food out by the pool. I thought we could eat outside as long as we're in the shade."

"I'll make sure we are," he vowed.

She looped her purse crosswise over her body, and he tried to ignore the way the strap showcased her breasts. He wouldn't be the only man to stare and secretly vowed to scowl when necessary. *She might not be for me, but she won't be hassled on my watch, even from a distance.*

As they left the room, he slowed his gait to match hers, then moved closer when they exited the elevator onto the much more crowded first floor. His trained gaze moved over the crowd of tourists, hotel guests, and those heading straight to the casinos. They wandered down several halls past shops and the spa until finding the doors leading to the pool deck. Once outside, the shouts of children in the water and the chattering of adults gathered at tables and in gazebos met their ears.

Diana moved closer, and he shifted his elbow

slightly in silent invitation. He sucked in a quick breath as her fingers wrapped around his bicep, and she allowed him to guide her through the throngs of people. A poolside café was easy to find, and as she ordered, he spied a small table for two off to the side under a palm tree. He walked her over, and once she was seated, he jogged back to collect their lunch. Patiently waiting was his strong suit—he'd built his sniper career around it—but now, while in line, he kept looking over at Diana to make sure no one bothered her.

According to Jerry, there wasn't an overt threat to her, but the concern was that someone would attempt to talk to her alone, using her visual limitations as a way to intimidate or coerce her into saying something confidential about their new technology. He snorted. After spending time with her, he knew she would never make that kind of error. But he wasn't about to take a chance on anyone approaching without him being by her side.

Finally, his name was called, and he collected the tray. With a chin lift, he indicated he wanted a server to bring the drinks, and without waiting, he headed straight to her. She sat under the shade with her sunglasses on, and he called out as he neared.

Her head jerked toward his voice, and her smile lit his world. Forcing his breath steady, he set the tray on the table. "I have the food right here. The drinks are coming."

The server placed their drinks down, and he tipped the young woman, noting her wide eyes as they stared up at him. She scurried away, and he shook his head.

Even when he wasn't trying to intimidate, he accomplished that feat.

"What's so funny?" Diana asked, unwrapping her burger.

"Oh, I think I scared the server. My ugly mug isn't what she's used to." He settled into the chair and reached for the fries. "I'm putting your fries at twelve o'clock. The ketchup is at three o'clock."

"Thanks." She grinned, taking a huge bite of the burger. They chewed in silence for a moment. She took a deep sip from her soda and leaned forward. "I can't imagine why you call yourself ugly. You don't strike me as a man with false modesty!"

He paused mid-bite and stared. Her gaze was on him, and sitting as close as they were, he was surprised at her comment. "You don't have to be polite, Dr. Olson. My self-esteem is intact and all based on my talents as a Keeper. Looking in the mirror doesn't have to stroke my ego."

Her eyes widened, and her glare hit him like a slap.

"I'm not trying to stroke your ego, Mr. Bennett! But I can't imagine how you don't see what others see!"

Her indignation caught him off guard. "People look at me and see a large man. They'd be right. I work out and work hard to make sure I'm in top shape, but I'm not a gym rat searching to be photographed. Others see someone with a stern expression. That's always been my look. Guess I came by it naturally. It served me well in the military, and as a bodyguard suspicious of everyone around, that expression still works for me. I don't have time to worry about my hair or clothes. So the hair stays short, and the clothes are what the mission demands. If that's jeans and boots, I'm satisfied. I'm not trying to be Hollywood's version of security. I'm just a tough son of a bitch and good with that."

She blinked, and he inwardly groaned. He'd just expressed more words than he'd spoken to anyone in a long time. They weren't particularly nice words, and they sure as fuck weren't said in a particularly pleasant tone. He opened his mouth to apologize, but his words halted when her hand landed on his arm, and once again, the heat seared a path straight to his chest.

"Well, Mr. Bennett, I think everything you said is true, but I also know what I see. I think you're beautiful."

Air rushed from his lungs as though hit in the gut by a sucker punch. He'd never been called beautiful in his life. The description would be laughable if it wasn't for the intense way Diana stared at him as though she saw something that he'd never seen.

His attention was snagged by an approaching group of men whose eyes were on Diana, and he shifted in his seat, standing as they reached the table. They glanced at him but then focused their attention on her.

"Dr. Olson?"

"Yes," she said, her voice firm, but Bennett could hear a slight tremor that he recognized came from her when she was uncertain. A quick glance let him know she didn't recognize them from the distance they stood. She stood, and he moved closer to her.

"And you are?" he growled, looking down.

The three men's gazes jerked up to him, their eyes widening before settling on her again.

"I'm Dr. Peter Voltov from ISEE. I work for NitroSabir at the Switzerland location of our Russian-based company. I haven't had the pleasure of meeting you but had met your father years ago. I was pleased to hear he was being honored this year."

"Thank you," she said, her smile back in place.

Dr. Voltov continued, "I'm with Dr. Lin Kang and Dr. Edgar Masterson, both with the ISEE."

She reached out, and the three shook her hand as she greeted them.

Dr. Kang said, "I'm from NaeGeo company. We're based in Korea."

"It's nice to meet you. I'm well aware of your company's excellent reputation."

"I was also sorry to hear about your accident. It's good to see you have recovered."

"Thank you," she acknowledged softly.

"I'm a great admirer of your work, as well," Dr. Masterson said, his voice booming and his handshake vigorous. "Too bad about the accident. Orica has those incidents happen, too. I guess it's just part of our industry."

If the men expected her to say more about her vision, they were disappointed. Bennett was about to shut down the conversation when another voice rang out.

"Hey, Diana!"

Bennett narrowed his eyes at Alex's approach with

two more men in tow. He felt the growl come up his throat.

Diana turned and smiled. "Hello, Alex."

"I met up with Dr. Kang's assistant, U-Gin. And this is Bart, one of the reps from OSHA. We're going back to the Ferris wheel tonight. The one with the bar. We wanted to invite you to come along."

"Oh, I don't think so, but thank you."

"We understand that a number of the conference attendees will be enjoying the casino tonight," Dr. Kang said. "If you want, you may certainly join us."

"You ought to come," Dr. Masterson said. "We'll make sure no one tries to flog you."

Diana's head jerked slightly, and the Australian continued, "You know. Steal from you."

Her brow furrowed as she looked up toward Bennett. He bent closer and whispered, "Do you want to go? If so, I'll be with you."

She gave a quick shake of her head, and he turned to the group. Smiling, he said, "Diana and I have plans for this evening."

He looked back down to make sure he'd read her right, and once again, her gentle smile hit him.

The others said their goodbyes, and when it was just the two of them again, they sat down to finish their lunch. She was quieter, and he hated that their time had been interrupted. *Our time? What the fuck? I'm here to protect her... not want her for myself.* Yet even as the thought struck, he knew something about the beautiful woman had already wormed her way inside.

8

Diana stood in her bedroom, close to the full-length mirror on the closet door. Her hands smoothed down the material on the front of her red dress. Leaning closer, she checked her makeup and hair, satisfied she looked appropriate for dinner. Terrance told her they would go through the art gallery and then have dinner.

She pressed her lips together, then loosened them in haste, not wanting to smudge her lip gloss. Instead, she closed her eyes, but the only thing that came to mind was him. How could he think he wasn't attractive? He was breathtakingly gorgeous, and she could only imagine the women lined up for his attention. Dropping her chin, she shook her head in derision. *Stop acting like a starry-eyed teenager with a crush. This is not a date.*

Yet, despite her self-talk, her feet stumbled to a halt when she opened her eyes and walked out of her bedroom. He stood nearby, facing her as though waiting for her to appear. She was close enough to see the black material of his pants stretched over his thighs, and the black dress shirt tailored to fit his body perfectly. A black tie and leather jacket completed the look.

"Wow," she breathed, allowing her gaze to rove over him from head to toe. "You look amazing."

"Hell, Dr. Olson, I was about to say the same thing. You're absolutely beautiful." Neither moved as they stared at each other. Finally, he crooked his elbow. "Ready?"

"Yes." She rushed and placed her hand on his arm. *Not a date. Not a date.* The repeated mantra didn't seem to make a difference as the tingle from her hand on his arm made its way through her body.

Once they alighted from the elevator and stepped onto the lobby floor, they moved past the throngs heading out to dinner, shows, or to the casino, and families heading back to their rooms from the pools or sightseeing. Coming to the art gallery entrance, she moved toward the counter to purchase two tickets when he reached into his pocket and pulled out two, holding them in front of her.

"Mr. Bennett," she scolded. "You're not here to buy everything! You bought lunch. This whole trip should be my treat!"

"I got it."

His voice rumbled, and the vibration moved through her. It struck her that if he ever spoke while she was pressed against his chest, she would feel the vibrations even more. Blushing, she simply nodded and turned to face forward. They walked down the first hall, and all thoughts flew from her mind except the artwork lining the walls and on the pedestals.

"Oh..." she breathed, moving closer to view the paintings.

"The showing is called Blooms," he said, pointing at the words on the wall.

She stepped forward to read more about the exhibit, and he moved along with her. She glanced over, surprised to realize she was still holding his arm. "Oh, sorry—"

"No worries," he said, tightening his arm to his side, clasping her hand close to him.

She smiled and turned her attention back to the paintings and sculptures as they wandered along together. Most, she was able to move close to, appreciating the colors and themes. She leaned forward for the ones behind a roped area, sighing when they were still too far away.

"This one sort of looks like a bunch of blue flowers. It says it's a meadow in Texas. 'Fraid I don't know much about art, but I can tell you what I see."

She turned, and her grin widened. "I think what you're describing is perfect."

They wandered along the exhibit for the next hour, and she never felt rushed by him. When they got to the end, she hesitated. "You know, I've been selfish with your time."

He dropped his chin to peer at her, his brows lowered. "What do you mean?"

Her shoulders hefted in a barely-there shrug. "You've just been so patient when you probably hated this."

"I'm here for you. I'm here to make sure you're not

in danger or taken advantage of. I'm here to make sure you're okay. Just because art shows aren't what I usually go to doesn't mean I didn't enjoy it." He jiggled her arm. "Are you ready to eat?"

Just then, her stomach gurgled.

He laughed. "I'll take that as a yes."

She snorted, then immediately clapped her hand over her mouth. "Good God, I can't remember the last time I laughed and snorted at the same time."

"Maybe you should do that more often."

Giving him a narrowed-eyed headshake, she said, "Oh, that would be attractive."

"I can imagine everything you do would be attractive," he said, guiding her out of the exhibit and down the hall toward the restaurant.

She stared straight ahead, afraid to look up at his expression. And at this closeness, she would have been able to see it with clarity. *He thinks I'm attractive?* While not a novel concept, she had found that since the accident, men tended not to be interested in a visually limited woman outside of work. It had been a long time since she'd been in a long-term relationship, and she'd hardly dated since the accident. It didn't help that she'd thrown herself into learning how to adapt at work, even hiding her despondency when she'd first been forced to give up the lab experiments. Little time was left over for joining the dating scene, and it was more exhausting than the rewards.

Past date memories slid through her mind. *"No, I wasn't born this way." "Yes, it's permanent." "No, I can't just have surgery and make it all better." "Yes, I still work." "No,*

I'm not totally blind." "Yes, I can see that you're staring at the woman sitting at the next table."

She smiled at the thought that a man as masculine as Terrance considered her attractive. It might be silly, but such a simple statement after seeing such a beautiful art exhibit filled her with a lightness of spirit that had been missing for a long time.

Before she knew it, they stood at the hostess station of one of the Bellagio's exclusive restaurants. Still holding on to his arm, she carefully walked as they weaved their way through the large room filled with diners, hating how the scene blurred all around, managing to keep her off-kilter. When they stopped, she gasped when she saw the two-seater table in a corner with tall, potted palm trees creating a natural barrier between them and the others.

"Oh, this is lovely. I made the reservation but didn't dream of asking for something special."

With one hand on the back of her chair and his other hand lightly on her back, he waited until she settled before he moved to sit. "I asked them for a private table away from the rest of the patrons."

His thoughtfulness filled her deeply, and she couldn't remember the last time someone had done that for her. Of course, her coworkers had learned what worked best for her on the job and had been accommodating, but this was memorable.

They perused the menu once the server left to get their drink of choice. She held the menu close, then once she gave her selections to the server, she leaned back and smiled.

Terrance was hard to read, and she was sure it was due to just him and not anything to do with her lack of vision. His rough hands gave evidence of a hard worker who had labored and not spent his career at a desk. His clothing choice indicated he was confident in himself and didn't pretend to be something he wasn't. His gaze moving over the others in the restaurant signaled that he took his security duties seriously. Yet there was an ever-so-slight nervousness to him as though he might feel like he didn't belong.

"Hey," she said, reaching over to gently touch his arm, drawing his attention back to her. "Are you seriously afraid someone will approach me here?"

The corner of his lips curled upward. "Professional habit." With a light scoff, he amended, "Or professional liability."

"Liability?"

"Always looking. Always suspicious. Always wondering. Guess it makes me a poor dining companion."

"It's fine," she assured. "It's who you are." As soon as the words left her mouth, she wanted to know more. "What did you do in the Army?"

His gaze shot to hers, but the depths hid any answers. He ran his tongue over his teeth as though pondering his response. "Ranger."

She stared blankly. "I'm sorry. I don't know what that means."

He chuckled ruefully. "No reason you should. I was an Army Ranger. It's a specialized operations team."

Blushing, she tucked a strand of hair behind her ear.

"I'm embarrassingly ignorant about the military. We have military contracts, of course, but I'm not involved in the sales or training. Just the development of products mostly used in the mining industry. I've heard of SEALs and Green Berets but realize they're all from different branches of service."

"Different and the same." He hefted his broad shoulders, not seeming upset that she didn't recognize his specialty. "Each is a bit different while often working similar missions. Ultimately, all that matters is that we fought on the same team."

"I'm sure you're being very gracious."

"Not at all, Dr. Olson. I can't pretend to know everything about your job, and I'd have to be a conceited jerk to be upset because you didn't know the details about what I did in the military."

A bubble of laughter erupted. "You put that very well, Mr. Bennett." Their meals were soon served, and they ate heartily for the next half hour with easy conversation between them.

When the server placed the coffee and dessert before them, he surprised her when he asked, "Tell me about your family."

Her fork halted on its way to her mouth. "I would have thought that information would have come up in your research on me."

His head inclined in a conciliatory nod but pressed forward. "Much does, but I'd like to hear about them from you."

She sipped her coffee, pondering his request. Seeing no reason not to talk about her family, she set her cup down. "I suppose it sounds so cliché to say that my upbringing was wonderful, but it's true. My parents were loving, and my childhood was filled with good memories. My mother had difficulties getting pregnant, and whether they tried for more children or not, I don't know. But they never made me feel as though I wasn't enough."

She leaned back, warming to the subject of her family. "My parents met in college. My mother was an English major who taught and wrote for many years. My father was a brilliant chemist, and along with his brother, who had financial acumen, they bought out an explosive company and founded Olson GeoTech. Within twenty years, it had become a force in the industry by hiring the best employees and encouraging innovation. People probably assume my dad pressured me to earn a chemistry degree and enter the family business, but my parents encouraged me to do whatever I wanted."

"And chemistry was it for you?"

She laughed while nodding. "How many children get to visit their dads at work and watch lab experiments and then go out into the field and watch explosions?"

His shoulders shook, resonating with mirth. "Guess not many."

"I thought my dad had the coolest job in the world. And it was something that interested me as well. Dad insisted I intern at other places after I graduated, but when it came time for a job, I wanted to work in the family business."

She smiled at the memories, then leaned back as her

grin slid from her face. "I worked with Dad while earning my master's and doctorate degrees, but was only twenty-eight when he died in a car accident. He was coming home late and hit a slick spot on the road. Spinning around, he slid into a tree. Dad died instantly."

"I'm sorry."

She looked up, her gaze searching, desperately wanting to see him clearly. He leaned forward, his forearms resting on the table, and she mirrored his movements, bringing them close enough for her to discern the sincerity behind his words of sympathy. *He knew. He knew I needed him closer.* That truth hit her, and she sucked in a quick breath. Swallowing deeply, she nodded. "Thank you."

Clearing her throat, she continued, "Mom and I were despondent. It had always been the three of us."

They were quiet for a moment, and she dragged her fork through her cheesecake, toying with it more than eating.

"I shouldn't have asked about your family."

Her chin lifted, and once again, she spied sincerity. "Oh, it's... well, I would say it was fine, but the reality is that I miss him. I'll always miss him. But you know what? You might think it was hard to return to work without him, and it was at first. I used to cry every day when I drove to work, but GeoTech was all I knew. And it was what I had left of my dad, so I realized how lucky I was to have had those years working with him. And now, I feel he's still with me, and I can continue his legacy. How many people can say they worked with their father and loved it?"

Terrance nodded curtly, but this time, she felt as though a cloud had passed over his face. He shifted in his seat, and when he looked up at her again, his face was back to expressionless. She wondered if she had imagined the cloud or if it was a trick of the restaurant lighting.

"And your mother remarried?"

She tensed slightly but heard no judgment in his question. A sigh slipped out as she nodded. "Honestly, I couldn't imagine my mother ever remarrying. I suppose that's a childish thought. Stephen Markham worked in the accounting division and had been a family friend. His wife had died a few years earlier from cancer. He and Mom bonded at first through their shared grief and then over a love of old movies and wineries. In truth, Dad wouldn't have wanted her to be alone forever. Now, I'm glad they have each other."

"You still close with her?"

She smiled and nodded. "I have dinner with Mom, Stephen, and Alex. Mom sold our family home when she married Stephen, and they bought a new house in a gated community with a golf course. It's lovely but lacks the sentiment of the home I'd grown up in. But I think that's good... a new start for them. Family pictures with my dad are in the house. Stephen doesn't want us to feel like Dad isn't still a part of us."

"And Alex?"

She smiled, thinking of her stepbrother. "Alex was a bonus sibling, although later in life. He was in high school when his mom died and then in community college when his dad and my mom got together. His dad convinced him to go into chemistry and work at GeoTech. He's young and enthusiastic. He's worked for a couple of years as my laboratory assistant."

"And how's that working out?"

She opened her mouth to answer his question with an, "Oh, it's fine," but something in his voice caused her to hesitate. His eyes were on her, searching. It struck her that Terrance gave all his attention to her when he talked, never wavering. Flippant, easy responses weren't what he wanted or deserved. "Sometimes it's a bit annoying."

He remained silent although one brow lifted.

She understood the unspoken question. In fact, she'd come to understand a lot of his quiet mannerisms in the little time they'd spent together. She appreciated the quiet. Too much noise was often overwhelming, especially when she couldn't see clearly. And many times, people overcompensated when they talked to her, chattering away to clarify things when she preferred shorter explanations.

Jerking slightly, she explained her comment about Alex. "As I said, he's young. Sometimes he seems more interested in telling his friends that he works for an explosive company and reminding his coworkers that he's *in the family business*." Shrugging, she waved her hand dismissively. "But he follows directions and is enthusiastic about learning what he can."

Cocking her head to the side, she now asked, "I'm curious. Why do you ask about him?"

"He seemed more interested in what he could do in Las Vegas than about being your employee."

Now her brows lifted. "Well, he did come a few days earlier for a vacation. Anyway, he's a young man who has a chance to cut loose here. Drinking, having fun, seeing some adult shows, and probably gambling a little. It's his first time here, so he'll live it up a little."

He dipped his head to the side, taking her point, but remained silent. It was easy for her to imagine that Terrance never did anything for fun. "What about you? What do you do besides work?"

"Work out."

Her chin jerked back slightly. "Oh... well, besides working out?"

"Run. Practice shooting. Lift weights. Go on maneuvers with the other Keepers. Kayak. Swim—"

Her hand shot upward. "Wait. I know you must do all that for your work, but I asked what you do besides work?"

"I just told you. That's what I do in my spare time."

"Mr. Bennett! Surely, you do something for fun!"

His mouth pressed into a fine line, and she was mesmerized by the tight muscles making up the hard planes of his face. He looked to the side, and his gaze seemed to move over the others in the restaurant before returning to her face. Finally, he hefted his shoulders before turning his palms up on the table. "I... well, I work on my house."

An air of uncertainty surrounded him, but she couldn't imagine the ultra capable Terrance being unsure about telling her what he enjoyed. Grinning, she said, "Tell me about it."

Brow lowering, he shifted in his seat before lifting

his coffee and draining the last drop. Setting it down, he sighed. "It's not fancy."

Leaning forward, she placed her hand on his arm and peered closely. "It doesn't have to be fancy. It should just be something you like."

Their gazes held, and time ceased to matter. For all she knew, it could have been seconds, minutes, or years. She couldn't look away if her life depended on it, needing to see the emotions in his eyes crashing like waves upon the sand.

He spoke, and she was riveted to each word.

"My house is small. Kinda remote. It was a cabin with two bedrooms and one bathroom, originally built by a man who wanted a place for his family to vacation. More than camping, but not with all the bells and whistles of modern accommodations. With the help of a contractor and my friends, I've added on to the back, so there are now three bedrooms and another bathroom. It's got a view of the mountains, and the ocean is only about a fifteen-minute drive. A couple of friends don't live too far, so I have privacy and company when needed." He looked down at her hand resting on his before lifting his gaze again and continuing. "There was an old garage, separate from the house, but I connected the two with the addition. Most of the work I do myself. I like working with my hands, creating something that's all mine."

Her lips curved more with each word. Terrance didn't talk much, but when he opened up, his eyes lit from a fire deep inside, and she could have stared into their depths all night.

9

Bennett waited in the hall outside the ladies' room, having escorted Diana there after the meal. His gaze moved up and down the hall out of habit, but his mind was firmly locked on the beautiful woman who'd once again wormed her way past the barrier of his professional interest.

Okay... I walked with her around the gallery, and we had dinner. Now I'll deposit her upstairs where she can go into her room, and I can spend the rest of my evening mentally preparing to take care of her conference security.

Pleased to have snapped back into security mode, he focused on the door across from where he stood, not caring if every woman who walked out was startled at seeing his hulking glare. *She's been in there for several minutes. How long is appropriate before I check on her?* He rolled his eyes. *That would be great... storm into a ladies' room when she probably has to wait in line.*

The door opened again, and this time, Diana appeared. She stepped hesitantly into the hall with one hand lightly resting on the doorframe. He rushed forward, his long legs reaching her in just a few steps. As soon as he neared, she smiled widely and let go of the doorframe to reach out toward his arm.

"You don't have to rush."

"I promised I'd be right here. Just didn't want to look like a pervert, but wanted to make sure you didn't have to wonder where I was."

Her fingers squeezed his arm, and his chest clenched. Sucking in a breath, he fought to find his resolve. When he guided her toward the elevators, the sound of music met their ears as the automatic doors near the back of the lobby opened.

She bounced on her toes. "Can we go outside and watch the fountain show?"

Staring down into blue eyes filled with hope, he couldn't deny her anything. "Absolutely."

He had no doubt he'd given the right answer when her face lit with excitement. They made their way outside to the huge pool and found a place along the fence perimeter to stand. The Bellagio fountain show was a major attraction and free to the public. As more people crowded around, he hated the idea that she was jostled. "Here. Hold on to the fence."

As soon as she placed her hands on the black metal fence surrounding the fountains, he stepped behind her and placed his large hands on either side of her much smaller ones. Now, his body encircled her. She twisted her head around, looked up at him, and smiled. He dipped his chin to hold her gaze, and her mouth was so close at this angle.

"Thank you," she whispered.

Sucking in a deep breath, he forced his lips to curve before jerking his chin forward. "You don't want to miss the show."

She nodded, then faced forward again, and he let out a long, slow breath, hoping he'd kept it silent. She had her back pressed to his chest, but he kept his hips angled away so she couldn't feel his response to her being so close. Drawing on the focused command of his body, he battled the desire coursing through his blood.

He tipped his head back and stared up at the night sky. With the multitude of lights from the hotels and casinos, it was impossible to appreciate any stars that might be visible. He missed the view from his home, where nothing marred nature. A vision of Diana being there whispered through his thoughts, but the music started again, jarring him back to the present.

The fountains burst forth into their intricate water dance, and she leaned forward, her fingers tightly clutching the fence. He wondered how much she could see or if it was all a blur.

As though she could hear his thoughts, she said, "I can see lights flashing and the movement of shadows. And hear the music, of course. But it's still beautiful."

While he stared at the water show over her head, his heart pounded faster than the rhythm of the music. "Not as beautiful as you," he whispered, glad that the music crescendoed and the crowd clapped, keeping his spoken words from being heard.

While other spectators nearby moved around, coming and going, Bennett continued to envelop Diana with his protective arms surrounding her. If he'd believed in magic, he would have sworn a spell had woven its web over the two of them. When the last musical note ended and the dancing water fountain silenced, he didn't move, afraid of breaking the spell, not wanting it to end.

Finally, her fingers slipped off the top of the fence. He remained in place, his feet rooted to the sidewalk and his hands still gripping the fence railing, bracketing her in. The instant it took his brain to catch up to what he needed to do, her head leaned back against his chest, erasing the hint of space he'd maintained. They stood in silence, close but barely touching. He had no idea what she was thinking, but he was certain his body wouldn't obey the command from his brain to move away from her.

Inhale. Exhale. Inhale. Exhale. Calling upon his training, he kept his breathing steady even as his heart rate increased. She sighed and turned, still within his arms. She peered upward and placed her hands on his arms.

"That was fabulous!"

He smiled at her enthusiasm, sure he'd never smiled so much in a day. "Yeah, it was. Thank you."

Her head tilted to the side, her blond hair flowing over one shoulder. "Why are you thanking me?"

Scoffing, he replied, "This isn't something I'd have done on my own. But with you, I got to enjoy something new and wonderful."

"Good." She looked around as though just realizing the crowd had dispersed. "I suppose we should head up to the room. Tomorrow's conference starts early."

Agreeing, he forced his hands to release the fence railing, and just as they fell to his side, he crooked his elbow once again. She accepted the gesture, tucking her hand against his body as they walked back along the pool and into the hotel. The casinos and floor shows were in full swing, and people rushed around, sending his smile to morph into a glare as he kept others from bumping into her.

"Looks like this place wakes up about the time I'm ready to go to bed," she observed.

Silently agreeing, he was on heightened alert. Hating unpredictable crowds, he led her to the elevators. Once on their floor, he opened their suite door and completed a sweep of the interior before breathing easier. Turning, he saw her grinning and walked closer so she could see his face before he lifted a brow.

"Sorry. I still can't get used to having security. It seems so over the top. But please don't be offended," she rushed to add. "I'm glad you're here."

He'd had clients thank him before. Men clap him on the back and offer him a drink—sometimes in genuine gratitude or to try to prove their cock was bigger. The latter he hated. No matter who he was or what he did, a real man had no need to prove anything. Women clients either shrank from his unsmiling expression and serious demeanor or, on a rare occasion, propositioned him. Those he always turned down. He wasn't opposed to a sex-only encounter but never with a client.

But Diana's simple words of appreciation, combined with her bright face as she peered intensely at him, had him long to reach out to tuck a wayward strand of hair behind her ear, just to see if it was as soft as he imagined.

But he was a hulk, and she was delicate. He was a former grunt who killed for Uncle Sam, and she was a brilliant chemist. And she was a client, and he was a Keeper. It didn't matter that his coworkers and even his boss had fallen in love on missions; relationships just weren't in the cards for him. He was much more likely to end up with his heart trampled.

Blowing out a long breath, he nodded. "You should probably head to bed, Dr. Olson. Tomorrow will be another long day."

Nodding, she stifled a yawn. "I'm usually in bed early, so I might be dragging tomorrow. But who cares?" Laughing again, she threw her arms out. "I got to stroll through an art gallery, have a delicious dinner, and experience the Bellagio fountains. All with a handsome man! I'd say that was a great day!" She patted his arm as she passed him and walked into her bedroom. Turning, she softly called over her shoulder, "Thanks again, Mr. Bennett. Sleep well." Then she disappeared into her bedroom, and the door closed with a click.

Bennett stood in the middle of the living area, his legs apart, his hands on his hips, and his chin touching his chest as he stared at his boots. *Sleep well.* He lifted one hand and rubbed his chest, wondering if indigestion from the meal caused the ache. Or if it was the woman in the next room. *Fuck.*

After checking the locks, he headed into his room. Perusing his secure email, he read the latest intel from LSIWC about the conference, both location and attendees. He'd sent a message earlier asking about Peter Voltov, Lin Kang, and Edgar Masterson.

He scanned the report provided by Natalie and Jeb. Peter Voltov: Russian, now living in Zug, Switzerland, at the NitroSabir industrial plant. Lin Kang: Korean, working for the Korean Explosives Company and living in ChungCheongbuk-do, Korea. Edgar Masterson: Australian company of Orica and living in Queensland.

Sitting in the chair, he flipped on the lamp and continued reading about the various companies and the ISEE. These global companies had developed the explosives used in mining and technology, had locations worldwide, and had exemplary reputations. They weren't involved in warfare or terrorism explosives. *Yet... all it took was someone working on the inside who wanted to sell technology to a foreign company or group.*

An hour passed, and he shut down his tablet, then headed into the shower. He stripped as the water heated and then stepped under the multiple showerheads. The water pounded his muscles, and he grabbed the soap. As he scrubbed his body, his mind drifted to Diana, and he wondered if she was already asleep.

Her blond hair would be spread over the pillow. Her eyelashes would form little crescents on her cheeks. Her lips would be parted just enough for little puffs of air to escape as she breathed deeply. She might be on her side, curled into a protective ball with her hands clasped under her pillow. Or she might be on her back, her arms and legs spread as she starfished in the middle of the bed. She'd wear a nightgown. Something feminine yet simple. Or maybe just a top and shorts.

Each image seared into his mind, and his hand lowered. He stopped and grimaced, with one hand on the tile of the shower wall. It seemed wrong to jerk off to her image. *She's a client. Not some barfly that had been shoving her tits in the face of any man who'd buy her a drink. She's special.*

Yet her image eased the tightness in his gut. Her gaze made him want to stand taller, be worthy, protect, and defend. And he knew that while she would only ever exist as more in his imagination, he wanted to allow himself the idea of being intimate with her for just one moment. Gripping his erection, he stroked the length, and with the image of her smiling up at him, a burn started in his lower back. His balls tightened, and his release shot out of his cock, marking the shower wall. Barely able to hold himself up as all oxygen left his lungs, he pressed his forehead against the tile. Gulping in air to keep from dropping to his knees, his chest heaved with each breath. Finally standing, he tried to remember if he shouted when he came harder than he'd ever come in his life. *Jesus, please don't let her have heard me!*

After rinsing off the shower walls, he turned off the water, stepped out onto the plush mat, and dried with the oversized towel. Listening carefully, he heard no sounds coming from the suite. *She was exhausted and was probably fast asleep, thank God.*

A few minutes later, he climbed underneath the cool covers and lay on his back, one hand under his head, and stared up at the ceiling. Thoughts drifted through his mind... the other Keepers, all friends of his, had found love on missions. How they'd somehow made relationships work with amazing women. Rachel always said it took someone special to be with a Keeper—and these women were.

Now Diana had entered his life. He'd only known her a few days, but her touch sent warmth throughout his body, and her intense gaze, as she brought him into focus, made him want to be worthy of that scrutiny.

Snorting, he closed his eyes. *Stop dreaming and keep thinking of the mission. Tomorrow, I need to be on point, not wishing for things that won't be.*

10

Diana lay in bed, unable to sleep. Her mind was filled with everything that had happened since waking that morning.

Picked up by Terrance. The plane trip where he agreed to describe the view. The drive into Vegas, where he'd detailed the area without being asked, seeming to have already learned what she liked. The way he allowed her to hold his arm when they walked through crowds. The upgraded hotel suite was unlike any she'd ever stayed in before. Lunch by the pool. Giving her an easy out when she preferred not to spend time with Alex or the other conference attendees. Surprising her with the gallery exhibition and then describing the items she had trouble seeing. Dinner in a corner so that it was easy to focus on just him while giving him a chance to make her feel secure. And then at the fountain show when he surrounded her with his body. She'd never felt so safe in her life.

He was so tall that her head fit under his chin when

she leaned back. *God, I can't believe I did that.* So broad he had no difficulty reaching around her to enclose her as she stood near the fence. Her own human shield.

She'd been so moved by the music, the lights, and the movement of water that she'd given over to the emotions swirling through her. And leaning into his strength just seemed natural. He could have stepped back and leaned away, but he remained in place, allowing his warmth to envelop her.

Would a man like that ever want to be with a woman like me? She rolled over and sighed. *I wonder what kind of woman he dates?*

An image of a tall, model-type with perfect makeup and a designer dress that draped on her willowy body while sipping a martini came to mind. Someone with a cool gaze who could scan the room and give Terrance a come-hither look from the other side, then appreciate every nuance of him as he walked over to her.

Or maybe a well-built woman with a deep laugh, tight jeans over a perfect ass, low-cut shirt showcasing a great pair of boobs, sitting at a bar drinking beer and then playing pool with him leaning over behind her as she made each shot.

But a chemist who spends her days at work with explosives and her evenings reading or watching TV alone? Don't think so.

She rolled to the other side and stared at the clock, knowing she would have trouble staying awake at the conference. But sleep was not coming. She'd heard the shower running in the other bedroom and had given in to imagining him naked with the water cascading over the thick muscles and warm skin.

Her body flushed, and heat pulsated from her core, sending tingles outward. Her breasts felt heavy, her nipples aching. Dressed in a camisole and silky sleep shorts, she cupped her breasts, tweaking her nipples, her need rising. Her other hand slid inside her shorts, not surprised to find her folds slick and her clit swollen. Gliding a finger inside, she reached the spot that always did the trick—the spot her few former lovers could never find, although she doubted they actually tried. Working her body, she pressed her thumb over her clit while tugging on her nipple. Crying out as her orgasm sent tremors throughout her core, she clamped her mouth shut, hoping her voice hadn't carried.

Panting, she slowed her breathing as she lay on her back once again. *I'll never have him, but oh my God... just imagining being with him made me come harder than I ever have.*

Body sated, she soon fell asleep.

The light was blinding, and she gasped, sitting up, her breathing ragged. She blinked, and her hand flew upward to cover her face.

"Diana!"

The sound of her name jolted her, but she was only able to squint to see the large shadow filling the doorway. She could still feel the heat from the flash of fire as though it was real and dropped her chin to her chest, trying to protect her face.

Her breaths came in pants, and she tried to steady her heartbeat, though the disorientation kept her off-kilter.

"Diana."

The voice came closer, and the side of her bed dipped. Opening her eyes, she peered at Terrance, and her world straightened. "Oh…" she muttered, her face now flaming. "It was… I had… it was only a dream."

"What kind of fucked-up dream has you screaming out in pain?" he asked, leaning closer. "A fucked-up nightmare, that's what."

She swallowed deeply, but her throat was so dry her breath hitched. He jumped to his feet and stalked into her bathroom. He wore low-slung sweatpants, and she could only imagine women lining up to volunteer to become a piece of material that would drape over his ass or cling to his thighs or cup his crotch. His torso was naked, debunking her assumption that male models were airbrushed to give them abs like she'd just seen. Not one inch of him wasn't drool-worthy.

Before she had a chance to melt into a puddle, he walked back with a glass of water in his hand. She reached for it eagerly, not stopping until every drop was drained. Wiping her lips with the back of her hand, she set the glass on the nightstand. "Thank you."

He sat on the side of her bed again, and instead of feeling odd, having him so close felt comforting. Strangely normal. She stared at her hands clasped on her sheet-covered lap, then lifted her gaze to see the concern in his eyes. "I'm fine, honestly," she assured. "I don't have those dreams often. In fact, it's been a while since one woke me up."

"Can you tell me what it's about?"

A little scoff slipped out. "It's a replay of the accident. You know how some dreams are weird and don't make any sense? Well, when I have this dream and wake up in a sweat, it's always a replica of what happened that day."

He leaned over her and snagged an extra pillow. Placing it behind her, he inclined his head, indicating for her to settle back against the pillows. She obeyed, finding it nice to have someone there when she woke up in terror. In the past, she was always alone, struggling to breathe after the nightmare.

"We were running tests on a variety of chemicals. The lab was secure. All protocols had been followed. Yet… sometimes accidents occur. I had prescription safety goggles but was in the process of changing to the ones that were darkly tinted when one of the assistants went ahead and set the charge off. Unfortunately, the blast was much more intense than anticipated, and a wall of fire blew out toward us. The firewall protected us from the heat, but I was staring straight at the light without my full protective lenses on. It felt as though my head had just exploded," she said, tightening the grip of her hands.

He reached over and placed his hand over hers, his fingers slowly massaging until she loosened her clench and allowed him to link his fingers with hers. He continued to gently rub his thumb over her tense digits, the movement sending warmth and ease throughout her body.

Licking her lips, she shrugged, still holding his gaze. "Anyway, I honestly don't remember much. I know Alex was there holding my hand. Someone hit the alarm that also called for emergency services. The lab soon filled with techs, assistants, other chemists, and firefighters. Jerry and Steven came bursting in. Someone wrapped bandages around my head to keep my eyes closed. I was transported to the hospital where I underwent surgery." She sighed. "And here I am, two years later, making the most that I could out of my career and life while sometimes struggling with the limitations."

"I think you're amazing, Diana."

She noted he used her first name again but couldn't tell if he had realized it. She liked it and wasn't about to draw his attention to the fact. "Well, I have some sight and can still do the job I love even if adaptations had to be made. And even if I have a few nightmares, I'd say I'm pretty lucky when all is said and done."

"Don't belittle what you went through. Or what you suffered. Or how your life changed. You're fuckin' amazing. Own that shit, Diana."

His expression was hard but gentle as he held her gaze. He didn't offer placating sympathy, but his gaze held understanding, making her wonder about his background. His words were sharp but not cutting, instead filling her with power. It *was* okay not to be happy with what had happened. It *was* okay to wish that life had not taken much of her sight. It *was* okay to sometimes feel sorry for herself. She wouldn't wallow in it, but she also didn't have to hide it. "Okay." She grinned. "I'll own that shit."

"Damn straight." He chuckled.

They sat for another moment as their mirth slowed, but their gazes never wavered. A part of her wanted to beg him to stay. To curl up with her, hold her, and not let her sleep alone for once. But how disastrous to discover how wonderful it would be to have that other person in her life only to have them walk away at the end of the conference. "Well…" she began.

He jumped up and looked down at her. "Yeah, if you're okay, then I'll see you in the morning… or rather in a couple of hours."

She nodded and forced the smile to stay on her face. "Sure. Thanks again for checking on me and then listening to me."

"My pleasure." He turned and walked to the door, closing it behind him. At the last second, he stopped and called out over his shoulder, "Sleep well, Diana."

He was gone before she had a chance to respond, but it was just as well, considering she had no idea what to say that wouldn't give him a peek into her heart. Sliding down under the covers again, she blew out a long breath. No longer afraid to close her eyes, she found sleep once more.

11

Bennett escorted Diana to the entrance of one of the ballrooms in the Bellagio where the conference was being held. He'd reviewed her schedule, starting with the keynote speaker and then various breakout sessions, which she'd insisted she was only interested in a few. Luncheon was in another ballroom. And then, more sessions were in the afternoon, with time for informal gatherings, cocktails, and dinner afterward.

Having provided security for conferences before, he found the best way to get through the tedious speakers was to blank out everything but keep his gaze and focus on the room's inhabitants, much like his days as a sniper. He wanted to know who was sitting near her, who tried to maneuver her into a private conversation, and who showed undue interest in her.

But then, who wouldn't show undue interest? He'd gone back to sleep with the image of her in her camisole, sleep-tousled hair, and large blue eyes staring up at him the previous night. And he damn sure knew that image would stay with him for the rest of his life.

Her attire was simple when she stepped out of her bedroom this morning. Black pants. Green blouse. Hair pulled back in a low ponytail. Just a hint of makeup. And black flats. And Christ, he wanted to drop at her feet and worship. If he felt that way, every man in the vicinity would too.

As soon as they entered the crowded room, her fingers clutched his arm. Determined not to leave her until she was seated and comfortable, he leaned down and whispered, "Where would you like to sit?"

"Diana!"

At Alex's voice, Bennett grimaced, unable to keep the growl from slipping out.

Her stepbrother walked over with a smile on his face. He glanced at Diana's grip on Bennett's arm and held out his hand. "Come on, sit with me." Looking up at Bennett, he added, "I've got her from here."

Diana lifted her face and smiled at Bennett. "I'll go with Alex. Will you be…?"

"I'll be near, I promise. Just over on the side of the room where I can see you." He speared Alex with a glare. "And I can see everyone else."

As she and Alex walked toward the side of the room, he watched as Alex talked animatedly, often stopping to greet others. Finally, they entered a row and sat. Bennett breathed easier, observing Diana sitting on the end of a row, easy for him to get to her if needed.

He leaned against the wall, both in plain sight and invisible. Someone might take note of a big man standing to the side, but a hotel like the Bellagio often had security personnel for the hotel and private individuals, so no one paid attention to him. Alex talked to Diana, but whatever he said made her laugh, so he shifted his gaze around the room of about five hundred other participants.

What he couldn't figure out was *why her?* She worked for GeoTech and was the daughter and niece of the founders, so she wasn't a security risk. She now concentrated on teaching courses in explosive theories and developed patents with the other scientists but spent little time actively in the lab or the field. She was working on expanding on the patent chemical innovations her father had started, but it was only in the early developmental stage. Her private life gave no fodder for extortion or blackmail. Anyone wanting to gain access to GeoTech wouldn't go through her. And he couldn't figure out how getting rid of her would make a difference either.

The keynote speaker began, and Bennett had no problem tuning him out. The only information on explosives that he cared about was what he'd learned in the military and what they used as Keepers. The global and mining explosive industry was not a topic he cared about. But even if he had been, his attention was riveted on the room and one occupant.

His gaze continually moved about, little escaping his notice, especially when it came to Diana. The keynote speaker stood on a stage in the front behind a podium with a wide screen behind him. Bennett knew Diana could not see the screen, much less the speaker. But her attention and respect were given, something he noticed Alex appeared incapable of doing. On the other side of Alex sat the two young men from the night before, and the three of them spent time whispering. At one point, Diana punched Alex in the side to shush him, and Bennett was torn between chuckling and wanting to go over and grab the entitled prick by the neck.

He had no problem with people earning degrees but held them in no higher regard than those with life experiences that gave them the education they needed to make their way in life. What irritated the shit out of him was the way Alex had ridden on his dad's coattails and now Diana's. She tried to make excuses for him, but Bennett was good at reading people. His take on Alex was that the young man wanted the prestigious career but wasn't always willing to work hard for it. And the fact that he'd been present when Diana's accident occurred made Bennett trust him less.

Shifting his gaze around again, he took in the multinational gathering. With the conference hosting international companies, over ninety countries were represented, all part of the ISEE. It had been a herculean task, but LSIWC had provided him with a short exposé on each company. All were highly respected, and all with exceptional security. Yet no industry was immune from espionage. And industrial espionage meant that what was stolen and placed on the black market was research, ideas, theories, patents, experiments, and knowledge. There was no bulky product to transport. And the idea that someone would try to get to Diana... *over my dead body.*

When the keynote speaker finished to rousing applause, Bennett walked along the edge of the wall so that he would be closer to Diana when she was ready to move to the next location. She turned her head, her gaze shifting, and he stepped forward. Once again, as soon as he moved into her line of sight, her smile broadened, striking him in the chest and causing his lips to curve upward.

Just over her shoulder, he observed Alex turning away from his companions, and a sour expression crossed his face when he spied Diana moving toward Bennett. Alex quickly covered his scowl, but Bennett had already clocked the annoyance.

Focusing his attention on Diana, he had already memorized her schedule as well as scoped out the smaller conference room locations. "Are you ready?"

Nodding, she reached her hand out and placed it on his arm. The touch felt natural, as though it belonged right where it was. For a man who didn't initiate physical contact other than an occasional handshake or clap on the back with one of his friends, it had taken him a while to become used to a hug from one of the other Keepers' wives or girlfriends.

When he'd taken this assignment, he'd assumed Diana would have someone to assist her physically from location to location. If he wasn't around, that responsibility probably would have fallen to Alex. But now, he couldn't imagine allowing anyone else the honor. His relationship with her might be fleeting, but as he got to know her, he was thrilled to be the one she relied on.

"Hey, Diana, I can take you to the next session since

it's in the room right next to mine," Alex offered, walking up to them.

She glanced at him and smiled. "Thanks, but I'm fine with Mr. Bennett. Anyway, you take the opportunity to hang out with someone new for a change. Enjoy yourself."

"Well, if you're sure…" Alex continued.

"She's sure," Bennett interjected. "And so am I."

Alex held his gaze for just a couple of seconds before glancing at his companions and then back at Diana. "Sure, sure. I get it. Uncle Jerry hired the muscle, so we need to make sure he gets his money's worth."

Not willing to give Alex his attention, Bennett still tamped down the desire to wipe the smirk off her stepbrother's face.

Diana glared at her stepbrother's back, but Bennett didn't want her to waste any more time on him. With so many people at the conference, the room was already a teeming mass of movement, and he wanted her away from the crowds. With her hand still on his arm, they made their way out of the ballroom, the path clearing as Bennett had no compunction about using his height and shoulders to part the crowds.

A soft sound of amusement met his ears, and he looked down to see Diana's free hand covering her mouth to hide her mirth.

"I feel as though I'm with Moses as he parted the Red Sea." She laughed. "Even when I had my sight, I was often the smallest one around and got stuck behind everyone. Once, when I was a child and had come to a conference with my parents, I got separated from them and was at the height of staring at everyone else's butt. Finally, I heard my name called and had to jump up and down shouting for them until people moved out of the way. When I was reunited with my parents, they made me promise to always hold their hand after that, even when I was way too old to do so. But after having been separated from them, I didn't mind!"

"Then perhaps the moral to that story is that I'll require you to hold on to me, as well."

She glanced down at her hand on his arm and squeezed. "I don't think you have to demand that. It seems to be happening naturally." As they moved to a hallway with smaller conference rooms on either side, her brow lowered, and she caught her bottom lip between her teeth.

He was just about to ask what was wrong when she suddenly blurted, "Is that alright? I don't want to take advantage of what you're here to do by holding you. I know, in truth, that's not your job. I can certainly have Alex—"

"It's fine," he stated brusquely. His words came out harsher than he meant when she jumped slightly. Sighing, he never wanted her to be afraid of a brute like him. "I'm sorry. I didn't mean to frighten you. The military drilled giving and following orders, so I'm not very good with gentle speaking."

"You didn't frighten me. In fact, I think you're very good at gentle speaking."

Bumped from the side by several conference attendees, he growled at the group moving past. They muttered their "sorrys" as they looked at him with fear in their eyes. "Fuckers," he groused.

Diana laughed again. "Okay, maybe you're better at gentle speaking with me and not so much with others."

Looking back down at her beautiful smile, his anger eased. "People should be more careful."

"I'm fine," she assured. Glancing at the nameplate by the door, she said, "Okay, this is my room. You don't have to come in if you don't—"

Without giving her a chance to finish her statement, he shook his head. "Let's go, Dr. Olson."

The breakout session was just as boring as the keynote for Bennett. *Jesus, will this ever end?* At least, in the smaller room with only about fifty conference attendees, he had an easier time keeping an eye on her and the others. He recognized Dr. Kang and Dr. Masterson sitting together, their gazes occasionally drifting to Diana.

The speaker droned on. "Attenuation modeling is now extended to transducers and sensors using eight-channel seismographs with sample rates up to 128K."

As soon as the hour session was over, he made his way to her in haste, wanting to escort her to the luncheon in the ballroom so she could sit where she was comfortable. Finding a table near the side door, he held her chair, scooting it in once she was seated. As he stepped back, she twisted her head around, her face scrunched in obvious concern. With one hand still on the back of her chair, he leaned closer.

"Can you sit to eat? No one will care if you're with the conference or not."

His fingers grazed her shoulder as he shook his head. "I'm fine. I'll just be to the side." Her face still held concern, so he added, "I won't be far."

"It's not that. I'm not afraid. I just hate to eat and have you standing during lunch—"

"Hey, Diana." Alex interrupted, sitting at the table, keeping a seat between him and her.

"It's fine, Dr. Olson," Bennett replied, once again keeping his focus on her while noticing Dr. Kang slide into the seat next to her. Straightening, he moved to the side but observed as she was joined by Alex's two friends, along with Dr. Masterson, Dr. Voltov, and another man, introduced as Dr. Hwan Parks. With his back against the wall, he faced the table and turned slowly. Looking at his watch, he tapped out the message to Jeb to check the audio receiver he'd placed on the corner of her chair while he listened, as well as the video from the miniature camera attached to his shirt.

The conversation centered around the conference's sessions and industry news, which was easy for Bennett to filter out.

"I was surprised to see that GeoTech felt the need for added security, Diana," Dr. Masterson said. "Is there something to be concerned about?"

She hefted her shoulders in a delicate shrug. "Mr. Bennett is here to assist me."

"Oh, so he is personal security?"

"In a way, yes."

"Just call him the hulking assistant." Alex laughed, already on his second martini just as the meal was served.

"Alex!" Her sharp voice drew the eyes of others at the table. A blush moved over her face. "My uncle felt that with a crowded conference in an unfamiliar city, it would be best if I had someone who could help me navigate while staying safe. Mr. Bennett is most assuredly *not* my assistant." She smiled toward the others at the table, then shrugged again, offering a light chuckle. "There's no threat other than me getting lost."

"I think you're incredibly brave, Diana," Dr. Kang said, leaning forward. "After an injury like yours... well, to come back so fully to work is miraculous."

"How do you manage?" Dr. Parks asked.

"I don't have to be the one performing in the lab. I have the knowledge and the theories and can direct the lab's research remotely. Alex is invaluable in stepping into the role of being in the lab. I'm certainly able to study the reports that come to me so we can make changes in our equations."

"It's good to know you've been able to adapt so well," Dr. Masterson said.

"That's our Diana." Alex grinned, lifting his drink in salute. "Capable as well as beautiful."

Diana blushed lightly but smiled at the others as they continued their meal. Bennett's fingers flexed into fists at his sides, the unusual emotion of jealousy sliding over him at the smiles she bestowed on everyone. The rest of the meal passed uneventfully, and several at the table left to mingle with others. Diana had eaten little, and he was about to walk over to her when Dr. Kang leaned closer to her.

"I hear that your contrasting energy experiments are soon to be considered revolutionary," he said.

Diana shifted in her seat, her gaze darting up. "Yes. We are proceeding with the first stages of testing soon."

"You know, there are those here at the conference who would love to have the results early."

Bennett watched as the lines around her mouth tightened. "I'm afraid you won't be obtaining that information before we're ready to release it. A great deal of research and analysis still needs to occur first."

"And patents to be obtained."

"Yes, Kin. Absolutely."

"Then I will just say that you need to be very careful here, Diana. Some would trample upon the ethics of this organization to obtain what they want."

A slight gasp was heard, and Bennett pushed off from the wall, his steps eating the distance to her. Tapping his earpiece, Jeb radioed, "Got it. Checking it out."

Bennett arrived at the table, his attention centered on Diana. "Dr. Olson, are you ready for the afternoon sessions?"

She looked up, and a rush of air left her lungs. "Yes. Yes, thank you." Turning back, she inclined her head toward Dr. Kang. "Have a nice day, Lin."

"You too, Diana."

Bennett speared him with a glare, then allowed Diana to place her hand on his arm. As they walked out of the ballroom together, they weaved among the attendees still mingling and the servers starting their cleanup service.

Neither spoke until they were in the hall. "Are you all right?"

She snorted along with her nod. "I'm fine. It was a boring conference lunch with rubbery chicken, asparagus, and chocolate mousse. Just like almost every other conference luncheon I've had."

"You ate very little."

Her brow lowered, and her nose scrunched, giving her a childlike expression. "I really didn't like it much."

"But what about the conversations? Alex? Dr. Kang?"

Her gaze jerked over to him. "How…? What…?" Cocking her head to the side, she stared intently. "Were you able to hear?"

"Yes." When she hesitated, he continued, "That's my job, Dr. Olson. I need to know what's happening around you to know if you're safe."

"And you take your job very seriously."

"Yes, I do. Does that bother you?"

"I… I'm not sure." She licked her lips, then turned, dropped her hand from his arm, and walked to the ladies' room door. Looking over her shoulder, she lifted a brow.

"You're safe in there," he vowed, realizing her concern.

She nodded, then disappeared behind the heavy, ornate door. He sighed, wondering if he'd just destroyed their trust and whatever other emotion seemed to swirl when they were together. He crossed one booted foot over the other and swept his gaze around the hall as he waited.

12

Diana headed straight into the bathroom stall, then hesitated with her hands on her waistband, glancing at the toilet behind her. *How did Terrance hear the conversation at the table? Am I bugged? He said I was safe here.* Shaking her head, she sat and took care of business. She trusted him.

She washed her hands and waited for the drying machine when another conference attendee stepped closer.

"Dr. Olson, I've wanted to meet you. I'm Suzanne Burns from Orica Industries. The Australia division."

"Hello," she greeted just before the whirring of the side by side hand dryers deferred their speech. Once they stopped, she said, "I've met Dr. Masterson. I believe he's from the same division."

"Oh yes, I know him well." Suzanne rolled her eyes. "We don't work together, but I know he's intensely envious of your company's progress. Between you and me, he's a chauvinist. I think it galls him that you, a woman, are such a success."

She blinked, her smile forced, uncertain how to respond.

Suzanne leaned closer as they walked toward the door. "Everyone knows you're GeoTech's star. I think it eats him up that he doesn't have the same prestige as you."

"Well, it's the company's projects, not mine alone." As she entered the hall, she immediately sought Terrance's gaze. Finding it on her as he approached, she smiled. Looking back at Suzanne, she said, "It was nice to meet you."

"Likewise. Maybe we can grab a drink later." Winking, she added, "And damn. You can bring him for drinks also!"

Watching the other woman walk away, Diana placed her hand on Terrance's arm and sighed. "Can we go outside for a while? I'd really like to get away."

He turned them in a different direction, and she allowed him to lead her toward the nearest exit, glad he acquiesced without hesitation. Once they stepped into the sunshine, she sucked in a deep breath and tilted her head back to bask in the warm sunlight on her face. He stayed near until she opened her eyes, and they wandered past the gardens near the pool. He didn't ply her with questions, for which she was grateful. She just wanted to breathe fresh air and let her mind ease. After a few minutes, they found a small, unoccupied settee under a palm and sat beside each other.

When the voices in her head quieted, she smiled. "Thank you. I needed this."

"What's going on, Dr. Olson? How can I help?"

"I've been to conferences and even spoken at several before, but this seems different. Maybe it's because this is the first one since the accident." She appreciated that he waited for her to gather her thoughts. "Having limited vision means I can't read other people's expressions. I hear their words and intonation, but are they joking? Being sincere with a compliment? Making a comment that could be taken as a threat? I'm off balance, and I'm not sure what to do about it."

She wasn't surprised the muscles in his arm tightened. Terrance's protectiveness was at an all-time high, and she wondered if perhaps she should have remained quiet. "I'm sorry. I'm probably just whining—"

"Don't say that," he ordered, his gruffness familiar. "You feel what you feel. Remember, you own it, Dr. Olson."

She chuckled, his words from last night coming back to her. "How much could you hear at lunch?"

"I placed a small transmitter on the top of your chair. It is quite sensitive, and I was able to hear Dr. Kang's comments. I also need to let you know that Alex needs reining in. If he's just immature, his actions, including excessive drinking, could put GeoTech at risk."

She opened her mouth to deny that Alex would do anything to hurt the company, but then snapped her lips together. Tucking a strand of hair behind her ear that had caught in the breeze, she glanced up at Terrance to see him peering intensely at her. His gaze penetrated through all the layers she forced into place with others she didn't know well. The ones who said, "Don't pity me," "I have visual limitations, but I'm not impaired," "Respect the work I do," and "Don't underestimate me."

But with Terrance, the pretenses were all stripped away. She had no idea how someone she had just met—a man unlike any man she'd been around—could make her feel things she'd thought long gone. He made her feel secure in a world that had taken her security. He offered understanding when others only gave sympathy. And she hadn't missed the way his eyes slightly dilated when she was close, giving her the idea that perhaps he felt a rush of lust just as she did when he was near.

"I know you're here on a professional basis only. I get that, truly. But is there any way you can go back to calling me Diana? I don't want to make you uncomfortable, but—"

"Yes."

She blinked, jerking her head at his instant agreement. "Yes?"

He held her gaze, and then his lips curved. "Yes, Diana."

She watched in fascination as the muscles in his face eased. "Just like that?"

Nodding slowly, he never let go of her gaze. "I... I felt as though I needed to keep things professional with you. Calling you Diana seemed to mess with my focus."

"Oh. I don't want to interfere with your ability to do your job." Her fingers flexed on his arm.

"I've never done this before," he admitted, a hint of

red covering his face. "Talking with you and getting to know you felt like…"

"A friendship?"

He chuckled. "Yeah. And I guess I talked myself into the need to back away. Calling you by your professional title seemed appropriate. But I'd really like to call you Diana if that's what you want."

"It is, Terrance. Mr. Bennett was so formal. I know you're here for a job, but you're the only person here who I like being with. I thought Alex would be okay, but now he's getting on my nerves. And everyone else is curious or dances around the accident since this is my first time back at the ISEE. Or I'm worried that someone is looking for industrial espionage and sees me as an easy target."

"Tell me about Alex."

"I want to defend him, but to be honest, I don't know what anyone is capable of. That seems sad, doesn't it?"

"Not sad. Unfortunately, many people aren't trustworthy. You're trusting with your team, which is undeniably a good thing, yet people can have hidden agendas we don't know about. Believe me, I've seen this happen in my line of work."

Her stomach growled, and she remembered that he hadn't eaten either. "When we were walking near the fountain last night, I thought I smelled a hamburger stand. Maybe a food truck?"

He twisted around and grinned. "Yeah, there's one just down the street."

She bit her lip, but her grin slipped out. "Hungry?"

"For a food truck hamburger?"

"Or maybe even a hot dog. Or a slice of pizza. Or a taco—"

Laughter belted out as he rubbed his free hand over his head. "Yeah, sure. I'd love to get something to eat with you."

They stood and walked through the crowds, his arm familiar underneath her hand. "I should feel guilty about skipping the conference this afternoon, but then, I only came for the final speech where they give out awards and accept the one for the company. I don't even know why Jerry insisted that I come."

They stood in a short line at the food truck. "Okay," Terrance began. "They have hot dogs, chili dogs, one or two-patty hamburgers, french fries, and onion rings."

"Oh my God," she moaned, now hungrier than ever. "I'll take two hot dogs and an order of onion rings."

Terrance stepped up and ordered for them both, then led her to the side as they waited. It only took a few minutes for their food to arrive, and they walked over to a bench near the fountains that was still in the shade. Spreading out the fare, she placed her mound of onion rings in the middle.

"If I share my onion rings, will you share your french fries?" she cajoled, batting her eyelashes.

Grinning, he dumped his fries in the middle as well. Soon, their conversation stopped, as the only sounds coming from them were chewing and moaning in pleasure. Struck with how their food enjoyment produced similar sounds to sexual pleasure, her face flamed with a blush that had nothing to do with the sunlight.

It had been a while since she'd had more than getting

herself off, and glancing to the side, she sighed slightly at the idea that Bennett would be just the kind of man she'd be interested in. *Protective. Caring. Attentive. Focused.*

"Is the sun too hot?"

Jumping at his voice, she swung her head around, seeing his brows lowered in obvious concern. "No, I'm fine." Suddenly, she blurted, "Do you notice everything?"

"With you? Yeah."

"Why?" As soon as the word left her mouth, she winced. *Stupid question! I'm his mission.*

He lifted a hand to rub over his head, then shrugged. "You're easy to notice."

That wasn't the answer she expected, but she remained silent, waiting for more. She'd learned that while he was quiet, he would always answer her, giving a well-thought-out response.

He looked away, his gaze moving over the crowds before returning to her. "Because you're beautiful. Not just on the outside but inside. You're smart, but don't try to make anyone else feel less. You're loyal. You want to see the best in everyone. You're special, Diana, so even if you're my mission, I'd still notice you."

"I'd notice you, too." The words were out before she could pull them back. That seemed to be happening more and more in his presence. She wanted to look away in embarrassment but discovered that being so close and staring into his face, seeing the nuances, was the only thing she wanted to do. His mesmerizing gray-green eyes zeroed in on her, holding her captive. His closely shorn hair, a look that totally worked for him, added to the way her heart leaped every time she saw him coming toward her. Each flex of his muscles drew her attention to his arms, shoulders, back, and thighs. And his lips. Those gorgeous, full, strong lips. *If I just leaned in a little closer...*

Her phone vibrated, causing her to jump, breaking the moment. She fumbled in her pocket and scrunched her nose at seeing Alex's name. "Hey, what's up?"

"Where are you? You disappeared."

"I decided to get some air, and we're sitting outside since there wasn't an afternoon session I needed to attend."

"We? You and your bodyguard?"

His petulant tone irritated her. "I'm with Mr. Bennett if that's what you mean."

"Come on, Diana. You know Uncle Jerry was just paranoid. All this cloak and dagger just seems over the top. Even Dad said so."

"You talked to Phillip?"

"Yeah, and your mom. Told them you can't even breathe without that bodyguard stalking your every move."

"You really had no right to do that, Alex, but be assured I'm enjoying my time here, just like you were with your friends. I hope you gain something from the afternoon sessions. I'll be sure to discuss them with you when we get together again." With that, she disconnected, keeping her gaze on her hands gripping her phone.

Terrance stood and tossed their trash before returning to the bench. "You okay?"

Jerking her gaze upward, she nodded. "You want to get out of here?"

"What do you have in mind?"

She grinned. "Let's check out Vegas."

She had no idea what his response would be, but the slow curve of his lips was met with a widening smile of her own. He held out his hand, and she took it eagerly. As his fingers wrapped around hers, she could swear the touch wrapped around her heart.

13

Bennett couldn't remember the last time he'd smiled so much. In truth, he knew the answer... never. He'd never spent an afternoon sightseeing, just walking around, window-shopping, people-watching, and ducking into a few hotel lobbies and casinos to check out the views. And he'd never spent an afternoon with a beautiful woman, her hand in his as he tried to ignore his body's response to her closeness. Focusing on describing what they were looking at, he loved how her face lit every time he guided her through the crowds.

He was still hyperaware of their surroundings, but with no one from the conference knowing where they were or what they were doing, he allowed himself to relax and enjoy the day.

"I can't believe what we've done today!" Diana enthused, jiggling his arm as she tugged on his hand. "I haven't done something like this since... wow, Terrance, I can't remember when. Probably not since college."

"I was thinking the same thing. I've never done this."

She twisted around and peered up at him as though searching. "Never?"

Shaking his head, he held her gaze.

"Never gone sightseeing? Or just walking through a crowded place, looking at people for the fun of it? Eating ice cream from a street vendor?"

"No, never. My family didn't… well, my family wasn't exactly the all-American family. I sometimes hung out at bars while in the military, but that was never really my scene. Since working for LSIWC, life's been about missions, my friends, and working on my house." He waved his free hand outward toward the Strip. "This is all new to me."

"So, um… not what you usually do on a typical date?"

Her face pinkened, and he battled a grin. He could tell she regretted her words as soon as the question slipped out. Yeah, they'd crossed the professional line, which no longer bothered him. Tightening his fingers around hers, he bent closer. "No. I don't date."

"Oh." Her eyes widened, then quickly narrowed. "Wait… why not?"

Now caught in her web, he realized she would naturally have questions. He ducked his head as his shoulders hefted. "Never found anyone I wanted to spend more time with than a hookup, and honestly, I don't do that a lot either."

"Oh." Her chin dropped so that her eyes were at his chest level, and he missed them on his face. She might not be able to see much out of her left eye, but when she held his gaze, he felt all her attention on him.

She always studied him so intently, and while he knew it was partially due to her vision limitations, it also was simply part of her—the desire to know and understand. And being the object of her view, he no longer felt like squirming away. Instead, he simply remained steady, a smile on his face, waiting. As usual, he didn't have to wait long before she tilted her head back and allowed her gaze to rove over his face.

"What now?" she asked softly.

"How about drinks?" Seeing she needed more of an explanation, he pressed forward. "At one of the nicer hotel bars. Like a date." The last words nearly choked him, but not because they weren't sincere… just rare and terrifying. He'd rather stare down a target for two days before firing off a kill shot than have asked a woman like Diana on a date for drinks. Time stood still as unaccustomed fear crawled up his throat. Just when he was about to blow it off as a joke, a smile filled her face, causing her to beam.

"I'd love to!"

The air rushed from his lungs. Grinning, he looked around and spied The Venetian hotel across the street. Moving to the intersection, they crossed with the crowd when the light turned. He led her carefully to the entrance and into the lobby.

The cool-blue lounge decor had sofas scattered about the middle, tables around the edges, and a long wooden bar against one side. Behind the bar, the mirror and glass shelves reached toward the ceiling, filled with bottles sparkling in the low lights. The tables lining the picture window at the front allowed patrons to view the bustling sidewalks outside. There were people inside, but most tourists were out sightseeing at this time of day, and the casino lounge lizards hadn't arrived yet.

Looking down, he asked, "Where would you like to sit? Over by the window to see outside? Or the inner glass wall so you can peer into a part of the casino?"

She nibbled her bottom lip as she looked around, her brow furrowed.

"Whatcha looking for?" he asked, uncertain what she needed.

"Is there a quiet corner? A place just for us?"

The left side of his chest jumped, and his fingers twitched against hers in his hand. "Um... yeah... that'd be great." Sending his eagle-eyed gaze around the room, he turned and led her to the far corner to a two-seater table with a few potted palm trees nearby. Offering the server a chin lift, he waited until Diana settled into her seat, then shifted his chair closer to hers before sitting.

The server came by, and Diana carefully perused the cocktail list. Finally, she grinned. "I'll have the watermelon martini."

He chuckled at her obvious exuberance. "This is the first drink besides wine I've seen you order."

"I usually don't drink at all when I'm out. Alcohol makes it harder to focus, but I feel safe with you."

It took a few seconds for her comment to hit him. With her visual limitations, she was never able to just let go without having to always be aware of how to move around. Her hand was lying on the tabletop, and he reached over to engulf it in his. "You'll always be safe with me."

The drinks came, and they listened to the music as he downed his whiskey and loved watching her enjoy her fruity cocktail.

When finished, they sat, their eyes only on each other. "Tell me something about yourself," she asked. "Something you don't usually tell other people."

At first, he wanted to deny her, only because he hated talking about himself. "I'm not very interesting." He hoped that might put her off.

"You're interesting to me."

As always, he felt sincerity pouring from her. He knew she wasn't just asking to pass the time. Or to fake concern. Or looking for him to be broken so she could try to fix him. The truth was, he was not so afraid of her finding out his demons but discovering he might not be worth her interest.

She leaned closer, her gaze assessing. "You know so much about me. There's not much I can hide. But I don't want you to share yourself with me just to feel like we're on equal ground. I really want to know more about you."

He allowed himself to consider that the time they spent together was almost date-like in a world where they might be together as a couple. But his story wouldn't fit her idea of a man to go out with. He scrubbed his free hand over his head and, for the first time, wished he had spent more time thinking about his appearance. His clothes and hair were always efficient and comfortable, not for style or looks.

Her thumb gently glided over his knuckles, the barest touch bringing his attention back to her. "No matter what you tell me, it won't change what I think about you," she vowed.

Her words were pretty, but he wasn't going to hold her to them. She was too sweet to be with someone like him. If only he could convince his heart that it didn't matter that they wouldn't see each other after this mission.

He allowed her touch to lull him into a blissful state where he didn't want to be afraid to share. *But when she realizes who I truly am... better that she learns now.*

"The politest version is that I grew up in a house that wasn't nurturing."

She chewed on the corner of her bottom lip. "How bad was it?"

"Hell."

She sucked in a quick breath as her fingers twitched against his. But she didn't let go. Instead, her grip tightened.

Emboldened to get his story out there so that if she was going to run, it would happen before he fell even more for her, he plunged ahead. "I barely remember my mom. I have a few hazy memories of her in the kitchen, but she hated to cook. I remember she'd yell about having to fix food for a brat and her ungrateful husband. Of all the memories I could have, that's the only one that comes to mind. No bedtime stories. No hugs. No walks in a park. Just her calling me a brat and hating her life. I guess she'd finally had enough. When I was four years old, she left and never came back."

"Oh God," Diana breathed, tears forming in her eyes as she clung to his hand.

"Dad? Well, he blamed me. Said they'd been fine before I came along, and my ugly, dumb ass was the reason she left."

"No! He didn't!"

"Oh yeah, he did. Of course, as an adult, I know he was a miserable, worthless piece of shit who was mostly wasted on alcohol. But as a kid, I busted my ass to try to make it all better. I learned to cook with a microwave. I cleaned the house. I did the laundry. I made sure I got my homework done. No Little League. No school activities. No trips. Dad was at work, or when he was at home, he was in the recliner, drinking. I figured if I were the perfect son, then he'd love me. But all I learned was that his belt hurt when it hit my back, and his fists hurt just as much when I got older."

He stopped looking at her and looked down at the table. Once started, the words flowed, but he sure as hell didn't want to see the rejection in her eyes. Her fingers twitched against his hand.

"Oh God, Terrance. I'm so sorry."

"Don't be, Diana. It is what it is. Eventually, I grew to my height and started working out. I was a lot bigger than him. He stopped hitting me, probably scared I'd hit back, but I never did. I'd seen what a lack of control had done to him and vowed never to do the same."

"Was there no one for you?"

He nodded. "An older couple in the neighborhood used to let me come over when my dad was on the rampage. Mable would make dinner and bake cookies. She'd let me read the books they had in their house.

Harvey would pitch to me and taught me how to hit a baseball."

"And other kids?"

"I was kind of a loner. Never really needed other kids too much." Pulling his bottom lip between his teeth, he sighed. "Harvey had a few old photographs from his days in the Army. I thought the uniforms and weapons were the shit, and that got me thinking about what I'd like to do when I grew up."

"That's why you joined the Army?"

"God knows my dad didn't give a shit what I did. By the time I graduated, Dad had spent more time at the local bar than at home. I joined right out of high school to escape. I had no false ideals about patriotism, flag waving, or fighting for my country. The recruiter had a big poster that said, "Be all you can be." Looking at it, I knew that I never had that growing up. There were no parental expectations for me to be anything, and Harvey told me the Army would teach me how to do something, pay me for it, and get me the hell out of Waco. I graduated from high school on a Friday night and was on the bus on Monday morning, having already signed up. Dad never even got out of bed to say goodbye."

His gaze had remained stuck to the table next to their linked hands. Hating to be weak, he lifted his chin, determined to accept whatever emotion she expressed on her face. Shocked, he found her blinking back tears unsuccessfully as one slid down her cheek. He immediately lifted a finger and wiped it away, his heart pounding. "Don't cry for me. Please, don't waste your tears on me."

"Oh, Terrance," she whispered. "If ever someone was worthy of having a tear shed for them, it would be you."

The background noise of the bar fell away, leaving only the sound of their breathing and hearts beating. He loved the way she stared at him—a mixture of peace and adoration in her eyes, yet he knew the story needed to continue.

"There's more. I got through basic training and discovered I had laser focus... an eagle eye, and no compunction about killing another person if needed. My range skills had me at the top of my class. They recruited me to go through Army Ranger and sniper training. I was a trained killer. Not just in the heat of battle but lying in wait to take out whoever I was commanded to."

The words fell between them, and he refused to look away, determined to see whatever she felt.

Her face softened. "You were a soldier. You followed orders."

His tongue ran along his bottom lip as he considered her words, as well as the gentle expression on her face. "That simple?"

She huffed. "Did you go out and kill people on a whim or just because you didn't like them?"

He remained perfectly still. "No."

"You were in the military. You did what you were trained to do." She sucked in a deep breath and let it out slowly, leaning forward. "I'm not naive. I can't pretend to understand what it was like to take a life, what your training entailed, or what your job was like. And more importantly, how you coped with the stress."

Her fingers traced over the calluses on his fingertips. "GeoTech is known for our geo-explosives used in mining and construction. But there are always uses for our products sought by other governments or regimes, other companies, and even terrorist groups. And I'd be stupid to think that some of our explosive products don't fall into the wrong hands. I'm not one to throw stones, even if that was my nature."

He leaned back, his gaze still searching her face, the oxygen thick between them as he tried to drag it into his lungs. He knew what he was. No illusions. But being with her made him long for things unspoken. Things unbidden. He opened his mouth to speak what was moving through his mind. *"You're beautiful. You're amazing. You're special. You make me feel more than I've felt in a long time. You make me want to be more. You..."*

But no words came out as he forced them down. Not willing to fuck up anything happening with something that might make her terrified of his feelings, he simply rubbed her fingers with his as they ordered another drink and listened to the music in the background.

"Tell me something about you that makes you happy," she suddenly demanded, her attention back on him.

Without giving it much thought, he replied, "I like to bake bread."

She startled, jerking back. "No way."

He tensed, wondering if she would laugh. Or worse, tease him. He should have known better.

"Oh my God! I do, too!"

Now it was his turn to jerk. "Really?"

"Yes. It started in high school when my chemistry teacher explained how cooking was just chemistry... different combinations of elements... ingredients and heat. We made bread one day as a lab project, and I was hooked."

He smiled, imagining a young Diana eagerly experimenting in the kitchen, searching for the perfect rise, the perfect timing, the perfect recipe.

"Can I ask how you got started?" she asked, her expression hesitant.

Shrugging, he nodded. "It's no secret. Mable would always make bread, especially on holidays. One Christmas, when I was about eleven years old, I went to their house. Dad was drunk, and we'd had no tree, no Christmas decorations, and no presents—"

"Oh God, Terrance. I'm so, so sorry," she rushed, her eyes glistening with more unfallen tears.

Trying to ignore the well of emotion she showed for him, he gently rubbed her hand again. "As soon as I stepped into their house, it was just what I needed. There was a tree in the corner of the living room and a couple of presents underneath with my name on them. And the house smelled fuckin' amazing. I don't even remember what the presents were because once I'd had a slice of her homemade bread, I was a goner. Begged her to teach me how to make it."

A smile replaced Diana's tears. "She taught you!"

"Yep. She showed me each step, and for the next seven years, until I left for the military, we would bake bread every chance we got. To this day, the scent of homemade bread brings back the best memories of my childhood." Shaking his head, he chuckled. "I've never told anyone that."

Her teeth captured her bottom lip as she held his hand. "Then I'm honored."

Wanting to lighten the mood, he leaned forward and grinned. "I have some yeast starters that I've had for a long time to tempt you with."

Eyes wide, she bounced in her seat. "We should get together when this trip is over and compare recipes. We could have a baking day."

Stunned that she wanted to spend more time with him, he nodded. "That'd be great."

She leaned back in her chair with a satisfied expression on her face. He couldn't help but stare, his heart beating just a little faster. Once more, they listened to the music before finally deciding they were ready to leave. He tossed money onto the table and stood. Carefully pulling her from her seat, he grinned. "Let's go exploring some more."

"Show me the way." Looping her hand through his crooked arm, she tossed her head back and laughed.

It was the most beautiful sound he'd ever heard.

14

Diana couldn't believe how wonderful the day had turned out. She'd come to the conference expecting to be alone, bored, and hyperaware of her visual limitations. And she never imagined meeting a man like Terrance Bennett. Not only meeting but talking with, drinking with, laughing with, and now, once again, walking hand in hand with him down the sidewalks of Las Vegas. She'd told him she wasn't naive but had to remind herself of that fact.

He's here for a job. I'm a mission. But it doesn't mean we can't enjoy each other's company.

The next several hours were filled with their leisurely stroll, something his height and build made easier. He never rudely pushed or shouldered people out of the way, but his size simply parted the throngs, allowing them to move past unmolested.

By late afternoon, she knew they needed to return to the Bellagio and the award dinner of the conference. She sighed, and guilt hit. *That's the reason I came to Las*

Vegas. Casting her gaze to the side and upward, she squashed the smile that threatened to explode across her face at the sight of Terrance. His gaze continually moved around, always looking out for her. If someone wasn't paying attention as they walked on the sidewalk and came too close, he would growl and throw his arm out to keep them from bumping into her. And when he looked at her, a little smile escaped, giving the impression that smiling was rare for him and, therefore, all the more precious.

"Are you getting tired?" he asked.

Shaking her head, she replied, "No. But I know we need to head back to the hotel. I have to get ready for the award dinner."

He inclined his head to the right. "I've been leading us back here, figuring you needed time."

She should have known he was in control and making sure she was where she needed to be. "Thank you, but I feel guilty. It's not your job to—"

"Shh," he said, pulling her over to the side of the lobby as they entered the hotel and walked toward the elevators. "My job is to keep you safe. How I do that is up to me."

He kept her tucked in close, once more throwing glares at anyone who came near them in the crowded elevator. His hand rested on her lower back, the feel of his fingertips like a brand.

Soon, they were on the floor and walked silently to the door. Once inside, he pressed her gently to the side, and she waited as he scoped out the entire suite. As he stalked back toward her, he came into focus, his outline and shape already so familiar to her.

"All clear?"

"You're good to go."

She started toward her bedroom, desperate for a shower, when she stopped and looked over her shoulder at him, finding his gaze still on her. "Tonight? You'll stay close?"

"I'll be right there, Diana."

"I wish you could sit with me at dinner."

"I do, too."

His simple confession surprised her, and she tilted her head to the side.

"But I can't. I would love to be right with you during the meal, but it doesn't allow me a full view of the room."

She nodded, then turned and moved into her bedroom, closing the door behind her. She luxuriated in a long, hot shower, scrubbing off the layer of sweat and dust from walking outdoors. As her short fingernails dragged along her scalp, she leaned back to allow the water to cascade over her body and rinse out her deep conditioner.

She practiced her acceptance speech, hating the idea of public speaking but glad to have the opportunity to pay tribute to her dad. But her mind drifted to Terrance, easily tossing out all other thoughts.

Finishing, she applied her makeup and dried her hair, curling the ends so a soft wave of blond silk fell over her shoulders. Once dressed in long black, wide-legged pants and a soft gray silk top, she walked out of her bedroom, her gaze down as she fastened her earrings.

She spied Terrance in his typical black outfit, but it wasn't until she neared that her feet stumbled on the plush carpet. He was wearing a long-sleeved, button-up, black dress shirt, the fit obviously tailored for his build, tucked into black dress pants. While black seemed to be his signature color, he was gorgeous whether dressed up or casual.

She searched for a word to describe him but realized how innocuous certain descriptors were. In the scientific world, definitive elements, combinations, and equations were ways to describe everything accurately. There was no guesswork. But when trying to describe the way someone looked, you couldn't help but project your own desires.

Handsome? Yes, but not in the Hollywood pretty boy way. Mesmerizing? Yes, because his gaze was locked in on her, and she found she didn't want to look anywhere else. Impressive? Yes, but not because of wealth or status, but in sheer physical strength. Sexy? Oh yeah. While he wasn't reminiscent of the typical man she'd once dated, she could only imagine what it would feel like to be surrounded by his embrace, having his full attention as he made love to some very lucky woman.

"You look beautiful, Diana."

His deep voice reverberated through her, and she quivered, blinking to bring her focus back to the moment at hand. "Thank you. And I have to say I was just trying to figure out what word used to describe you, but nothing seemed to fit. Suffice it to say, you look amazing."

She watched as he checked his weapon before holstering it and pressed her lips together. His actions were a stark reminder he was there for a purpose, regardless of how much she felt a threat was minimal. When he was ready, he waved her in front of him, and they exited their suite, once more moving to the elevators. The evening at the Bellagio was different from the daytime. People still milled around in crowds, but many wore evening clothes to the bars and restaurants. Masses moved toward the casinos. And with the ISEE conference having its gala dinner, those attendees were evident as they made their way to one of the ballrooms.

She plastered her usual smile on her face, unable to clearly see those around her. Hearing her name called, she recognized Alex's voice and smiled as he came closer.

"Hey, Diana. I'm glad I saw you. Can I walk you in since we'll be seated together?"

She glanced to the side and caught Terrance's nod. Turning her smile back to Alex, she agreed. "That would be lovely."

As they walked away, she glanced over her shoulder, seeing Terrance follow closely. Just knowing he was nearby made her feel more secure.

"I wanted to apologize, Diana," Alex began. "I didn't mean to sound so petty when I talked to you earlier."

"Thank you, that means a lot that you apologized."

"I knew you wouldn't participate much in the conference, but I thought you might enjoy talking to some of the other ISEE members. A few of them have asked me about you, and I got stupidly pissed when it seemed that you preferred Mr. Bennett's company."

She patted his arm. "You're here for the conference and to enjoy some time in Vegas. I really only came for tonight's awards dinner but have been able to enjoy some time in Vegas, as well."

"You know I would've escorted you around," Alex said as he leaned closer, a contrite expression on his face.

"Are you kidding? You're young and single, and this is your first time in Vegas. You need to be with your friends and enjoying yourself, not hanging out with me."

They made their way to the table near the front, and as he glanced over her shoulder, she was sure he was looking for Terrance.

"I just don't understand why a bodyguard is needed," Alex said. "It keeps some of the other conference attendees from feeling like they can approach you."

"With the possibility of someone at the conference wanting trade secrets to sell on the black market," she whispered, "it just seemed prudent."

"Well, it's hardly like anyone here would try to do that to you."

They reached the table, and he held her chair while she sat. With others around nodding their greetings, she refused to continue to justify to him. Perhaps it was his youth, although he was only six years younger than her. But somehow, he seemed much younger. She often wondered if he was genuinely interested in the explosive industry or was just glad to have a ready-made job when he got out of college.

She'd never doubted his work ethic and knew she could be a taskmaster. Scientifically curious, she always sought a better solution, new information, and a hypothesis to study. And Alex had been exceptional at following her directions. *But does he want more?*

As the gathering around them grew, she could not discern individual faces, keeping a pleasant smile plastered onto her face so no one would notice. She glanced to the side, and while she could only see the tall, dark shadow of a man standing by the wall, her smile was now genuine, knowing how close Terrance was.

The dinner service began, and soon the cacophony of sounds rose in the air. Voices, laughter, the clinking of silverware and plates. Alex had turned slightly away, chatting with the person on the other side of him, leaving her to make small talk with the person on her right.

She was glad when the dessert plates were whisked away, and they were served coffee and wine as the speeches began.

Several awards were presented, acceptance speeches were delivered, and applause was offered. Finally, the Master of Ceremonies announced the posthumous lifetime achievement award for James Olson, founder of Olson GeoTech. As she pushed her chair back, it suddenly struck her that she needed assistance up on the stage and started to turn toward Alex.

A large hand gently cupped her elbow, and she jerked around to see Terrance standing at her side.

"Dr. Olson. Allow me to escort you."

Heart light, she walked to the side of the stage and up the steps, her confidence in place with his proximity. As soon as she reached the presenter, Terrance faded away, but she knew he was close. Holding the plaque, she stood at the podium and looked across the large room, her vision only allowing her to view a sea of colors swirled together but no individual faces.

As she looked down at her speech cards, a memory slammed into her. *She was practicing for her doctorate dissertation defense when nerves were getting the best of her. Groaning in frustration, her mom came into the study and smiled. "You know, your father once got this nervous, too."*

Staring incredulously, she scoffed. "Dad? I don't believe it!"

"Oh yes. It was at our wedding. He was terrified that he would mess up the vows."

She burst out in laughter, joined by her mother. "What did he do? Practice?"

"Oh no. That made him more nervous. We asked the minister to break the vows down into tiny half sentences. At least then, he could get through them without making a mess of them."

"Did it work?"

"Yep!" Her mother stood and walked over, hugging her. "Your dad and I are so proud of you."

She closed her eyes for a few seconds, and her mind filled with her father's smiling face with his glasses pushed up on his head as he worked on something intricate and then popped them back on his nose as he scribbled the equations into his notebook.

Smiling, she opened her eyes and no longer cared that in front of her were faces she couldn't see distinctly. All that mattered was that she gave voice to a man who could no longer do so.

"On behalf of Olson GeoTech, and in memory of my father, James Olson, I accept this prestigious award for his lifetime achievement in industrial explosives. My father spent his career fascinated with the technology of explosives but determined to find new and innovative ways to harness energy safely. He believed in increased productivity, a safer environment, and, most of all, the safety of those using our products and technology. He was proud of the work of the ISEE's commitment to the integrity of our profession. We know some would use our ideas, research, and ultimately our products in unintended ways. But my father proudly believed in the integrity of the employees at Olson GeoTech. He is no longer with us, but we are continuing his legacy and, within this year, will launch the expanded and improved contrasting energy project. And while tonight we honor the lifetime achievement he attained, for me, he was not only my mentor, my boss, but mostly just my dad. I was lucky. And for those of you who knew him, you were, too."

She turned and walked toward the stairs to a standing ovation, knowing that Terrance would be waiting. His hand reached out and carefully guided her down the steps. He escorted her back to the table, where he held her chair, then disappeared over to the wall, where he took up his sentry again.

The others at the table congratulated her. Alex's

expression held a slight pinched appearance just before he leaned forward, patted her shoulder, and smiled, making her doubt what she thought she'd seen.

She barely remembered the rest of the award ceremony, ready to enjoy the evening with Terrance. After the final announcements, she moved to gain Alex's attention. "I'm heading up to my room after this, so go out tonight and have fun."

"Are you sure? I was just going to hang out with some of the guys from the conference."

"Go." She laughed. "Go to a bar. Go dancing. Tomorrow's the last day of the conference, so enjoy Vegas while you can."

He laughed and leaned forward, kissing her cheek. She stood, not surprised, when Terrance appeared again, and she placed her hand on his arm. Her breathing slowed as his intense gaze penetrated her shell. *Enjoy Vegas while I can. Good advice for me, too.*

This time as they walked out of the massive ballroom, he didn't push past the crowd but walked slowly, allowing the conference attendees to shake her hand as they thanked her, and many had an anecdote to share about her father. Appreciating their words of kindness, she was still anxious to escape the crowd.

Finally, they made it into the lobby, and he bent to quietly ask, "What would you like to do now?"

She turned and placed both palms flat on his chest. Tilting her head back to hold his gaze, she smiled. "I'd like to go upstairs to our suite."

15

If Terrance was disappointed in Diana's answer, he didn't show it as he simply escorted her to the elevator. Once in their suite, they repeated the now familiar arrival maneuvers, and she waited until he had checked to see that everything was safe. Once the door was locked and secure, she slipped off her shoes and walked toward her bedroom, calling out, "I'm going to change into something more comfortable. You didn't have a chance to eat during dinner, so why don't you call for room service now that we're here? I'd love a glass of wine."

She quickly brushed out her hair in her bedroom and pulled it back into a low ponytail. Stripping, she showered again, then pulled on sleep shorts and a camisole with a shelf bra. As she stared in the mirror, her outfit was comfortable but certainly showed more skin than she was used to. Grabbing a mid-thigh length kimono, she slipped it over her shoulders and belted it loosely. Now, with her makeup washed off, wearing comfortable clothes and bare feet, she walked back out into the main area of the suite.

The room was empty, but in a moment, he appeared from his bedroom in black sweatpants with Army embroidered on one leg, showcasing his thick thighs. A short-sleeved gray T-shirt stretched across his chest, the arms barely containing his biceps.

Her gaze drifted down to his feet, surprised to see them bare like hers. It dawned on her that she had not seen him in anything other than boots, but the sight of his toes sticking out from the bottom of his sweatpants struck her as sexy. And she was quite sure she'd never thought feet were sexy before. In fact, from his toes, all the way up, his strong body to the masculine planes and angles of his face, and the intense eyes, the entire package was sexy.

As the word package ran through her mind, her gaze dropped to his crotch, and she swallowed deeply. While it didn't appear that he was sporting an erection, she could tell he was impressive all over. *And the lady lucky enough to enjoy his erection would know just how impressive he was!*

"You're staring, Diana."

Her gaze jumped to his eyes, finding his focus on her. "So are you."

"My reason makes sense. You're fucking gorgeous. But I don't know if I should be nervous or not."

Pressing her lips together, she tried to steady the erratic beating of her heart. "I think instead of being nervous, you should be flattered by my thoughts."

His brows lifted, surprise etched on his face as though her compliment was not something he heard often. Shaking her head, she waved her hand in his direction. "You know you're hot."

His hand scrubbed over his shorn hair, then he gripped the back of his neck and squeezed. She recognized his telltale signs of uncertainty but couldn't imagine why.

"I'm glad you think so, but…"

"If you say I need to have my eyes checked, I'll smack you."

He jerked as his mouth opened before snapping it shut. Laughter burst forth from her at his incredulous expression, and he soon chuckled as well. Drawn by a magnetic force, she stopped just in front of him when a knock on the door halted her movements. He hesitated, his chest heaving with a deep breath before turning toward the door.

He kept his body in the doorway as he tipped the server and rolled the cart in by himself. When he neared again, she asked, "Why didn't you let him come in?"

His gaze swept from her head to her feet before grousing, "Not about to let him see you like that."

Considering she was much more covered than most women at the pool, she furrowed her brow. "Like what?"

"Half naked."

An inelegant snort escaped, and she immediately clapped her hand over her mouth. "Half naked? Terrance, you're crazy. I'm completely covered!"

"Yeah, well, I just didn't feel like sharing."

Her humor fled at his words, and she was glad his back was turned as he set the tray on the table. *Didn't feel like sharing... sharing me?*

Before she had time to consider his words, he had turned to hold a chair out for her. Curious, she moved closer to see what he had uncovered, finding the scent of steaks with baked potatoes smothered in butter filling the air. Jerking her gaze up to him, she stared wide-eyed.

"You didn't eat much of your dinner downstairs."

"You noticed?"

"I notice everything about you."

The air seemed to still around them as their gazes locked. "Oh..." For a moment, she wondered if he would lean closer, but he jolted as though just remembering where he was and sat quickly in the chair. For several minutes, they ate in companionable silence, relishing the meal. She hadn't realized how hungry she was, but in only a few days, it seemed he had noticed everything about her.

And taken care of her.

That part was hard to get used to. Before the accident, she had been more outgoing, enjoying her job, her friends, and her life. But now that the world was blurry, trusting what she could see was harder. Driving was a thing of the past. So was biking, theater movie watching, and wandering in unfamiliar places without an abundance of caution. Her career was still as important, but it had changed based on what she was able to do now. And while adaptability was key to her existence and happiness, she missed her old life.

"You're thinking very hard over there."

His rumble sent her gaze up to find him staring. "Yes, I suppose I am."

"Care to share?"

She looked down, then stood and made her way to the bar to fill another glass of wine. He gathered the dishes, loaded the tray, and set it outside the door. Securing the door again, he walked over to the bar to stand near her.

Turning, she set her wineglass down, gathered her courage, and stepped closer. "I want to kiss you."

She watched him carefully, but other than a slow blink, he didn't move a muscle. "I want to kiss you," she repeated.

"Why?" he whispered in a low growl.

"Why? Because I've been attracted to you since the first moment I saw you." She lifted on her toes and, with her fingers gripping his shoulders, lightly touched her lips to his. At first, his mouth was pillow soft, enticing her to press her mouth closer, discovering the firm muscles underneath. He held himself completely still, but she was determined to break through his reticence. Pulling even closer, she angled her head so that her mouth sealed over his as her tongue darted out to trace the outline of his lips. Just as she felt his resolve slip, his hands gripped her upper arms, and he gently pushed her back just enough to force their lips to separate.

"No..." she groaned.

"I don't want... Taking advantage of you would be the worst thing I could do."

"How would kissing a willing woman be taking advantage of me?"

"Because you're... you're..."

Just as water slowly froze into ice, her blood ran cold until she wasn't sure it still flowed through her veins. Lowering her heels back to the floor, she stared up. "If you dare say that I don't know what I'm doing or give any indication in the slightest that I'm not thinking straight due to my vision, I'll kick you out of this suite faster than you can draw your next breath."

He blinked a deep crease, now marring his forehead. "No, that's not what I meant—"

Her fingers let go of his shoulders, and she pushed back before whirling around. "God, I can't believe this." Sucking in a deep breath, she started toward her bedroom, then stopped and turned to face him. "I apologize, Terrance. I never meant to make you feel uncomfortable. I shouldn't have come on to you when you were trying to do a job. I thought there was interest, but it was wrong of me to—"

"Diana, no, that's not it. I work for you. I can't..." He sighed, the lines around his mouth deepening.

She jerked slightly, taking in what he seemed to be saying. "So... if you weren't on this mission, you'd be interested?"

"Absolutely. No doubt."

Her teeth landed on her bottom lip before she pressed her lips together. Her gaze searched his face, finding his intensity still focused on her. Clearing her throat, she said, "We're two adults, Terrance. There's no reason we can't make this decision if there's interest on both sides."

Time stretched into eternity as the silence filled the space between them. She refused to move, determined that whatever happened would be his decision. She had made her stance clear, but now it was up to him, and as disappointed as she would be, she had to respect his dedication to his job. He didn't move. In fact, she wasn't sure he was still breathing. Remembering he had been a trained sniper, it hit her that he could probably still his entire body for long periods of time, just waiting for the right moment. *Is this going to be that moment?*

Finally, she realized the moment had passed, and he wasn't going to change his mind. Accepting his decision, she felt her chest squeeze, and escape was necessary. A sigh slipped out as a sad smile barely curved her lips. Inclining her head in defeat, she turned toward her bedroom again.

Suddenly, a hand grasped her arm, and her body slowly rotated back toward him. His grip was so soft she barely felt his fingertips, yet she had no doubt she was ensnared. He drew her body closer, and she was barely aware of moving until they stood in front of each other, the barest hint of space between them. She wanted to place her palms back on his chest but kept them down at her side.

With her gaze locked on his, she searched to find some hint of his thoughts. A flash of anguish moved over his face, and her heart squeezed again, this time in response to his inner battle. Wanting to know what he was thinking, she waited, breathing lightly.

He opened his mouth several times, but no words came out, and when she couldn't take the silence anymore, she lifted one hand and cupped his jaw. He closed his eyes and leaned into her simple touch.

The words that seemed to be pulled from deep inside his chest flowed.

"I'm out of my element here, Diana."

Her brow furrowed at the comment, but she didn't speak.

"I look in the mirror, and I know what I see. Some scars. My nose broken a few times. A man who doesn't give a fuck about looks or clothes. I wear black and gray because I don't have to figure out what the fuck to put on. I keep my hair buzzed so I don't have to give a fuck about what it looks like. I shave when it suits me, and then when it doesn't, I'll let my beard grow. I'm smart but not college educated. I'll do any mission my boss wants me to do, and I would never turn down a request from one of my fellow friends or Keepers. But I don't give a fuck what anyone else thinks about my job or career path. I'm not the man who captures a woman's attention unless they're just looking for a body."

His words scored through her, and she lifted her other hand to his shoulder, holding tight, locking her knees, so the power of his words wouldn't drop her to the floor.

"From the moment I saw you, it was obvious you were beautiful, brilliant, educated, and more than all of that, just a good person, Diana. Was I attracted? Hell yeah. I would have to be dead or dumb not to be attracted, and I'm neither. But I figured you were so far out of my league that even if we weren't working together, I would've never gone there. Believe me, I understand self-preservation. My wanting to protect you has nothing to do with your visual ability, but maybe it's more wanting to protect myself."

Again, the air swirled around them as time stood still. Swallowing deeply, she continued to hold him, refusing to look away. "When I look at you, Terrance, all I see is strength and beauty."

He scoffed, his head shaking back and forth slowly.

But she wasn't finished. "I can't change your past or how it's affected you, but I want you to see what I see. Strength, not only of body but of character. Beauty, not only deep inside but, Jesus, Terrance… you're gorgeous. Being with you the past couple of days has transformed my life. I want to see things again. Feel things again. Go places again. You've given back a part of me that I thought was lost. And when I look at you… I want to kiss you more than my next breath."

His gaze stayed laser-focused on her, and she felt the intensity of his perusal, praying he wanted what she wanted. With reflexes faster than she could have imagined, his arm snaked around her waist and pulled her to his chest. His other hand dove into her hair as he gripped the back of her neck. Then with a gentleness she could have only imagined a man with perfect control could have managed, he brought their lips together.

And her world stopped spinning as life ceased to exist outside the bubble of their aligned bodies. His mouth sealed over hers, the kiss sending shock waves throughout her core, making her want more of him. Her fingers grasped at his shoulders as her knees buckled, but she remained steady with his arm banded around her. And at that moment, when his tongue slid inside her mouth, she knew he would always catch her if she fell.

16

Bennett's brain short-circuited. All rational thoughts were obliterated. All objections were overruled. His entire being was centered on the feel of her petal-soft lips, sweet breath, the delicate scent of vanilla, and the way her fingertips dug into his shoulders.

Her words scored through him. *I want you to see what I see. Strength, not only of body but of character. Beauty, not only deep inside but, Jesus, Terrance... you're gorgeous.* Hell, he'd never been called beautiful by anybody. Women called him hot when they looked at his muscular build, assuming that would make sex better or different or... whatever the fuck they thought might happen.

But Diana... her gaze never left his face. Her warm eyes searched his, her longing for a connection evident, and damn, he couldn't deny he felt it, too. She was everything he'd ever longed for but never thought he'd find or, if he did, never thought he'd have a chance. He'd tried to refuse her but was now powerless to deny her anything.

Her knees buckled, but he kept her body pressed against his, holding her steady. She was so much smaller than him, yet they fit together like two pieces of an intricate puzzle. His cock reacted, swelling painfully, making him glad he was in sweatpants. But the last thing he wanted to do was scare her, so he shifted his hips back even though his body cried out in protest.

But it seemed Diana had other ideas as she dropped her hand from his shoulder to his lower back, pulling him tightly toward her to press their hips together once again. She groaned, and as her mouth opened, his tongue slid inside, slowly dragging through her sweet warmth.

As their tongues tangled, he refused to rush. He was a man of infinite patience and had no desire to give in to his body's urgency. He wanted to take his time and savor each sensation. The taste of sweet wine... the velvet smoothness of her tongue... the tingle shooting straight to his cock as he explored her mouth, committing it to memory.

While his body reacted, wanting more, he would have been satisfied with just a kiss. Something to carry with him like a memory that was etched deep inside and would be easy to pull out and savor again and again. He never expected more.

But just like before, she had other ideas as she began to rub herself along the ridge of his cock, and her breathing became labored as their kiss became more desperate. "I want you, Terrance," she begged against his lips.

He lifted his head, needing the separation to think

straight and peer into her eyes. It was easy to recognize the need in her gaze, but he hesitated. *Need for what?* A man? A cock? A fuck? *Can I give her just that?* The uneasy answer was yes, but at what cost? The answer was clear. *My heart.* But he would have sold his soul for a chance to be with Diana on any level she was willing to give to him. His heart was a bauble compared to the memory of her that he would carry for the rest of his life.

"What do you need?" he whispered, still holding her gaze. Her short robe now fell open, exposing the swell of her breasts and the hard pebble outline of her nipple.

Her lips curved. "I want all of you. Please."

Bending, he scooped her up into his arms, barely feeling her slight weight as he moved with purpose toward the bedroom doors. Halting, he looked down, a silent question moving between them.

She blinked, then laughed. "I don't care which room. I don't care which bed. As long as we're in it together, it doesn't matter."

Without overthinking, he stalked into his room and placed her on his bed. He wanted her scent to linger on his sheets. He wanted her image to remain after she left. He only wished it was at his house and not a hotel suite that they'd leave in another day so that her image would stay with him in a place where he could keep it forever. But this was the next best thing, and he knew how to appreciate what came his way.

Her arms didn't let him go, so he crawled over her body, keeping his weight off her with his hands planted on the mattress next to her.

Her gaze bore into his, and he lowered his head until

their lips were a whisper apart. Terrified of making assumptions, he sucked in a deep breath and let it out slowly. "I need to know what you want, Diana. I need to know so there are no misunderstandings. No mistakes. No hurt. It would kill me to do anything that caused you pain and would break my heart to misinterpret anything you need."

Their gazes never wavered, and her top teeth pressed deeply into her bottom lip. Finally, she nodded as her fingers clutched him again. "I want you to make love to me." Her voice sounded more like a confession than a demand. "I want to feel all of you. On me, around me, in me. I want to feel connected to you so that when you walk out of my life, I'll never forget our time together, even if this is all I'll ever have of you."

Her words nearly knocked the strength out of his body, and he forced his elbows to lock to keep from dropping down on top of her. She made it plain that she wanted sex, but he could swear it sounded like she wanted more. A connection. He also wanted that with every fiber of his being. But if all he had was tonight, he'd take it, memorize it, and store it in a secret place close to his heart.

"Christ, Diana, I want you, too." Bending his elbows, he closed the space between them, his lips landing on hers once again. This time, there was no hesitancy. No timidity. He angled his head and sealed his mouth over hers, kissing as though she was needed for his very next breath, something he was fairly certain was true. They kissed, not caring how messy it was. Noses bumped, tongues tangled, and teeth nipped while they tasted and tempted.

With his weight now held up by only his forearms, he kept from crushing her delectable curves pressed against his hard chest. Her legs slid open, and his hips fell into the space, his cock nestled against her core. She lifted as he angled down, and his brain short-circuited as the electricity jolted between them.

He cupped her face, his thumb moving over the softness of her cheeks. He wanted everything all at once but was terrified of moving too quickly.

Pressing her chest against his, he slid one hand down to hold her breast in his hand. Gently massaging, he filled his palm with her plump flesh, and her nipple, like a hard bead, taunted him. Sliding his hand under the bottom of her camisole, he tweaked her nipple as her skin was like satin under his rough fingertips. He suddenly jerked his hand away, afraid of hurting her.

"No. Don't stop, please," she begged.

"My hands are calloused."

"I know. I want you. All of you. Do you think I care about something like that? It just makes you, *you*."

Like a balm, her words soothed over the rough edges of his heart. His fingers moved back over her breasts, and now as her breath hitched, he knew it was from desire and not pain. Kissing a path from her lips, he moved over her jaw, then down to suck on the fluttering pulse at the base of her neck. He took his time as he continued the path until his mouth pulled her nipple deeply.

Gently slipping his fingers underneath the waistband of her shorts, he pushed them down until his fingertips found her slick folds, and the scent of her arousal floated around him. And with his forefinger covered in her juices, he circled her clit, loving the way her gasps told of her pleasure. Inserting one long finger inside her channel, he pressed his hips forward, not only in desire but hoping to stem off his impending orgasm, hating for things to end too soon.

He'd always been able to control every part of his body, but now with just the feel of her against his hand, he was about to come like a teenager fumbling on his first date.

He worked her body, carefully watching each expression on her face, hoping to draw out her pleasure. Bennett had never considered himself to be a master of sex, a Lothario, a man destined to make women come with just the crook of their finger, a wink, or a smile. In the past, if the woman had reached release before he came, he was satisfied. But with her, he wanted everything. He wanted her to feel as good as he did. He wanted to take her to heights he'd only dreamed about.

Her core tightened around his finger, and she was so responsive that he felt her fall apart in his arms, with her head thrown back and his name on her lips.

It was the single most beautiful moment of his life.

He dragged his finger out of her warmth, hating to lose the connection. Her eyes fluttered open as her fingers gripped his shoulders like she was waking from a dream. Her lips curved as her gaze remained focused on his face.

Lowering his body again, he kissed her smile,

knowing his mouth had never touched anything more special. Still not wanting to move too quickly, he was willing to take things slow, even halt if she wanted. But her hands clawed at his T-shirt, jerking it upward. Unable to keep the grin from his face, he shifted onto his knees as he straddled her hips. Reaching behind and grabbing his T-shirt, he pulled it swiftly over his head before tossing it aside.

Scooting back, he stood with his hands on the waistband of his sweatpants and hesitated. "I need to know what you want again, Diana."

Her smile remained, and she sat up, whipping her camisole over her head and freeing her breasts as they bounced lightly in front of her. "All. Of. You."

They moved together—he shucked his sweatpants and boxers down, kicking them away as she slid out of her sleep shorts. Now, both naked, their gazes feasted on each other.

She was perfection. Creamy skin. Perfectly proportioned curves. Hair flowing over the dark comforter, creating a halo.

She kept her gaze on him, and her smile beamed. "Jesus, Terrance, you're gorgeous." She lay back, spread out for his perusal, and lifted her fingers, wiggling them in invitation.

Crawling back over her body, he nestled the tip of his cock at her entrance. Gasping, he halted with a jerk, his eyes widening. He didn't have a condom with him. He wasn't a man who carried one with him all the time, and he sure as fuck never expected to need one on this trip.

"What's wrong?" Fear moved through her expression.

"Christ, I'm sorry, Diana. I don't have a condom."

"Oh…" She hesitated for only a second. "I'm clean. I can show you on my phone."

"Same. I'm clean, too," he rushed. "We're tested all the time for work." He hesitated again, then ventured, "But…"

"I'm on birth control." Her brow furrowed as she shook her head. "I can show you the pills in my bathroom—"

"I trust you."

Her smile returned. "And I trust you too."

Now, with no barrier between them, he pushed gently until his cock was seated inside, her tight inner core sheathing him completely. Rational thought fled as he fought the desire to thrust with abandon. But determined to give her nothing but pleasure and to make it last as long as he could, he pulled out slowly before starting a gliding rhythm that pushed out all other thoughts but her underneath him.

She met his movements and pressed her hips upward. While he wanted to take things slow, the speed increased with their need for each other. He linked his fingers with hers, holding her arms above her head as he pressed her hands into the mattress. A flush covered her breasts, moving upward over her face, making her blue eyes sparkle.

As he continued to thrust, he alternated between kissing her lips and moving lower to circle her breasts. He wanted her to come again. He needed her to come again. And just when he thought he might lose the battle to hold off his own release, she cried out as her body grew taut just before her inner muscles milked him.

At the end of his control, his jaw clenched as a grimace tightened his face when his orgasm slammed into him. He emptied deep inside her body with no barrier between them. Continuing to thrust, her channel now slick with their combined releases, he stared down at her face, seeing her glow as she smiled up at him.

He was now ruined for any other woman. Ruined for thinking a random hookup would ever satisfy him again. Ruined for trying to imagine a life with her not in it. But he wouldn't have changed a thing.

Once again, he knew *this* was now the single most beautiful moment of his life.

17

Diana stared at the awestruck expression on Terrance's face, knowing it mirrored her own. Her heartbeat pounded in her ears, and her chest heaved with the exertion of breathing. He rolled as he dropped, his arms snaking around her. The movement was so swift that her head rested on his upper arm, with their faces close together before she realized it. Breaths mingled. Legs tangled. Hearts pounded an erratic rhythm.

"Are you all right?" he whispered, his breath puffing over her cheeks.

She nodded, uncertain her voice would work. Swallowing, she replied, "Never better. Never."

Her answer must have given him the assurance he needed as the fear leeched from his eyes and was replaced with warmth.

"Me, too."

Now it was her turn to heave a sigh of relief mixed with the afterglow of passion. She had been sexually active before her accident, but looking back, it was always with carefully chosen men. She realized she'd always played it safe, and while sex had been pleasurable, it lacked enthusiasm. From now on, she wanted nothing less than what Terrance had just given her. In truth, she couldn't imagine being with anyone other than him.

She leaned in, burying her face in his neck, her lips touching his skin. She craved the closeness, but more, she craved hiding the grimace. She knew she could not contain her thoughts. This was a vacation fling. Something physical. Sex between two people who found each other attractive and liked each other. She wanted more but needed to bury that desire. The last thing a man like Terrance needed was a clingy woman who didn't understand the rules.

She felt the sting of tears. He shifted back and gently pinched her chin between his knuckle and forefinger, moving her head to see her face. Concern etched deep in his expression.

"Diana, what's wrong? Did I hurt you?"

Unable to hide the tear that escaped, she smiled and shook her head. "You'll think I'm so foolish, but I can't pretend to be cool. What we just shared was so beautiful that it's almost overwhelming."

Uncertain of his reaction to her honesty, she felt her heart squeeze when he smiled. He kissed each cheek, erasing the salty tear tracks.

"I couldn't agree more. You are the most exceptional woman I've ever met."

They lay quietly for a few more minutes as her fingers traced the tattoo of a lighthouse on his shoulder, and she thought of the lighthouse necklace resting against her chest. "Is this because of who you work for?"

"Yeah. There's a tracker embedded underneath the skin at the light."

A slight gasp fell from her lips as her eyes widened. "Wow, that's... that's... I don't even know what to say."

"The man who started the Lighthouse Security Investigations firm in Maine grew up near a lighthouse, and it had significance to him. He calls his employees Keepers as a tribute to the old lighthouse keepers who used to guide others to safety during storms." Shrugging, he added, "That's what our missions mean to us."

Shifting so she could peer into his eyes, she smiled. "That's so amazing. Beautiful. So special. Just like you."

He held her gaze in silence, then unwound his arms and slipped from the bed, heading straight into the bathroom. She blinked, hating the heat he took with him. Wondering if her words had embarrassed him, she scrunched her nose in frustration.

Now wishing she had directed him to her bedroom earlier, where he could've just left after the sex, she was uncertain if she should grab her clothes and leave now. Wanting to be covered before he came back, she sat up and reached for her camisole top at the end of the bed.

As she lifted her arms to slip it over her head, he stalked back into the room, his magnificent body on full display and a washcloth in his hand. He reached her and gently pushed her back, pulling the covers down. Before she could ask what he was doing, he placed the warm washcloth between her legs, and she gasped as he cleansed her with great care.

When he finished, he went back to the bathroom, and this time, she lay still, comforted by his care yet still uncertain of what to expect next.

The toilet flushed, and he returned a moment later. He slipped under the covers and pulled her body to him. With his arms enveloping her and the covers pulled up, she breathed in the scent that was uniquely Terrance. Not questioning what sleeping together meant, she vowed to simply enjoy each experience with him for as long as it lasted. Closing her eyes, she drifted off into a dreamless sleep.

When Diana awoke, the sun was already peeking through the slit in the blackout curtains. She stretched her arms above her head and then jolted awake at the feel of the sheet against her naked body. Eyes snapping open, she gasped at the realization she was still in Terrance's bed but also that she was alone.

Her face scrunched, and she shook her head quickly, embarrassment filling her. *Oh God, he awoke, and I was still here, so he had to escape.*

She slid from the bed, snagged her robe, and belted her kimono around her tightly. Unable to hold her bladder until she could get into her own bathroom, she hurried into his. After taking care of business, she washed her hands.

Grabbing her sleep shorts from the floor and her camisole on top of the covers, she ran to the door, hoping she could make it into her room without being seen. But just as she exited, she spied his back as he bent over the table.

She should have known she couldn't escape the notice of a former Ranger, but when he turned around and spied her, his smile was so wide that she could see it despite the blurriness. He moved directly to her and pulled her in for a hug. Her arms encircled his waist, thrilled for the connection while still confused.

He leaned back, his hands on her shoulders, keeping his face nearby. It dawned on her that he'd quickly learned how close he needed to be so she could truly see him, and she smiled. Whatever he was thinking, he certainly wasn't treating her as a vacation fling.

"I didn't know how long to let you sleep," he said. "It's late in the morning, but truthfully, I didn't want to get out of bed with you still in my arms."

His words surprised her, and her cheeks hurt from the wide smile that burst forth. Her attention was snagged as the scent of deliciousness wafted past. "Oh my God! Is that bacon?"

He threw his head back and laughed, pulling her into his side as he led her to the table where he'd ordered room service breakfast. The plates were piled with scrambled eggs, bagels, cream cheese, jam, bacon, sliced tomatoes, and a particular weakness of hers—fried potatoes. A pitcher of freshly squeezed orange juice and a steaming pot of coffee, along with a platter of pastries and a bowl of fruit, completed the massive meal.

"This is so much food! I'd love to say I can't eat at all, but I'm so ravenous, I'll certainly do my part."

He held her seat and then bent to kiss her lightly

before settling into a chair so close their knees touched. Everything about the morning was going completely differently than she had feared, yet, completely aligned with how she'd dreamed it could be.

"Has your agenda for the day changed since we slept so late?" he asked.

It took a moment for her to remember what was on her original schedule, wanting to scream that instead, she'd prefer to spend it in bed with him. Taking a sip of juice to cool her parched throat, she shook her head. "No. I was only going to attend one session this morning. Since this meal will serve as lunch, I'll just go to one other session early this afternoon."

"How about we plan to eat out somewhere once your session ends?"

Her breath caught in her throat, and she hoped she could remain outwardly calm while inwardly twirling with joy. "That'd be great."

"And then, this evening? We could see the fountain show again?"

Giving up on any pretense of calm, she laughed. "I'd love that!"

As they ate, she wasn't surprised at how much food Terrance could put away, knowing he worked out to maintain his powerful physique, but looking down, she scrunched her nose.

"What's that face for?" He tilted his head to the side as he awaited her reply.

"This," she exclaimed, rubbing her food baby. "You eat, and it all goes to muscle once you work out. I eat this much and get a tummy—"

With a light tug on her arm, he pulled her from her chair, settling her on his lap. Her arms wrapped around his neck, and she nuzzled his ear.

"This body is gorgeous," he proclaimed.

That caused her to jerk upright, her gaze searching his.

"I'm serious, Diana. You are fucking gorgeous. And you eat what you want when you want, and how much you want. Never starve yourself, babe, because every inch of you is beautiful."

Her hands snapped to cup his cheeks, and she held him tight. Her gaze roved over his face, once again committed to memorizing each nuance. "Your eyes see *me*," she breathed, her voice hitching.

He nodded slowly. "And your eyes see *me*."

They closed the scant space, their lips barely touching, then separating for an instant before slamming together again. The kiss became wild as need coursed through her body, and desire overcame all other thoughts.

He stood with her, held easily in his arms, walking into his bedroom, where they quickly discarded their clothes. This time, in the light of the last full day they'd be together in Vegas, they gave in to the passion that had ignited the night before.

Several hours later, they walked through the hotel to the conference rooms. She'd hesitated to place her hand on his arm as they walked, suddenly self-conscious. He'd reached down and snagged her hand, settling it on his forearm, winking before his professional mask slipped into place as his eagle eye scanned the area.

Leaning closer, she whispered, "I think we can safely assume that with the conference ending soon, there's no chance of any threat to me. I'd feel foolish for Jerry hiring you, except I'm so glad we met."

His lips curved at her words, missed by anyone not tuned in to them, but she was very aware. Smiling, she turned to face Terrance. "I shouldn't have had that second cup of coffee. I'm going to need a quick break before the presentation."

Not letting her go alone, they walked together. His phone rang, and he watched as she headed inside. "I'll just be over here."

A few minutes later, she exited the restroom and stopped in the hall. Looking to either side, she searched for the tall, dark figure but couldn't see over the crowd now that another session had let out and most attendees were hustling to the bathrooms. Not wanting to walk far but feeling the need to get away from the line gathering outside the ladies' room, she placed her hand on the wall and moved down the hall. Still not seeing Terrance, she walked around a corner, finding that hall almost empty. Realizing she was going in the opposite direction of the lecture rooms, she was about to turn around when a door opened. Peering inside, she saw movement and shapes of people, their voices coming to a halt. She was about to ask if anyone there knew the way to the main conference area when the door slammed closed in her face.

Embarrassed, she turned and walked back around the corner, the space just as crowded. But suddenly, the blurry masses parted, and a tall, dark figure headed directly toward her. Smiling, she reached out her hand, not afraid when the familiar, rough fingers snagged it.

"Shit, Diana. I turned to answer the phone, and the hall filled with women all rushing to the ladies' room. I couldn't find you. Fuck!"

"Hey, it's okay. I just got a little turned around when I came out, which almost never happens. It's all good."

Now that she was close, she could clearly see his tight jaw and grimace. Touching him, she drew his focus to her face. "Seriously, Terrance. It's all good."

"I shouldn't have taken my eye off the door."

"Well, you getting arrested for stalking a ladies' room wouldn't help me." She shoulder-bumped his side. "Come on. Let's get this last lecture over with, and then we can sneak out of here."

Those words seemed to placate the beast, and he escorted her to a chair before moving closer to the door of the room.

As the presenter droned on at the podium, her mind wandered to the man standing at the side of the room. His presence had become something she craved. It was hard to imagine returning to her staid life even though she loved her job. Now, she'd realized how much more she wanted. How much more she deserved. But it wasn't that he'd opened her eyes to passion with just anyone. No… she knew she'd found a life-changing passion with him. Sucking in a deep breath, she let it out slowly, hoping no one sitting near her noticed the blush covering her face.

Suddenly, everyone was clapping, and the lecture was over. She stifled a grin at the realization that, for the first time, she hadn't listened to a word and didn't care. The only thing she cared about was moving toward her, his familiar face and intense gaze becoming clearer with each step. She sucked in a quick breath. She had no idea what would happen when their time together was over. Giving a little shake of her head, she refused to allow any thoughts to drag her down now.

Taking his hand, she lifted on her toes and bypassed his lips as she placed her mouth near his ear. "How about another meal at the food truck down the road?"

His laughter surrounded her, and they walked into the sunshine once again.

18

Bennett walked along the sidewalk with Diana's fingers linked with his. As soon as they exited the Bellagio, he reached down, wanting a connection more than just her hand resting on his arm. He wanted to claim her as more than just a bodyguard, but his mind whirled with the changes in their relationship in the past twenty-four hours.

In fact, the only reason he took the phone call when he did when Diana was out of his sight was that it was from Dolby. And if he'd ever needed advice from a friend he trusted, it was now.

"Hey, Bennett. I got your message. I know Jeb is digging into some of the names you've sent us, looking for any connection to terrorist groups or the black market. Actually, there's so much information to dig through, Carson has several of us on it."

"That's great, man." He grabbed the back of his neck and squeezed.

"But your message said you wanted to talk to me. What's going on?"

Having no idea what to say and afraid that Diana would walk out of the ladies' room before he had a chance to get his courage up, he blurted, "How did you know Marcia was the one?"

The silence only lasted a few seconds but stretched interminably. Squeezing his neck again, he was about to withdraw his question when Dolby hooted loudly.

"Are you fucking shitting me? You? Damn, Bennett, I should have known you'd finally give in as soon as you found a woman who would break down that damn wall you've built."

Snorting, he glanced down the hall, still not seeing Diana. "It's got nothing to do with walls coming down."

"Then maybe she'll get you to see what the rest of us see."

"Hell, in truth, I'm not worthy enough for her."

"Shut that shit down, Bennett."

"What I don't know is how to combine the mission with the desire to be with this person." Thinking about Dolby and Marcia's relationship, he added, "Of course, Marcia wasn't your mission when you met and started falling for her."

"True," Dolby agreed. "But if you're asking how I knew, then that tells me you've already been struck with a feeling you've never felt for any woman before. And you're not some twenty-year-old fucking around at bars near a base. You're old enough to know what you want, but more importantly, you need to know what you deserve. And if she does, then don't doubt the feelings."

Dolby's explanation made sense, but it still didn't help how to combine a mission and feelings. Leo and Natalie had known each other for ten years before they got together. Hop had also known Lori since they were kids before they got together. Both women became missions, but not initially. Same with Rick and Abbie. It struck him that the only Keeper that would truly understand was their boss, Carson. The thought must've hit Dolby at the same time because he said, "I'm here at work. I'm passing you to Carson. Just remember, bro. Don't fuck this up. And I'm not talking about the mission. I'm talking about the chance with the woman you found."

Grimacing, he squeezed his eyes shut, wishing Dolby hadn't taken the initiative to hand the phone to his boss. He could hear hushed voices in the background before Carson came on the line.

Carson chuckled, then said, "If I know you, the last thing you want to do is talk about this. But if you're asking if it jeopardizes your job with me for you to fall for a mission, the answer is no. Hell, look at the original LSI Keepers in Maine. Almost every one of those men fell for their missions."

"That helps, boss, but I guess it still worries me."

"That makes you a good employee and a good man, Bennett—something we've known all along, but maybe you just realize that you are more than the job. If Dr. Olson... Diana is the right person for you and shares your feelings, then you'd be a fool not to see how far the relationship can go. And Bennett? I've never known you to be a fool."

With those words ringing in his ears, he disconnected as the hall filled with women swarming from the conference rooms toward the ladies' room. With so many people pressing around, even with his height, he couldn't see Diana. And for the first time since he started the mission, he wondered if he was allowing the relationship to put her in danger. As soon as his gaze landed on where she walked along the hall with her hand on the wall, his heart kicked inside his chest. Yeah, she was the mission. And, yeah, she was the woman he wanted in his life.

Now, walking along, his heart was light as they made their way to the line of food trucks. "What's it going to be today? Tacos? Kabobs? Korean Bibimbap—"

"Oh, I'd love kabobs!"

"You got it." He led her to the truck, where the scent of cumin, smoky paprika, and grilled lamb filled the air. Giving their orders, they soon collected their bags and drinks and walked to a bench near the fountains.

Chatting while eating was comfortable with Diana, something he'd never found with other women. Natalie, Abbie, and Rachel were easier since they worked for LSIWC also, and work dominated their conversations. As Diana groaned in delight with her meal, he looked over and shook his head. When she was standing in the ballroom accepting the award, it was hard to imagine that she'd want to be with him. But sitting here now, he felt such ease. And as soon as she groaned again, sounding so much like the noise she made just before she came, he shifted on the seat, his cock reacting.

Once finished, they walked along the Strip for a while until it was time to head back for the show. They found a secluded spot along the fence, glad the crowd was smaller than the last time they'd viewed the display. She leaned forward, her forearms resting on the top of the fence rail, her gaze riveted to the fountains as soon as the music started. He was more fascinated by her expression of wonder than the brilliant musical fountain presentation. He knew she was unable to clearly see the movement of each fountain arc, but her appreciation shone through.

"It's beautiful, isn't it?" she asked, her gaze never wavering.

"The most beautiful thing I've ever seen," he admitted.

She twisted around to look up at him, seeing him staring at her, a smile playing about his lips. Even in the evening shadows, he could see the blush rise up her neck and fill her cheeks. Chuckling, he leaned over and kissed her before whispering, "Yeah. I'm talking about you."

A crack sounded out just as a small, leafy limb from a nearby bush scattered. Instinct kicked in, and he grabbed her and shoved her to the ground, covering her with his body as he ignored her yelp of fright. "Get down. Stay down!"

Rage coursed through his veins, recognizing the sound of rifle fire. *Fucking aimed at Diana! I was fucking kissing her instead of watching, and she was fucking shot at!* Her body shook underneath him, and as he looked around, he realized no one else was reacting. The rifle fire had occurred when the fountain music crescendoed, camouflaging the noise except for someone like him who'd recognize it no matter what extraneous sounds resonated.

"Terrance? Terrance? What's happening?"

Leaning down, he whispered, "You were shot at. No

one else noticed because of the show. We've gotta get out of here. Come on. Stay with me, and do exactly what I say." He crouched low, pulling her to her knees before lifting her higher so that her feet were firm on the ground while still keeping her bent over and covered with his body as they raced along.

Seeing a taxi, he rushed her over, opened the door, and hustled her inside. "Take us to a strip mall outside of town. Any one. An extra hundred cash is yours if you get us there ASAP."

His gaze shifted all around, making sure no one lingered nearby with a weapon. Instead, all he saw were other spectators and tourists wandering leisurely about, not aware a weapon had been fired nearby. He grabbed Diana and tugged her torso over his lap. "Stay down."

Pulling his phone from his pocket, he called LSIWC's emergency line.

"Poole here."

"We were fired upon while outside the Bellagio. Dr. Olson is fine. We're in a taxi getting out of the area."

"Calling the others," Poole responded.

"I have to make a change in vehicles."

Diana twisted around and peered up, her eyes wide. Rage still coursed through him, but he coped by shoving all other thoughts to the side except getting her to safety.

"My luggage?" she whispered. "Can't we go to the hotel—"

"No. They'll be looking for you." He glanced at the cars on the road, then called up to the taxi driver. "Drop us off here. This is good." The driver whipped off the main road and pulled into a strip mall. "Park next to the black SUV," Bennett ordered.

As soon as the taxi came to a stop, he tossed the wad of cash into the man's hand. "Leave the second we're out." He threw open the door. Shifting out from under Diana, he exited first, then turned and grabbed her hand. Pushing her up against the side of the SUV, he watched as the taxi sped out of the parking lot and down the road. Her chest heaved, dragging his attention back to her. "As soon as this is open, hop in." He quickly used an LSI fob and opened the door.

"How did you—?"

"Get in."

She obeyed without more questions, for which he was glad. Once behind the wheel, he started the vehicle and pulled out of the parking lot. On the road, he turned to view her pale face and large, blue eyes darting around. *Fuck... she's got to be terrified, considering she'd been shot at and can't clearly see anything.*

He'd gone into bodyguard mode and was so focused on getting her safely away that he'd pushed her visual limitations to the background. "Diana?"

She still faced forward even though she couldn't see what was outside the window.

"Diana? Babe?"

That brought her head swinging around to him. "Terrance, I don't understand. What's happening?"

"You were shot at. I… I was focused on you and never realized the threat was there."

Her gaze never wavered. "It's not your fault."

He remained quiet, not willing to waste energy arguing about what he knew his responsibilities were.

"Why did you…?" Confusion crossed her face. "Wait… you stole this!"

"I couldn't trust that someone saw us take the taxi."

She opened her mouth, then snapped it closed. He wanted to apologize and explain, but his phone rang. "Talk to me."

Poole answered. "Got Carson, Hop, and Adam here. Chris, Leo, and Natalie are on their way in. What do you need?"

"Heading to the private airport, but the Olson plane won't be there. Need Hop to fly in."

"You got it," Hop responded. "I'll be in the air within forty minutes. Hang on, Leo and Natalie just walked in. They were outside when your call came in."

"Check on the movements of the ones I had you check on earlier. I want to know where they were and what they were doing," he ordered.

"On it," Jeb called out.

"We'll get to the airport and wait. It might be mostly closed this time of day, but we'll hide out until Hop arrives." He looked outside the window and exited the highway. "We should be there in approximately ten minutes."

Headlights shone through the back window, and Bennett twisted around to see a pickup truck closing ground. Narrowing his eyes, he continued to monitor it. "We've got company."

"Natalie here. I have your location pulled up. Take the next right. Small road but not secluded."

"Who are they?" Diana cried out, twisting in her seat to look behind them.

"Stay down. Keep your head down!" he ordered while his hand darted out to cup the back of her head and push her forward.

"Bennett, talk to us," Leo radioed.

"They must have been on our tail the whole way," he growled.

"Or she's being tracked," Poole tossed out.

Darting his gaze to where her crossbody purse strap was still visible even as she half lay on the seat, he slammed his hand against the steering wheel. "Goddammit!"

She whimpered, and he hated scaring her. "Diana, pull your purse over your head. Lay it on the seat."

She squirmed around, jerking the strap over her head while managing to keep her head down. He was glad it was a small purse as his fingers dug inside and wrapped around her phone. "Tossing her phone."

"Good," Leo said. "But they could have another tracker."

"Take this," he said, shoving her wallet into her shaking, outstretched hand. "Grab your driver's license." Then radioing, he added, "Have Jeb monitor her cards and shut down any use. Her bag is going out the window with the phone."

Once again, he was grateful that Diana followed his instructions. Without complaint, he tossed her purse out the window. Following Natalie's instructions, he made several more turns until they were the only ones on the road.

"I'm trying to pull up a satellite view of where you are, but I'm not getting anything right now," Natalie said.

He crested a small hill but was unable to see in the desert at night. "What have I got around me?"

"Flat land. Some hills. Mostly desert. I can't tell if anyone's following you but turn left at the next intersection. It takes you a little farther into the desert, but it'll eventually bring you around the backside of the private airport where Hop will come in."

Suddenly, headlights from behind flashed through the vehicle again, soon followed by the sound of a high-powered rifle being fired. Jerking on the wheel, he cursed as he radioed their situation. And with another round of fire from behind that managed to pierce one of the back tires, he struggled to maintain control. "We've been hit. Back right tire. God-fucking-dammit!"

"I have your location. A team is coming in," Natalie reported, her voice now uncharacteristically shaky.

Diana whimpered again, but there was little he could do to comfort her. Hanging on to the wheel, he calculated his plan if they needed to stop so he could return fire.

Losing speed, he watched the headlights grow brighter. "Diana, stay down. I'm gonna turn this around and take care of these bastards. Keep your head down."

In a deft maneuver, he jerked around so that the SUV spun ninety degrees, giving him a perfect shot out the window. Grabbing the weapon from his holster, he remained steady until another set of headlights crested the hill. "Another vehicle."

"Diana. Do not fight them. If something happens to me, don't fight them. Go with them. They want you… they need you alive."

"No!" she cried out, her hands darting forward to clutch his thighs.

He had limited firing power but was determined to take out whoever he could. *I'm not willing to be a sitting duck.* He pressed the accelerator again, shooting them toward the oncoming vehicles. Catching them by surprise, they darted to either side as he plowed through the middle, managing to get off several shots toward the driver of the vehicle closest to his side. Checking his rearview mirror, he watched the headlights shimmy back and forth before coming to a stop.

The other vehicle circled around and closed the gap with haste. He fired off several more rounds before they were hit again, and this time he was unable to keep the SUV from careening off the road. Hitting the upper edge of a small crest, the SUV flipped on its side. Throwing his body over Diana's, he tried to protect her, still shouting over the radio to LSIWC. Once they stopped, he instantly oriented as he unbuckled her. "Follow me!" He kicked out the remaining glass of his broken window as their vehicle lay on its side before climbing out. Turning, he gently pulled her forward. With her hand in his, he glanced behind them to see the headlights approaching. If he was alone, he would easily be able to travel in the dark night over the desert, but Diana needed assistance as well as protection.

Not willing to chance her falling, he gave her his

back and said, "Climb on," as Natalie radioed, "North. Head due north. There's an old mine a few miles away."

Diana scrambled onto his back, her arms encircling his neck as her legs wrapped around his waist. He was once more grateful she followed his orders without argument or hesitation. He looked at the compass on his watch and then began jogging. Their only hope was to get away enough to stay hidden until the Keepers could reach them.

19

Diana had often heard the phrase "hold on for dear life," but until this moment, she'd never understood the concept. As she bounced on Terrance's back, she clung to him like a spider monkey. Praying that she wasn't too heavy, that his boot steps were steady, that she didn't fall off, that her hands on his neck didn't choke him, and that she didn't get them killed, she continued to cling. Fear kept the words from forming—that and knowing he needed to focus.

She could tell he was listening to his coworkers through his ear radio and trusted they guided him as they jogged along. A flash of light crossed the path in front of them, and her body jolted as he knelt on the ground.

"We gotta keep going but need to stay out of their sight," he said, barely breathing hard.

She couldn't imagine how he had the breath to speak, much less carry her, but just as quickly as he had knelt, he stood, and they kept going.

Another flash of light hit them, and he cursed. A pinging sound rang out, and he stumbled as his body jerked. She screamed as they tumbled down, her hands flying out in an attempt to keep from falling face-first onto the ground.

"What happened?" she cried out.

"I'm fucking hit."

Hit? As in shot?

"They got me, not her. You decide. Superficial."

Diana's brain struggled to catch up to his words, then realized he was still radioing their situation to his coworkers. She'd scrambled off his back, running her hands over him, trying to find the wound. When she reached his left side, slick met her fingertips instead of just the material of his shirt. "Oh God. Oh God."

"We have to keep going."

She started to argue, but the words died in her throat. He might have wanted them to keep going, but there was no way he could carry her now. And in the dark, unfamiliar desert terrain where she couldn't see anything, there was no way she'd be able to do what he needed. Fear gathered in her throat, choking her like a vise grip, but as much as she desired to do anything he said, she was helpless.

Another flash of light crossed them, and he pulled her behind him, his weapon in his hand. Kneeling in the dirt, her fingers, now covered in his blood, gripped his shoulders. "Let me go, Terrance. They want me. Let me go."

"No fucking way, Diana."

She knew he'd never give up. She knew he'd never

give in. Whoever was after her and whatever they wanted, they needed her alive. The sound of footsteps neared, and she leaped to her feet, her hands in the air.

"Diana! Get down!" He growled, twisting to pull her down with him, a painful grunt leaving his lips.

"Dr. Olson."

She swung her gaze to where the voice originated, unable to see anyone. "You want me. Leave my bodyguard alone, and take me."

"We were surprised you showed up to the conference with a bodyguard. And such an attentive one, at that. His presence has certainly made our objective more difficult. But he is no longer needed."

Slipping around Terrance, she stood in front of him, her hands lifted in front of her. "I'll go with you, but only if you leave him alone and alive."

"He is of no consequence to us. Come."

"Diana, get the fuck back here. You can't do this!" Terrance bit out.

Turning, she looked down, unable to see his expression clearly, but knowing he was furious with both her and himself as well as the situation. "You've done so much for me. I have to do this for you."

Anguish passed between them, filling the air like storm clouds gathering in the distance. She swallowed past a lump in her throat before whispering, "I can't walk away without letting you know what I feel. We've only met, but you mean everything to me."

"I will find you," he whispered-growled in return.

Forcing her body to turn away from him before she changed her mind and flung herself into his arms, she walked toward the shadowed image of three men. As soon as she was close enough, one reached out and grabbed her arm.

"I understand you need assistance," he said, guiding her over the rough terrain toward the headlights. If the situation was not so bizarre and dangerous, she would've thanked him for his help. As it was, she battled the desire to jerk her arm away from his hand and go down fighting, kicking and screaming. Her body quivered, but she refused to turn around and look at Terrance, not wanting to give the kidnappers any more reason to think of him. He'd find a way out, and the Keepers would make it to him. And then, she knew they'd come for her.

She was forced into the back seat of the black SUV. One man climbed into the back with her, and another slid behind the wheel. The vehicle turned, and as they started away, a shot rang out, reverberating over the desert.

"No!" she screamed, her body jerking around to stare out the window at nothingness.

"I told you," the man sitting next to her said, his tone bored. "The bodyguard has no more use."

Still screaming, she launched across the seat, her fists raised. The man grabbed her and pinned her arms to her side. Her nose was covered with a cloth, and a sickly, sweet smell assaulted her senses. Then every muscle in her body relaxed, and her eyes closed.

Diana's eyes blinked open. Every morning her world was fuzzy, and she'd grown accustomed to lying for just a few seconds, continuing to blink, expecting to see clearly before remembering her change in vision. Today was one of those days. She blinked again, but the darkness wouldn't abate.

Her stomach lurched, and a strange odor lingered in her nostrils, reminding her of college days when a party lasted too long and involved too much alcohol. She'd never imbibed too often, but the occasional hangover always reminded her why she didn't drink heavily. Breathing deeply, she dragged oxygen into her lungs, willing her mind to return to the land of the living. But as the sleep fog lifted slowly, the bed underneath was hard, not at all like her mattress. When she rolled to the side and her palm landed on dirt, she sucked in a hasty breath as she blinked more to see where she was.

Darkness surrounded her, allowing only the barest hint of shadows and shapes. The strange odor had now been replaced with an old, musty smell, much like the old mines she had explored when studying the history of mining and the use of explosives. Gasping, she dug her fingers into the rock and dirt underneath her. *A mine? I'm in a mine?*

With no time reference, she had no idea how long she'd been asleep, but as the cobwebs continued to clear, she remembered snatches of her last memories. In a vehicle… headlights flashing across… being chased. Struggling to bring more to focus, she closed her eyes. Terrance was behind the wheel. *Terrance!*

Her eyes popped open, and she gasped again.

Looking around, she heard nothing except her own breathing. "Terrance? Are you here?" Then another memory slammed into her, causing her to bend over in pain as though gut-punched. He had been shot while carrying her. And then, when she left so that the men would leave him alone, there had been another shot as her kidnappers drove away. "Oh God," she cried as her chest heaved and fat tears welled in her eyes. Her chest caved as her heart shattered.

She curled in upon herself, drawing her knees up and wrapping her arms around her legs. With her forehead pressed on top of her knees, she let the tears fall. Nausea and dizziness battled with heartbreak and fear, none creating a place where she could escape the horror of what was happening. For several long minutes, no sound could be heard other than the hitching sobs managing to wrench from her lungs. *Please let the Keepers find him.* Even if it was nothing more than to bury him, Terrance didn't deserve to lay unfounded in the desert.

The idea of his friends coming to claim his body sent the awareness straight to the front of her mind that they would also look for her. *I cannot let anyone else die for me!*

Lifting her head, she swiped her hand over her cheeks and wiped her nose on her sleeve. Her now swollen eyes worsened her vision, but she cast her gaze around, searching for any clue as to her location.

Crawling forward, she discovered a rock wall and pulled herself to her feet. Moving slowly, with one palm against the side of her prison, she tried to discern if it truly was a mine. She tamped down the panic of how far underground she might be and continued to force her legs forward. With her fingertips dragging along the wall for reference, her hands snagged on a protrusion. Now with both hands exploring the object, she identified a wooden pillar about eight by eight inches square. Kneeling, she discovered it went from the floor to as high as she could reach. *For support?* Miners would dig or blast downward, then add wooden support beams to provide stability as they continued their search or extraction of ore.

The idea that she was now being held in a mine made her wonder if it was the same one she'd heard Terrance mention. But then, there were untold abandoned mines in the area, and she could be in any one of them.

Determined to find a way out, she kept her slow pace in the pitch darkness until her right eye became a little more adjusted to the dark, seeing more shapes and shadows. Somewhere a light must be shining.

"I see you're awake."

She jumped at the sound of a man's voice, his accent pronounced. Squinting, she could barely make out the form behind the slats, but the accent was familiar. "Who…" Clearing her parched throat, she tried again. "Who are you? Where are we?"

"I'm so sorry, Dr. Olson. I realize this is difficult for you, especially given your handicap."

A lantern flared, and she squinted again as the small light blasted out into the dark space, causing pain. She lifted her hand and rubbed her forehead, trying to ease the ache. Finally, she was able to watch the shadow of a man as he opened a slatted door and moved closer. Once he was in front of her, she could see his face. Even then, she stared in stunned silence for a moment, unable to reconcile the face with the circumstances.

"Dr. Masterson?"

"I see you're surprised."

Sliding her tongue over her lips, she struggled to force her brain to work at its usual capacity, unable to filter the various pieces of information, all trying to vie for dominance as her mind worked at a turtle's pace.

"I don't..." She shook her head. "I'm not..."

"I'm sorry for the chloroform effects." He reached into a pack hanging over his shoulder and pulled out a water bottle. "Here."

Wary, she reached for it, discovering the cap was still intact. Unscrewing, she tilted the bottle and drank thirstily. As the cold water hit her throat, she felt instant relief, and the chill also served to help jump-start her brain. Draining half the bottle, she lowered it and licked her lips again, not willing to lose a drop. "Thank you."

As soon as the thanks left her lips, she shook her head. It seemed ridiculous to thank her kidnapper for anything, but under the circumstances, staying in his goodwill as long as possible would only serve to hopefully keep her alive until she could find a way to escape or be let go.

"I'm sure you have questions."

"I think that's an understatement, Dr. Masterson. I'm afraid the effects of today's events and the drug have made me slow to reason things through, but I have no idea why you have taken me."

His hands were lifted to the side, palms up as he shrugged. "The answer to that is quite simple. I've wanted your newest technology for years. In fact, from the first time your father announced his work on GeoTech's contrasting energy project, I wanted his knowledge. It's unfortunate that his *untimely* death made my wait even longer."

She blinked, uncertain that she'd heard him correctly. His voice had remained so casual, as though he were simply having a conversation. Yet… the oxygen rushed from her lungs, making her light-headed again. "You're responsible for my dad's death?"

"It was an accident, I assure you. We had no desire for your father to die. Quite the contrary. We wanted his knowledge. We were prepared to take you as collateral if he refused to work with us. But unfortunately, the man hired to run into your father's car was a bit overzealous."

She leaned back against the dirt wall, uncertain that her legs would continue to hold her upright. Lifting a hand, she clutched the material of her shirt over her heart, her fist pressing inward to massage the pain slicing through her. Forcing her breathing to steady, she pushed thoughts of her beloved dad back into the box of grief she was so accustomed to. For now, she needed to gather every scrap of information she could. *Because I promise, before this is over, I'll bury you.*

"That was over four years ago."

"We were unable to get the intelligence before it was

released, but we've had our eye on your company. We had no doubt that as you followed in your father's footsteps, you would be on the cutting edge of more technology that our buyers would love to have."

"You work for Orica. Why would such a legitimate company face ruin by selling on the black market?"

"Orica?" He snorted, shaking his head. "They're satisfied to stay in the mining outback. They are hardly the most progressive. But there are always those who not only want the cheap, reliable explosives but are also willing to pay very well for innovative technology."

"For all this time, you've just been waiting until you could get your hands on me? That doesn't make any sense."

"No, you're right. I've had others persuaded to work with me. NitroSabir has been profitable, but with the war in Russia now, that has proven to be less than optimum."

"Why now?"

"What you alluded to in your speech. What you've devoted the past year to working on. GeoTech is ready to release their new technology, and my buyers want it first."

"My research isn't for sale. And no one at GeoTech will ever work with you."

"Don't be too sure. Everyone has a price." He shrugged, adding, "Plus, we had to act fast after you saw us."

"Saw you? When?"

"When the door opened at the conference. You looked in and caught me and several of my compatriots together. One of them said you couldn't see that far, but I wasn't going to take the chance. I knew your bodyguard needed to be taken out, and we needed you."

His words slammed into her, and she nearly bent over with the pain. Tears sprung to her eyes as she thought of Bennett's death because of her. She pressed her lips together, dragging them over each other, trying to keep from wailing.

Finally, Edgar moved, drawing her attention back to him. She tried to hold his gaze, but her insides quivered. Sucking in a deep breath, she released it slowly, uncertain how to escape this nightmare. She glanced to the side, hoping as the light chased more of the shadows away, she might be able to discern a way out. The room was nothing more than an opening in what had been a hallway leading down to another level. It was closed off with a wooden slatted gate.

He smiled, rubbing his chin as his gaze moved around the space. "We're in a mine. Of course, there are hundreds of thousands of abandoned mines, so in case you're wondering if your former bodyguard's company will be able to find you, they won't. But I thought this was a fitting place to bring you."

Unable to keep from asking, she sucked in a deep breath, then let it out slowly. "What is your plan? What are you going to do with me? I confess, Dr. Masterson, I don't understand what you hope to gain at all."

"For now, this is simply a place to hold you. Private. Secure. Giving us a chance to make sure you agree to our terms."

"But you know I won't do that. You know I would

die before giving into industrial espionage against my own company. Especially for anyone selling on the black market to terrorists."

"Dr. Olson," he said, his chiding tone grating on her already taut nerves. "How do you know we're selling to terrorists? Perhaps we just want the information to share with underprivileged countries who need your technology for their mines."

Now it was her turn to snort as she shook her head. "Oh, I hardly think you're looking to steal knowledge for benevolence. You'd make a lot of money with GeoTech's cutting-edge technology in the explosives industry on the black market. Maybe the terrorist groups wouldn't be able to use it initially, but you'll have buyers to develop it for them."

He chuckled, the sound reverberating in the empty space. "True. So true. But as to your not cooperating, you will find that the darkness closing so deep below the surface will eventually drive you mad. Plus, I'll leave you to it for a while and then bring another enticement. I'm sure you and I can work out an arrangement."

Before she could protest, he snagged the lantern off the dirt floor and walked away. He backed away from the gate, and she could see a padlocked chain wrapped around the top of several vertical slats. The light dimmed as he walked back up the tunnel, and the darkness threatened to swallow her. She worked to steady her breathing, terrified of hyperventilating or passing out.

Inhale. Exhale. Inhale. Exhale.

She was determined to get out. She'd been unable to

save Terrance, but she'd avenge his death if it was the last thing she did. Dr. Masterson was wrong about one thing. She could go for a long time in the dark without going mad. After all, she'd been doing that for almost two years.

20

Bennett lay on the ground, rage still coursing through him as much as the blood flowed through his veins and dripped down his side. He'd been forced to watch as Diana walked away when she was convinced that her acquiescence would guarantee his safety. Her arm had been grabbed by the fuckers who'd chased them before shoving her into the vehicle. As they drove away, he was furious that he'd been unable to stop them. And now, one vehicle remained behind, the lone occupant standing nearby wearing a stupid grin.

Inhale. Exhale. Inhale. Exhale.

Consistency. Steady. Positively identify target. In front of target. Behind target. Assess. Evaluate. Focus. Breathe.

Just as the man approached, Bennett lifted his weapon and fired. One shot rang out. One direct hit through the heart. One man dropped to the dirt.

Pushing to his knees, Bennett sucked in a painful breath, then made his way over to him.

"Bennett!"

Hearing Leo's voice, he radioed, "I'm here. Just took out the man left behind to finish me. But they got Diana. Goddamn fuckers got her."

He crawled over to the man and searched his pockets. "Got his keys and vehicle. Going after her." Sucking in a painful breath, he recognized the bullet that had hit him when Diana was on his back had been more than superficial. It was straight through on his side with an entrance and exit, but only going through the muscle. "Shit," he groaned, leaning over to pull a knife from his boot. Slicing off the man's shirt, he lifted his and wrapped strips around his middle to stem the blood flow.

"How bad is it?" Carson called out.

"Straight through. Only muscle. Other than that, not bad. I'm going after her."

"Wait. I can get backup to you—" Carson began.

"If the fucker I just killed doesn't show up, they'll suspect something anyway."

"You're right but go slow. Buy some time."

"Not sitting here while I wait for you," he argued in return. "No fuckin' way."

"Understood," Carson replied.

Carson's understanding came from what Bennett had confided about his feelings for Diana. He knew the others would now know. He held no acrimony—secrets among Keepers, especially with missions, could only lead to disastrous consequences. Diana's safety was more important than trying to keep his feelings for her hidden.

"Follow at a distance. Natalie has satellite imagery

now, and we can track you. Hop is on his way with Poole, Chris, and Dolby. The kidnappers need her alive, so that gives you time. Stay close but wait on backup."

He sighed heavily. Everything Carson said made sense, but not being able to rush to her ate at his gut. But Carson was right—whoever took her needed her alive. They could only get whatever knowledge they were hoping to obtain from Diana. "Okay, but if I get the opportunity to make it to her before you arrive, I'm going in."

"Understood," Carson acknowledged again.

"Abandoned mines are notoriously unstable. The ground can plunge underneath you without warning. Try to see where they are going in and out," Adam added. "If they've got her inside one, or especially deep in one, then you've got to exercise caution and care getting her out."

He headed to the Jeep and climbed inside. With the headlights on, he circled around until he was driving in the direction of the SUV that had left with Diana. "Direction?"

"Northwest. There are at least three mines close by that they could be heading to unless they are traveling farther," Natalie radioed. "I have her tracker locked in and will let you know."

Following the road, he slowly drove even though the desire to floor the accelerator was hard to battle. He had to use the headlights, but his long-distance vision was acute, and he could tell that the vehicle with Diana wasn't in sight, so they wouldn't see him. The terrain was hilly, and he was glad for the Jeep, considering a new layer of loose rock covered the ground, and small scrub brushes and pine trees dotted the area.

Anxious to find out more, he barked, "Where the fuck are they?"

Natalie's steady voice responded in return. "They're slowing. Wait... they've stopped. It looks like they're outside the abandoned Walker King Mine."

"Give it all to me." He slowed to a stop after pulling off the road.

"It's an old copper mine. Goes down about five levels. The lowest level is probably underwater or at least partially underwater. It's on protected land, so not privately owned. The entrance has a wooden shaft that leads down to the second level. I'm trying to check out the latest video posted by some explorers. Chances are the kidnappers are only using it to hold her and hide out for a very short time."

"Okay, it's got tracks and a few old mining carts," Rick said. "Abbie is pulling up the schematics."

"Got it," Abbie cut in. "Yes, the bottom level is flooded according to the latest intel, and the tunnel leading to it has been inaccessible since a fire in the 1950s. Some mine explorer groups have checked it out over the years, but a scheduled group hasn't gone through in over two years."

"Why did they bring her here? If it's protected land, then they don't own it," he growled, hating that she was inside a dangerous, abandoned mine. She'd be terrified and unable to discern her surroundings.

"My guess is that it's just a temporary holding place

until they can obtain what they need from her," Leo surmised.

"You asked me to check out Alex and his connections with the Korean engineer or guy from OSHA that he's been hanging out with," Jeb said. "So far tonight, they're still in the casino. Doesn't look like he's even aware something has happened to her."

He digested that information but wasn't willing to take Dr. Kang and the Korean company off the table as the ones wanting to get to Diana. "I'm going to check it out. Just to see how many are here."

"Stay in contact," Carson ordered unnecessarily.

Slipping from the Jeep, he moved with stealth up a desert hill toward the light in the distance. His boot steps were silent, as was his breathing. Memories of the Afghanistan terrain came to mind, making his present location appear familiar. Two vehicles were now in sight at the edge of a wooden structure built against the side of a hill. Only one man was visible standing at the entrance, a rifle loosely hung around his shoulders as he lit a cigarette, the smoke curling in front of his face.

Abbie radioed, "The entrance tunnel still has the wooden supports and a small building. It's not the original, but it's been many years since anyone has worked on it. An elaborate ore bin with a grizzly on top goes into a hopper and then down. The grizzly is the large grate near the end of the tall. According to the schematics, there would be the mining cart tracks leading down, but also a separate shaft with a ladder, so miners could go up and down without having to go around."

Bennett was already considering how to find Diana

when Abbie added, "If they have her inside, they probably went down the tunnels following the rail tracks. I can't imagine they'd want to put extra stress onto a wooden ladder since someone would need to be right with her."

"Chances are she's on the second or third level," he surmised aloud. "If they're using this as a temporary stop, they don't want to make it more difficult on themselves to get her in and out." He sighed. "Unless they want to ensure she doesn't escape, and then she might be held lower."

The idea that she was in even more danger of being three or more levels below the surface had his fingers curl into fists.

The man outside suddenly snapped to attention, his spine straightening as he turned to look toward the entrance. Another man walked out, a hat pulled low over his forehead, followed by another.

"Go back and find out why the fuck Jake isn't here yet."

The Australian accented voice hit Bennett. Tapping his earpiece, he whispered, "Australian." He knew that was the only word necessary for the Keepers back at the compound to start digging.

"Jake probably just got lost," the man with the rifle said.

"That's why I told you to go back and find him."

"Can't I wait till daylight? I won't be able to see anything now!"

The Australian stepped closer. "You're not paid to think. You're paid to do exactly what I say. Now get out of here and go find Jake. And while you're at it, check on that guard's body. I want to know that there won't be any evidence left over by the time the wildlife gets through with him."

The man with a rifle grumbled but turned and walked toward one of the vehicles. Bennett slipped a little closer, hoping to see the man in charge. Another man walked up behind the Australian.

"Don't you think daylight would be better?"

"We're not fuckin' going to be here in the daylight. We'll give her a little more time to let the fear convince her to give us what we want. Then we're getting the fuck out of here." The man turned, and Bennett recognized the Australian engineer, Edgar Masterson, just as one of the other men acknowledged him.

"Well, you're the boss, Dr. Masterson."

"Yeah, and don't forget it. You stay out here and guard until the others come back." With that, Edgar turned with the remaining man, and they walked back into the tunnel.

Whispering again, Bennett radioed, "Edgar Masterson. He's got Diana." As much as he wanted to find Diana instantly, he knew he needed to take out the man who had just left to keep his presence a secret. After radioing his intention, he slipped back to his Jeep, climbed behind the wheel, and headed in the direction of where he'd been shot. Driving with as much stealth as he had walked earlier, he parked at a distance. Slipping back through the desert, he spied the man leaning over the body in the dirt, seeing the exact second the man realized the body was Jake and not Bennett. He raced forward and tackled him, ignoring the white-hot pain slicing through his side.

It only took a few seconds to knock the man out, and while his instinct was to kill him, he locked that desire down. Ignoring the bleeding that his tackle had renewed from his wound, he sliced off this man's shirt and bound the man's wrists behind him. Stuffing a gag into his mouth, he left the man propped against a rock, not caring if the coyotes got to him before the Keepers arrived.

Once more, reversing his movements, he drove back and parked at a distance from the mine entrance. Now, with only Dr. Masterson and the other man there, he was determined to get to Diana. Moving over the same terrain as before, he stopped closer to the mine's entrance.

"What is Hop's ETA?"

"They'll land at a private airstrip in twenty minutes. Delayed due to going around a storm area through Death Valley. They'll have a bird waiting when they land and then get to you within forty minutes."

"I'm going in."

"I'll guide you," Abbie vowed.

Staying low, he crept to the door and peered through the wooden slats, where a lantern sat in the middle of the dirt floor. The small structure was empty, and there was no noise coming from the mine entrance. With his weapon tucked in its holster, he soundlessly hastened to the tunnel leading into the rock wall.

Abbie radioed, "Follow the path. It will be only a

slight downward grade, and then you'll pick up the rails."

With the illumination coming from the lantern behind him, he bent low, the ceiling close to his head. The gray rock walls surrounded him, and soon the light had faded to the barest hint, making it more difficult to keep his footsteps quiet with the loose gravel on the path. Just when he was ready to use the light from his watch, his foot slid across the rail track used for the mining carts that would have hauled the copper from the depths of the earth. Soon, he noted wooden crossties running underneath the tracks.

"I've made it to the wooden tracks."

"Keep going. The incline will become a little steeper. You should come to a main junction line, and you want to go straight ahead," Abbie instructed.

Even though the light was almost gone, he could make his way by keeping with the tracks. Although stepping carefully to keep from tripping over the rails or wooden slats slowed his progress.

Unwilling to chance making a mistake in the darkness, he flipped on the watch's light, beaming it downward and forward so that his footsteps were sure. Coming to the junction, he could see a movable switch in the tracks below, allowing mining carts to go straight or to the left.

The sounds of footsteps on gravel and heavy breathing met his ears, and he hustled down the left track, pressing his back against the wall as he flipped off his watch light.

After a moment, a light could be seen in the

entranceway to his tunnel, but he was sure whoever was walking along had no idea he was hiding to the side. The man who'd been with Edgar Masterson walked past, his flashlight focused downward as he shuffled along toward the exit.

Instantly assessing, Bennett didn't want to give the man a chance to alert Edgar of his presence but still preferred to take him out of the equation so one less person could impede Bennett from getting to Diana.

Once again, he covertly slipped from his hiding place and followed, keeping his footsteps paced with the other man's to mask his presence. Just as the kidnapper stepped out of the mine entrance and into the wooden shack, Bennett wrapped his arm around the man's neck, and with a quick, carotid restraint, he disabled the man as he fell unconscious. Hefting him over his shoulder, he ignored the pain and prayed the loss of blood wouldn't hinder him as he carried him out to the vehicle that had been used to transport Diana. Finding a length of rope, he efficiently bound and gagged him, as well.

Now, no longer wanting to waste any time with hopefully only Edgar still inside, he retraced his steps, letting LSIWC know his plans. With the man's flashlight, he hurried back through the tunnels and passed the junction, anxious to find where she was being held.

21

Diana's legs were tired from standing, but she hated to sit on the ground, even with her back against the rock walls. She felt more vulnerable on the ground. Somehow standing would give her a fighting chance when Edgar returned. Her chin dropped to her chest, and she sighed heavily. The room was pitch black, so she would have been disoriented even if she had perfect vision. Instead, she steadied her breathing and listened for any change in sounds that might indicate his return.

She'd tried and failed miserably not to think of her dad's death being more than an accident. "Dad..." she whispered, swallowing deeply while blinking to keep the tears from falling. Her father had completed his work on contrasting energy at the time of his death, and Olson GeoTech was in full trials. The industry was anxiously waiting on the results. It would certainly cement their company as a world leader in explosive technology for the geology and mining industry. They were all so excited. She'd worked alongside him as she finished her doctorate, thrilled to know she was part of the cutting-edge industrial science of explosives.

When he'd died in the car accident, her world had stopped. She grieved the loss, not only as her father but also mentor, boss, co-researcher, and friend. She'd even wondered how she could go on, but it had been her mother and Uncle Jerry who had insisted that she could honor him by making sure Olson's contrasting energy came to fruition. And after a year of that success, they'd encouraged her to take the next step her father wanted to work on. She'd made it her reason for getting up each day until her accident.

Thinking about the loss of her father caused Terrance's image to fill her mind, and her chest depressed as the air rushed from her lungs. Squeezing her eyes tightly shut, she could no longer hold back the tears that dripped down her cheeks, falling to the rock floor below.

It was hard to imagine the ache in her heart at the loss of someone she'd known for less than a week. But he wasn't just someone she met and spent time with. He wasn't just a hired bodyguard. And he wasn't just a man she'd slept with. In the week since she met him, he'd become so much more.

He was the man she felt safe with. Emotionally as well as physically. He was the man who didn't seem to be taken aback by her lack of visual acuity. He was the man she confided in, opened up to, and shared with. He was the man who so easily walked with her and talked with her, guiding her without taking over, describing without making her feel like a burden.

Yes, they'd slept together, and while she'd tried to convince herself it was just sex—really good, fun, amazing sex—she was more connected to him than with any other man she'd ever been with. He made her feel and experience things she'd wondered if she'd lost forever.

It was strange since they came from such divergent backgrounds and experiences, yet perhaps, just like magnets, the attraction drew them together, making it easy to stay connected and difficult to pull apart.

"I wanted more time with you," she whispered into the darkness. "I wanted everything with you."

And just like she expected, the silence remained, and no answer came back to her. Blowing out a long breath, she battled a sense of dizziness. Inhaling deeply, she tried to blank her mind from all that stole her away from the moment, knowing both her father and Terrance would want her to escape.

Edgar. I need to focus on Edgar.

What does he want? My latest industrial research is still at the trial stage, and without all the necessary data, selling it to a terrorist group that doesn't have the equipment or products means they won't be able to use it.

She sifted through the information she knew about him. Edgar Masterson. Chief explosive engineer for the Australian company, Orica. *Who does he really work for? NitroSabir? The Russian government? Australian miners? The Koreans? Or some terrorist group that he simply profits from?*

She was taught to think rationally through a problem, analyze possibilities, test theories and hypotheses, research, and discover. And while her exceptional ability to do so made her top in her engineering class and an asset to her father's company, she had found that sometimes understanding people was not nearly as easy or productive. Trying to work through the *why* of Edgar's actions, she was coming up empty.

Then I'll simply focus on getting out of here! I refuse to give in, and I refuse to give up!

She skimmed her way toward the wall, heading in the direction where Edgar had left. Her fingers came upon the wooden gate. Feeling all around, she discovered it was just as she discerned in the light of the lantern he'd had with him. It was a slatted gate and not a solid door. There was a chain around part of it, and she could touch a padlock dangling from the chain. Not wasting her time on the lock, she knelt, touching the wooden slats near the ground. They were firm but not closely set together. With no other implement other than her body, she sat on the ground with her knees cocked in front of her. *There's no leverage for me here.*

Still crawling in the dark, she shimmied to the side so her back was against the rock wall and angled her legs toward the gate. Cocking her knees again, she pressed her back against the wall and kicked out, making sure the soles of her shoes were flat against the wooden slats. Pain upon contact reverberated through her legs and lower back, but she felt the wood give ever so slightly. Not willing to stop, she kicked again and again, finally hearing a crack from the gate. Buoyed by the possibility of success, she ignored the pain of the rocks digging into her back and lifted her legs again, kicking out twice in succession.

Finally, the wood splintered, and the bottom slat broke. Smiling, she scrambled forward, her fingers ignoring the splinters of wood jabbing at her as she pulled several pieces of the broken slats away. The space she created from the bottom of the gate to the ground was about twelve inches. It would be tight, but she preferred to try to squeeze through than risk Edgar hearing her as she attempted to kick out another slat.

Lying flat on her stomach, she pressed her cheek against the dirt floor and inched forward. The bottom slat rubbed against her head, but she managed to get through. Her breasts pressed flat against the floor, but she shimmied forward with her upper arms, slithering underneath the gate like a snake. She was afraid her hips would catch, but adrenaline rushed through her body, giving her the strength to keep going. Grimacing, she clamped her jaw tightly to keep from crying out and managed to squeeze her ass underneath the wood. Bruised and battered, she was nonetheless elated once free.

While she was out of her prison, she had no idea what to do from here. Without light, she was at a complete disadvantage. *What if there was more than one way to go?*

Scrambling to her knees, she stood slowly, her hands holding the rock wall. Gliding along one side and then moving past the gate and feeling the other, she determined that the room she'd been held in was at the end of this particular tunnel. Still afraid she might run into Edgar, she was grateful she didn't have to choose which way to go right away.

With her hands gliding over the hewn stone, she moved forward, inching along but afraid to go too fast. She'd been inside many mines, having studied the industry. Some of her fellow graduate students had loved going exploring in abandoned mines, and she'd joined them on numerous excursions. She'd loved the knowledge gained from seeing what the miners of old had to do to conquer the earth to bring forth the ore and minerals. She imagined their lives and work, often in primitive and dangerous settings. She'd never explored the mines as a hobby, preferring to focus on the industry's future and how to make it safer.

There would be shafts in the floor or ceiling leading to other levels with ladders to traverse. *Excellent if I could see where they were before crashing through and possibly tumbling to my death or being maimed!*

Continuing to inch along, she had to glide one foot forward at a time to ascertain if the floor was still solid rock while never being certain it wouldn't crumble underneath her. The pathway led upward at a slight angle, giving her the courage to continue knowing she was heading out. But it had become evident that she was not on the ground level and likely lower than the second level.

She had no idea of the passage of time but could only imagine that Edgar would soon return. If he came across her in the middle of the tunnel, he would have the advantage. But going back was not an option. And while she knew there would have been no chance of staying in the room he'd locked her in, her circumstances didn't feel as though they had truly improved.

Jerking when her hand snagged on a piece of wood coming down from the wall, she noted it was different from the support timbers she'd encountered. Grabbing hold, she discerned a ladder going up the wall. Since ladders were often used for quick access between levels, she was hyperaware that a hole in the floor probably went down with a ladder, too. While going up the ladder was a possibility, she wasted precious time deciding whether it was worth the risk.

Going up a level quickly only to become turned around at the top and then traveling the wrong way down the tunnel would be disastrous. Popping her head up to the next level only to run into Edgar would also be devastating. *But then, standing here debating with myself while also being a sitting duck is stupid!*

Her foot had discovered more wooden slats on the floor underneath the ladder, giving proof that it was a perpendicular shaft going up and down. Kneeling, she listened and heard the barest hint of water dripping from below. Many mines filled with water, or at least the lower levels flooded. The idea of plunging to her death made the decision to climb up even more tenuous. She couldn't remember a time in her life when every possible action could be met with devastating results.

Sucking in a deep breath and firing off a prayer, she

gingerly placed one foot on the bottom rung of the ladder leading upward and tested the weight. The wood held strong, not yielding a creak or a crack. Now, more determined, she began the slow upward climb, still surrounded by darkness, unable to see her hand in front of her face, and her feet no longer on solid ground.

She inched upward, testing each rung before giving it her weight. The time in the hospital after her accident came to mind. She'd held out hope that the darkness that met her would only be temporary. And while the doctors had not wanted to take away her expectation, she was grateful that they also gave her the truth.

"We feel certain that your left eye will regain no more than the light and dark shadows you currently can see. Your right eye has near vision, with objects becoming more blurry at a distance. A retina transplant is always a possibility, but we will discuss that down the road. There is the possibility that over time, the distance you see clearly will increase."

At the time, the words had seemed harsh and unyielding, a definitive change in how she saw her future. But if her parents had taught her anything, it was always to look for the next solution, the next theory, the next way to make something work. And she learned that her career would not be defined by her vision loss. Changed... absolutely. But it did not end.

Climbing carefully, she tested out each rung, but not being able to see where it led was unnerving. She'd experienced darkness before, but knowing she was deep underground made this darkness even more claustrophobic. *Keep going. Don't give up.* The air smelled less musty with each step as the level she was moving toward had more airflow. Once again buoyed by that new possibility, she continued to climb.

Suddenly, voices met her ears, and she halted on the ladder, her fingers gripping tightly onto the wood as the bottoms of her shoes balanced close to the side rails to support her weight better. It only took a few seconds to recognize Edgar's voice, but she couldn't tell who he was talking to. She hated that he was between her and possible freedom.

When no one answered his questions, but he continued to speak, she realized he must be on his phone. Still hidden in the narrow shaft, she could see the barest hint of light coming from his cell phone on the far side of the space as he leaned against the rock wall. While nothing was clear, she reveled in the tiny illumination that cut through the piercing darkness that had engulfed her for the past hour.

Surprised he got a signal in the mine, it hit her that they must be closer to the ground level. Trying not to make a sound with her breathing, she listened to his side of the conversation.

"I can't believe the fucker didn't come back. I paid for men who would do what I asked. Is that too much to expect?"

"Yes, I've got her. She's not cooperating, which shocked the hell out of me, but I have her locked down in the mine, so she'll talk real soon."

"No, no, she's not hurt. Not yet. Hell, dead or injured doesn't get me what I want."

"Well, if my inside contact had done the job, we would've already had the information."

"I have at least three buyers lined up, and no... I'm not telling you who they are. Do you think I'm stupid? Suffice it to say, I'm tired of working for a company that refuses to make the most of what they have. And with the money I'll have, I won't have to stay there."

"Yeah, well, I need to go back down to her. I want her scared but not freaking the fuck out once I start threatening her family. She'll cave. Then I'll take her to the airport, and you make the arrangements to get us out of here. As soon as she coughs up the research, we won't need her anymore."

His words stopped, and her heartbeat almost did at the same time. *She'll cooperate. Scared. Threaten her family. She'll cave. We won't need her anymore.*

Hearing that Edgar was ready to go back down to the room she'd been held in meant she had precious few minutes left to escape. She heard his footsteps move away, fading into the distance. Not able to tell which direction he went, she could only assume he was going back down the tunnel to the level she'd just left.

Scrambling up the ladder, she crawled on her hands and knees out into the tunnel hallway where he had stood. The ladder had extended up another level, and she was uncertain if it went to the top floor. Turning in a circle, she clenched her hands together, the combination of fatigue and fear keeping her from quickly analyzing the best course of action. She'd come this far but knew his discovery of her escape would have him racing back up the tunnel.

Turning, she skimmed along the wall again until her hands came to the next shaft and ladder, and heaving a deep breath, she began climbing upward again. She had no idea where it would lead, but right now, she could only depend on herself to escape from Edgar. And up was the only way to go.

22

Bennett hastened down the same path he'd taken earlier, following the old mine-cart rail tracks. Once down on the second level, having passed the junction, he slowed, hearing voices from ahead in the tunnel. Now that he stopped and listened, it appeared the voice came from below. A faint glow illuminated a hole in the floor at a widening in the tunnel. He'd passed ore chutes, but now a shaft appeared with a ladder going straight down to the level below.

With each step he crept closer, the illumination grew. Staying out of sight, he leaned forward just enough to peer down, hearing Edgar. His heartbeat pounded a staccato as he thought Diana might be with him, but listening to the one-sided conversation, it became evident that Edgar had placed her on a lower level, locking her in somewhere.

Bennett's anger raged to a degree he'd never felt before. Not when his father heaped abuse on him or when his mother left. Not when he'd been in battle with the enemy, fighting for his life and the lives of his team, only to lose someone in the end.

This was a wave of anger born from deep inside his heart for a woman he'd known less than a week. He couldn't explain the connection and wasn't about to waste time trying to give it a definition. His emotions were just as real regardless of the length of their time spent together.

Diana meant something to him, and while he had no idea what her feelings for him were, he'd take whatever he could get. If it was friendship, he'd be the best damn friend she'd ever had. If it was a travel companion, he'd described the wonders of the world to her. And if he was lucky enough for her to have feelings for him, too, he'd devote the rest of his life to making sure she knew that she had his heart.

And with that realization, a strange calm moved through him, chasing away the remnants of rage. A soldier thought best when his anger was tempered with a quiet, resolute determination. Edgar not only had Diana fired upon, but he'd also caused their car accident, kidnapped her, dragged her into a dangerous abandoned mine, and now locked her in a dark prison. As far as Bennett was concerned, Edgar never needed to see another dawn.

He tested the wooden ladder with his foot to check if it would bear his weight. A large man, he had to consider that it might be too old or too rotten to hold him. When it appeared to remain steady, he scaled down the ladder to the level below where Edgar had just left. Looking around with his watch light, he could see the widening of the tunnel. A small sound came from the shaft as it continued to the level below, and he hesitated, wondering if Edgar was now just below him. With his watch covered, he was in darkness and remained perfectly still.

Leaning ever so slightly to the side, he could tell someone was in the shaft. *Fuck!* He thought he'd taken care of all of Edgar's companions. Without making a sound, he plastered his back against the wall, waiting to see which direction they went.

The shuffling sound indicated the person moved up toward him. He could barely make out a small hand lifting to the next visible rung on the ladder before the back of their head moved into sight.

Diving to the rock floor, he whipped his hand out to the person just as they emerged. With one hand clamped over their mouth and the other around their middle, he lifted, stunned at the slight weight. A whiff of vanilla hit his nostrils at the same time her body crashed into his. *Jesus Christ... Diana!* At the last second, he twisted so that when they fell back onto the floor, he landed first, protecting her. He grimaced in pain but kept his grip secure. She recovered quickly, kicking out and clawing at his arms. Grunting, he was sure his wound was once again re-injured.

"Diana," he whispered, "it's me."

Her body jerked then stilled, each muscle locking. Her rigidity had him fear she was about to have a seizure. His arms tightened, then eased off her chest while still covering her mouth. "Diana, baby, it's me."

With his grip less tight, she managed to flop around

until she faced him. With the barest hint of lighting from his watch, her gaze searched his face with disbelief and pain etched into her expression. Her face crumpled, and a tear fell as a wail attempted to escape her lips.

"Oh, babe, please don't cry. We've got to stay quiet. We'll get out of here. I swear you can fall apart later, but you're so strong, Diana. Please, baby, hang on."

She attempted to swallow several times, then jerked her head up and down.

Keeping his hand over her mouth, he said, "I'm gonna move my hand, okay? You okay?"

Again, she nodded as the fight had left her. He slowly lifted his hand over her mouth, and she gasped, sucking in a ragged breath.

"I… I… thought… you were dead." His arms squeezed around her tightly again, hating that she'd suffered not only the kidnapping but thinking he'd been killed.

"Injured but not dead, baby."

She blinked, seeming to take longer to process his words than normal, and then jerked again. He grunted but remained on his back with her protected against his chest. She scrambled to the side, her eyes and hands searching.

"Oh God," she breathed, and he looked down to see renewed blood on his shirt.

"It's fine. We can't worry about that now. We need to get out of here."

A roar sounded from deep within the mine, and they stared unblinking before he scrambled to his feet, pulling her upward along with him. "Looks like he's discovered you were smarter than he gave you credit for."

Her face, which just a moment before had been crumpled in grief and shock, now morphed into a wide-eyed fright, then morphed again into resolute determination. Her chin lifted as she wiped her tears, mouthing, "I'm ready." Bennett couldn't help the grin that slid across his face at the woman in front of him that held his heart.

Heavy, fast-approaching boot steps crunched on rock and echoed through the chamber.

"You can't escape, you stupid bitch!" Edgar called out, his voice bouncing off the rock walls. "You, of all people, should know I have this place rigged. You have no choice but to work with me!"

Not wanting to waste a second, Bennett grabbed her around the waist and hoisted her onto the ladder going up to the next level that he'd just come down. "Up! As fast as you can go!"

Still gaining strength from his presence, or perhaps it was just adrenaline rushing through her body, she scrambled upward at a pace much faster than he'd seen her use a few minutes earlier. He hesitated for a few seconds, debating whether to follow her immediately or wait for Edgar to arrive so he could take him out once and for all. But with the possibility of explosives rigged along the tunnels, chutes, and shafts of the old mine, he didn't want to leave Diana unprotected again.

Making his decision, he radioed, "We're heading up from level three to level two through the shaft.

Masterson says the place is rigged with explosives. He's right behind us."

Not waiting for any instructions from LSIWC, he grabbed the wooden ladder and hoisted his body upward, closing the distance between Diana and himself. By the time he got to the next level, she had stepped off the ladder and stood with her back plastered against the rock wall. He cursed, realizing she needed more light to see clearly but was hoping to keep their location a secret from the ever-approaching Dr. Masterson.

Abbie radioed in return, "There's a chute at the next widening. It's closer than the next ladder shaft. It'll go up to the first level if you want."

"If he sets off an explosion, what's safer? Chute, shaft, or tunnel?"

"Chute. It'll be fortified."

"Fuck," he breathed. He hated to have Diana crawl up an ore chute, but there was no time to make a different plan. Turning, he leaned closer and clamped his hands on her shoulders. Bringing his face close, he whispered, "We've got to hurry. Can you climb up an angled chute?"

She nodded, her eyes boring into his, although he had no idea how much she could see. He held up his watch light and spied the opening to the wide chute, glad to see it was almost five feet wide and about three feet tall. With his hands spanning her waist, he hoisted her upward until she grabbed the wooden slats and pulled forward until her knees and toes could find purchase. "Go as fast as you can, babe. I'll be right behind."

In typical Diana fashion, she immediately followed his instructions, and even though a layer of dirt covered the chute, she scrambled upward, her feet slipping occasionally. As soon as he had room, he jumped and grabbed hold of the bottom of the wood and pulled upward using his arm strength. It was harder for him to maneuver in the space, but he ducked after hitting his head once on the upper rocks that formed the ceiling of the chute.

He caught up to her and dodged her feet as she crawled. Another roar of fury met their ears from below as Edgar reached the level they'd just left. Needing them to hurry, Bennett climbed closer to her and shoved his shoulder under her ass, boosting her upward. Like a trooper, she didn't say a word but continued to hoist herself up the forty-five-degree angled chute until she whispered, "I'm at the top!"

"We're here, man," Hop's voice called out over his earpiece radio. "Coming up on the top level, out inside the mine entrance."

Before he could respond, a blast resounded in the tunnels, reverberating throughout his body. Diana cried out, her body sliding back but stopping when he threw his arms and legs out, pressing them against the rock and wooden walls to keep himself from moving back down the slide. "Explosion!" he called out but knew it was unnecessary. The Keepers would have heard it already.

Rocks pelted them as he tried to move her upward

to the next level. She bent over, her head and torso now flat on the ground, and he shoved harder to force her legs to make it out of the chute. Just when his head and shoulders made it free, the rock and wooden walls of the chute filled with debris, trapping his lower half. Unable to move his legs, he cursed, banging his fist against the solid floor.

Dust and gravel filled the air like a thick fog, coating everything and filling his mouth and nostrils. Squinting, he tried to protect his eyes, feeling around with his hands until his fingers wrapped around her ankle. She choked and coughed, gasping in air, but he knew she was still alive.

"Are you hurt?" he growled, trying not to suck in the debris.

"No," she replied, her voice sounding far away after the explosion had dimmed their hearing.

"Keep going. I can't come right now but keep going. Keep going up. The Keepers are here, and I'll get to you."

She twisted around until her face was directly in front of his. Her hands clutched his cheeks. "Why can't you come?"

"The chute caved in on the bottom part of my legs—"

"Oh my God, Terrance! Oh my God!"

Hearing her panic, he assured her, "I'm not crushed. It's just the rock has filled the space. Once gravity can shift more, it'll go on down the chute, and then I'll work my way up."

"Here, I'll help!" She scrambled to her knees, and he

heard rocks shifting as her hands clawed beside his body.

"Stop, there's no time. I don't want you breathing all this shit. Get out and then—"

"I'm not leaving you! I'm not going to leave you!" Her voice bordered on hysterical even though her movements were steady as she shoveled more debris away.

The idea that the walls could cave in and kill her was more than he could bear. "Diana, babe, listen to me. I need to know you're safe. I need to know you're getting out of here."

A sob ripped from her lungs, and she clutched his filthy face. As the dust settled a little more, the light from his watch allowed him to see they were covered in thick, gray, powdered rock dust.

"I don't care what you say, Terrance Bennett. I am *not* leaving you! Save your breath and help me get you out of here!"

Not willing to waste time arguing, he joined her efforts as he fought through the rubble that had filled in around his waist. Scooping handfuls of rocks to the side, they made headway, but he still couldn't move his legs. Focusing his energy on wiggling his feet, he felt a slight shift as some of the rocks below his body appeared to be loose enough to slide down the chute. It wasn't much, but he would take any inch of freedom he could manage.

"I don't know how long this is going to take," he choked out as they continued to shovel rocks from his hips and toss them up. A pile had gathered next to her, but she was unfailing in her continued efforts.

"I don't hear anything," she muttered. "I wonder what happened to Edgar?"

"With any luck, he blew himself the fuck up," Bennett growled.

A snort erupted, and he looked up. As more dust settled, his watch light could pierce through the haze, and her face became visible. Her entire body was covered in a thick layer of gray dust, with only a few swipes around her eyes, giving life to the zombie effect of living through a mine explosion. "You're beautiful."

Another snort erupted from her, and she shook her head. "You're crazy. If you keep talking like that, I'm going to wonder who has the vision problem."

Their fingers bumped into each other as they hauled out the rock by handfuls until his hips were visible. He wiggled his feet a little more, finding that he was now loose at the other end from mid-calf. "We've got about two feet still around my thighs to get out of here," he reported.

"We got this." Her chest heaved from her exertion, and her movements were halted in between coughing at the dust they inhaled.

He searched beyond her to see what he could discern of the tunnel's integrity. While their section of the tunnel had not caved in, he had no idea if the way was blocked to the outside.

Her thoughts must've followed the same as his when she asked, "Will the Keepers be able to get to us?"

"One way or the other, babe, I guaran-damn-tee you that they won't leave without us."

She held his gaze, a tremulous smile playing about her lips. "Then let's keep going. I want to meet your friends."

Now the chuckle came from deep inside him as he nodded. "You got it." Looking back down, he pulled more rocks from the trapped chute. Together, they could do anything.

23

The soot-like dust filling the air had coated every inch of her being, and Diana wondered as she coughed again if she would ever be able to wash it all off, sneeze it all out, or get it out of her throat and lungs. Terrance was just as covered, but on him, he just appeared more rugged instead of bedraggled like her.

Rugged and alive. *Alive.* Her heart was slow to catch up to her mind, and the realization that the man she'd fallen for wasn't dead after all, settled deep inside. Maybe if they'd had a slow reunion, time to talk, and find out everything that happened, it would've seemed more real. But instead, he'd swooped in, catching her off guard and sending her mind into a tizzy. And it had been nonstop since that moment.

She was amazed at how instinctively he'd adapted to each change, making instant decisions. Tunnel or ladder? Go up the ladder. Is Edgar coming? Take the chute. She knew someone was helping him through his earpiece radio, but Terrance made the split-second decisions that kept them alive.

She was used to methodical analysis of research. Test, analyze, reevaluate, change, then test again. But Terrance was able to assess and move into action while she was still trying to get her bearings.

"Diana? You okay?"

Her head jerked up from where she stared at the rocks, her mind all over the place. *Christ, stop thinking and just dig!* "Yeah, sure. How are you doing?"

He reached forward with his arms and grabbed the top of the wooden edge of the chute and pulled. While he tried to wiggle his thighs free, she continued to lean down and pull rocks away. At this angle, she had her face plastered against his stomach, and she could only imagine what they must look like.

Suddenly, his body moved, and the sound of more rocks sliding in the distance met her ears. He shouted triumphantly as he shimmied upward, forcing more rocks around his thighs to fall away. His chest heaved as he hoisted himself up, and she threw her arms around his neck. They clung to each other for a moment, simply glad to be alive and together.

He shifted to his knees, his hands clutching her face as his thumbs swiped at the thick dust covering her. "I can't believe you got me out of this."

She shook her head, her heart full. "We. *We* did it together."

He stood and gently pulled her up to her feet. Using his watch's illumination, he swung it around the area, giving evidence that the entire section of their tunnel was coated in dust and loose gravel, just as they had feared. But next to them, the cart rails were still visible.

"Let's go," he said, linking fingers with her. He took off, and she was determined not to hold him back even though her feet stumbled over the now even rougher terrain of the tunnel floor. "There are the switch rails," he said, pointing downward.

She had no idea what he was talking about, so she remained quiet, allowing him to pull her along.

"It shouldn't be long now. The exit should be just up ahead."

The area was still dark, only illuminated by his watch, making her wonder why the light wasn't coming from the outside. "Is it still nighttime? I have no idea how long I've been down here."

Before he could answer, they rounded a bend, and he came to a halt, causing her to run into the back of him. "Fuck!" He cursed as she grunted, bouncing off his back.

She had been staring down at the rails, finding them the easiest thing to focus on besides his body as they stumbled along by the pale light from his watch. But now, she could see what caused him to stop. In front of them was a pile of rocks and wooden rubble covering the end of the tunnel.

"Oh God, we're trapped!"

She wanted to sit and weep, but he radioed, "We've got to be close to the exit, but the area has caved in. Can you work it from outside?" After a few seconds, he replied, "Got it."

She waited as he turned and looked down, holding

tightly to her hand. "Don't worry, babe. I'm gonna get you out of here. The Keepers are on the other side, having just discovered this cave-in. I'll work it on this end, and they'll work it on the other. We're going to make it out of here."

With a nod, she sucked in a deep breath to steady her heartbeat. Instantly regretting that, she coughed some more. He gently pushed her to the side. "Sit here. Rest. I'm going to start on the right side of this to remove some rubble, coordinating with what they're doing on their side."

Leaning back, she rested against the rock wall for a moment, catching her breath and trying to clear her mind of the panic of being trapped in an underground mine. But standing there worrying wasn't going to get them out any quicker. She felt around, barely able to see his shadow in the scant illumination. "Show me what to do. I'm not going to just sit."

He looked at her, and if he thought to argue, he decided better of it. "Okay, come on. We're going to start pulling some of the smaller rocks out, and then I can shift larger ones and let gravity allow them to roll down."

Working in tandem just like before, she pulled out all the smaller rocks she could handle, giving him room to haul out the larger pieces and toss them behind them. Unable to see clearly, she heard his grunting as he lifted heavier rocks and could only imagine the strain his muscles were under to work so hard and fast. She lost track of time but kept going, and while she knew he was injured, neither of them wavered in their task.

They had not heard any more noise or voices from Edgar, and she could only assume his attempt to trap them trapped himself as well.

"Stop!" Terrance's hand shot over to her, stilling her in the middle of tossing a rock to the side.

She startled, her body jerking, but halted, her head turning toward him.

"Poole?" he called out.

"Hey, man," a voice replied from the other side of the rubble. "We're close. Hang tight."

"I'm near the edge on the right side. You keep going on your left, and we'll be through."

With renewed vigor, she dove back into the rock pile with him, digging until her fingers bled and her ragged nails tore even more. Suddenly, as he pulled a rock from the top and let it roll down, a ray of light beamed into their tomb.

The sudden light cutting through the foggy darkness caused her to blink and look downward even though her heart leaped at the sight.

"Bennett?" a male voice called out.

Terrance grinned widely and stuck his hand toward the hole, clasping another hand coming through. "Thank fuck, guys. Glad to see you."

"Dr. Olson?"

"She's right here with me."

"Are you all okay?"

"We will be. Let's keep going."

He turned his gleeful expression toward her, and a similar smile hit her face. Chest heaving, she looked back at the wall before bending to move more rock. He stopped her and shook his head. "Hang on. It's getting dangerous here with us taking this down from both sides. A heavy rock could roll down on you."

This time, she didn't object but stood slightly to the side as the light grew larger with each rock that fell from the pile. When a hole was large enough for them to slide through, he turned and held out his hand. "You ready?"

"Hell, yeah," she said, nodding while staring at his face. After such darkness, the ability to just see him even a little more clearly brought tears to her eyes.

"Okay. Up you go." The hole was at the top of the pile of rubble, and he once again grabbed her around her waist and hoisted her up. She reached out, uncertain where to grab since some of the rocks were loose. But strong arms reached through the opening, and hands clasped around her forearms.

"Dr. Olson, just let us guide you out but make sure not to let us pull you too hard."

"Okay," she grunted as rough rocks dug into her chest and stomach. Terrance cursed from behind as he tried to guide her body through the hole. She still had to shimmy over the rock fragments. She looked up at the man holding her, and it appeared his face was contorted into a grimace.

"Shit," he said before focusing on her face. "Hey," he added in a softer voice. "I'm Dolby. It's good to see you, Dr. Olson."

She nodded again, and then with a final tug, he managed to pull her enough so that other hands reached out to take her by the waist and then the legs.

She was scooped into the arms of another man who turned to carry her outside.

"No! Terrance! I want to wait on—"

"Dr. Olson," he said with kindness. "Bennett would have my balls if I didn't take you out of this and into the fresh air. I'm Poole, by the way."

She twisted to observe Terrance now being assisted out of the hole as well. "I need to see him…"

"He's coming—"

"No, I need to be closer to see him," she choked out, her voice now as shaky as her body.

Poole turned and carried her swiftly toward him. Terrance offered chin lifts to his friends, but his gaze pinned on her. He was right there in two steps, shifting her from Poole's arms to pull her against his body. Quivers threatened to overtake her, but his arms only tightened, offering her strength and comfort.

"Shhh, babe, we made it. You and me, we made it," he shushed gently.

She nodded, unable to speak. Finally calming, she lifted her head and peered into his eyes. Only then did it really hit her that the air they were breathing was cool and crisp and fresh. Letting out a massive, chest-heaving sigh, she smiled. "We made it. Together."

Diana sat in the back of a long, white panel van, the outside so nondescript it could have belonged to any local delivery business. But the inside was filled with a long table against one side with computer equipment and monitors and two people in front of them as they typed on keyboards. On the other side were several chairs, currently occupied by her and a man introduced as Landon Sommers from the FBI. He seemed friendly with Terrance and the others, but now that the adrenaline had left her body, she was barely hanging on.

"Dr. Olson–Diana. I know you're exhausted. We're almost finished with our initial interview."

As nice as Landon was, she didn't miss the word *initial*, obviously indicating she would be interviewed more at a later time. But she understood. She had been the victim of numerous crimes and the witness to even more.

When she and Terrance were first pulled out, his coworkers had made sure they were away from the mine entrance in case there were more reverberations, explosions, or cave-ins. They both drank from the water bottles provided, grateful there was enough for her to wet a cloth to wipe the thick rock dust off her face. It was still on her body and clothes, coating her hair, and she had no doubt it lined her nasal passages, too. But to feel as though she could breathe clean air, clear out her throat with the water, and see without blinking more dust into her eyes, she felt better.

She had been introduced to the other Keepers, grateful that each one stepped close so that she could see their faces as she shook their hands. Somehow she'd imagined that Bennett's size would make him stand out among his fellow coworkers, but it was obvious that his boss recruited men who could easily be bodybuilders as well as cover models. She was dwarfed but so grateful they had the combined strength to rescue them from the mine. She had no doubt she and Bennett would have met with success by themselves, but having the others allowed the rescue to proceed much quicker. And once out, they made all the difference in getting the medical care Terrance needed.

She'd fussed over him, worried about infection, blood loss, pain, and whatever else she could think of. He'd tried to assure her that he was fine but must have finally given up and let her worry since she'd made it evident that she wasn't about to stop. Somehow, focusing on him kept her mind from wandering down a path leading to hysteria.

Hop had an easy smile and an all-American boyish charm, which was amusing on the body of a man so large. Chris was also over six feet tall, but he had a more slender build and a serious expression on his face. He was the one who, immediately after greeting her, had stitched Terrance's wound, binding it with clean bandages and giving him a shot of antibiotics. Dolby, like Hop, had a boyish charm, along with a twinkle in his blue eyes. Poole was as tall as the others, but with a thick beard that didn't hide the way his lips quirked upward when he smiled.

It was evident by their mannerisms and camaraderie these were good men. And now they hovered outside the van, their conversation low and indistinguishable. Terrance had stayed right with her, his hand holding hers. She looked down at their connection. The dirt that covered both of them from head to toe was almost laughable. Yet neither Landon nor his coworkers had thought twice about ushering them inside the air-conditioned van for comfort even though they were like the Charlie Brown character Pig Pen where dust was flying off them constantly, landing on all the furniture around.

Terrance had also given his statement, and now it seemed they were just waiting to be given permission to leave.

"What's going to happen now?" she asked.

Leaning closer, Terrance whispered, "Landon will let us go soon, and Hop will fly us back to California."

"And then…?"

He didn't answer her but instead held her gaze, and she realized that her rather simple question was open to a great deal of interpretation. Landon had also gotten off the phone and turned his attention back to them, so she thought it was a good time to elaborate.

"What I mean is that I've given you all the information that I know. I have no idea what happened to Edgar, but I don't expect to see him again. And I assure you that I will speak to the board of directors and my uncle as soon as I return. Our next level of contrasting energy will no longer be there in my head but ready to test. The information will be out there soon, and the patents will already be applied for. So whatever Edgar was looking to do as far as selling my initial research, he won't be able to do anything even if he's alive."

Terrance continued to hold her hand, but it was Landon who spoke. "Those are all good ideas, Diana. At this point, Olson GeoTech should be protected, but it's important for you to continue to have protection, as well. We know Edgar wasn't acting alone. And because this is international, that's also why Cody is working with us from the CIA. We've contacted Orica and are waiting to hear back from them. We have no idea who his black-market contacts are, but he's being investigated to the fullest."

She nodded slowly, hating the idea of the black market in their industry, but it was naive to imagine that despots and terrorists didn't want explosive technology as well as explosive products. And that didn't include the other *legitimate* companies who were willing to steal the research of others in the industry.

Terrance's voice cut through her musings. "She'll be protected."

Looking over, she wasn't sure what he meant but didn't want to press the issue now. Whether LSIWC considered her uncle's contract over since the conference was ended, or if they would continue, or if Terrance would provide personal security… she had no idea. Looking down at their connected dirty hands again, she felt the squeeze from his fingers and was willing to go on faith that he would take care of her. And she wanted to take care of him.

24

As soon as they finished their interviews, the Keepers drove them back to the helicopter Hop had landed nearby. Bennett was glad it was a six-seater, giving them plenty of room, even though it was a short flight to the airport. Once at the airport, he made sure he and Diana had time to shower in the small airport lounge and have something to eat.

"Will you stay close?" she'd whispered.

He hadn't wanted her to feel embarrassed and was grateful when the other Keepers disappeared for a little while. The two of them couldn't fit into one shower, but he waited outside to ensure she had everything she needed. While the water washed away all the dirt that covered her, there was a light tap on the door.

Opening it a crack, he found Dolby outside with a small bag. "Natalie called ahead and arranged to have your luggage picked up from the Bellagio and brought here. It's already stored on the plane, but I figured you'd need clean clothes since you'll probably want to burn the ones you're wearing now."

More grateful than he could express for Diana's sake, he took the bag and held his friend's gaze. Finally, with a chin lift, he simply said, "Means everything, bro."

A chin lift was returned before Dolby walked away. The water turned off, and Diana popped her head out, her eyes wide. "I feel a thousand times better, but I just realized I have no clothes!"

Holding up the bag, he grinned. "Don't worry. My people have already taken care of everything." When he explained what they'd done, and she peered inside the bag to see a clean pair of leggings, panties, a tank top, and a bra, she was thrilled.

His brow furrowed at the idea of anyone handling her underwear, but she popped him on the shoulder and said, "Stop grousing. It's just underwear!"

While she dressed and exclaimed over the lotion that she was able to use, he jumped into the shower and eagerly washed the nasty mine dust, dirt, and sweat off his body as well. Glad that he had short hair, it didn't take long to get scrubbed clean. Rejoining the others, they were thrilled with the sandwiches, water, soda, and chips. Diana ate ravenously, and the Keepers made sure they had their fill.

Once they were on the plane, and she was safely buckled, he sat next to her. He wondered if she would like him to look out the window to describe what he saw, but almost as soon as they were wheels up, she leaned her head over to rest against his shoulder and fell asleep.

He'd caught the looks the other Keepers sent his way and, at first, stiffened, ready to defend their closeness. But as soon as his gaze met the eyes of Hop, Dolby, and Chris, he knew they understood. He'd fallen for a mission... not just any mission but with an amazingly strong woman who made him want things he'd never realized he was missing.

Poole just grinned, and now Bennett wondered when the next Keeper would fall. With that, he closed his eyes and leaned his cheek against the top of her head. As soon as they landed, he knew decisions would need to be made. He just had no idea how Diana would feel about those decisions.

Bennett didn't care that the CIA, FBI, Interpol, or whoever the fuck else was working on either finding Edgar Masterson or his body. He didn't feel that Diana was safe. And even if Carson had not wanted him to continue, he would have done so anyway. But luckily for him, he worked for a boss and with a group of men and women who didn't believe that the mission was over until the mission was *over*!

By the time they landed, Diana was rousing awake. She moved to each Keeper, offering a heartfelt hug, and Bennett listened as each sincerely thanked her for helping save him. She'd waved off their appreciation, but when they called her a badass worthy of a Keeper, she'd blushed and laughed.

Once in his SUV, still parked from when they'd flown to the conference days before, they drove down the road.

"It seems a lifetime ago that we were here," she said, her voice showcasing her fatigue.

"I know." His hands tightly gripped the steering wheel before he lifted one and rubbed it over his head, then squeezed the back of his neck.

"What has you worried?" she asked. When he glanced to the side, she chuckled. "I can tell you're thinking hard about something when you squeeze your neck."

Snorting, he was secretly pleased that she'd noticed that about him. "We're heading to my house."

"Your house?"

"Yeah. It's safer until we figure out what our next step is."

"Safer?"

He glanced over again. "Are you going to keep repeating what I say?"

She blinked, a crinkle forming between her brows. "No, but then nothing you're saying makes sense, so I'm a little lost."

He sighed and nodded. "Okay, we're almost at my house. How about we get there, settle, and then talk it out." Satisfied when she easily agreed, they were soon pulling down his drive. He wondered what she thought of his house when she stared out the window but knew she would need to be closer to see it fully.

Once inside, she wandered around, giving it her full attention. He looked around, trying to see it through her eyes. It wasn't large, but having ripped out a few walls to open up the living and kitchen areas, and with little furniture, it gave her a chance to walk without stumbling over things in the way.

She turned and smiled. "I like your place. It's cozy."

A chuckle caught in his throat as he grinned in return. "Cozy? Can't say I'm much of a decorator but guess I never thought cozy was a word that would describe a place I lived in."

She moved gracefully until she was right in front of him, her head leaned back so her gaze stayed on him. Recognizing her subtle cues, he could tell the instant his face came into clear view for her. It was in the way her lips slightly relaxed as they smiled. Not that it was fake before but just that it was now more natural. He wrapped his arms around her and held her close, lowering his chin so their gazes remained locked together.

"I think cozy just means that it's a place you've made your own. A place you're comfortable in," she said. "I like it."

"I want you to be comfortable here." He hadn't planned on the words, but once they'd slipped out, her smile widened even more, and his chest squeezed at the sight. Bending, he kissed her lightly at first, but as soon as she angled her head and allowed his tongue to glide over hers, the kiss flamed into the all-encompassing territory. They had things to talk about, but right now, he just wanted to pretend they were a couple with no issues or problems and nothing to be concerned about other than if they could make it to the bedroom.

Her fingers flew to the bottom hem of his shirt, grasping at the material as she tugged it up his torso. He hated to lose her mouth but separated for the instant it took to jerk the T-shirt over his head. Their mouths sealed again, and her hands danced over his shoulders, down his pecs, and traced along the ridges of his abs. A low growl came from deep inside her, and he quickly swallowed the sound, wanting more.

His hands fisted the material of her shirt, and he lifted it, gently pulling it over her breasts. Then once again, separating his mouth from hers as he tugged the T-shirt over her head, he tried not to snag her hair. His movements were the desperation of a starved man with water in his grasp.

She reached behind and unclasped her bra, jerking the straps down, allowing her breasts to bounce slightly with their freedom.

He bent and wrapped his arms around her hips, then lifted her easily into his embrace. At this angle, her nipples were at the perfect level, and he buried his face between her breasts before trailing kisses from one nipple to the other.

Her back arched as she wrapped her arms around the back of his neck, holding on. And when he pulled the nipple deeply into his mouth, circling the hard bud with his tongue before nipping slightly, her head fell back, and another delicious groan rumbled from her chest.

"Bed," she muttered, her pretty voice reaching his ears. As he continued to feast on her breasts, she kissed his forehead, then commanded again, "Bed."

Her nipple fell from his mouth with a pop, and he looked up with a smirk. "You got it." It took no time with his long stride to reach his bedroom, and as he stalked inside, he was glad that while the room was starkly furnished, he'd kept it neat. The king-sized bed was covered in sheets and a blanket, but as soon as he bent and laid her back on top of the covering, he gave no more thought to the room other than the woman gracing his bed.

Standing, he lifted one of her feet and slid off her shoe. Repeating the action with her other foot, he then tugged her leggings and panties over her hips and down her legs, leaving them in a pile on the floor. Now, staring down at her naked body spread out like a feast before him, his chest depressed as the air left his lungs and words failed him. Finally, uttering, "Christ, Diana, you're beautiful."

Her smile softened, but she only lifted her hands toward him. Not willing to waste a moment, he toed off his boots and shucked his pants and boxers.

Her gasp caused him to halt, seeing her gaze pinned on the bandage covering the side of his abs. He had a corresponding one on his back, but it was out of her view for the moment.

Tears welled in her eyes as she crawled to her knees on the bed and leaned forward to place a soft kiss over the bandage. "Oh, sweetheart, I'm so sorry you got hurt trying to protect me."

He gently pushed her back onto the bed as he crawled over her body. "Babe, I'd give my life to protect you."

They held each other, neither speaking, their eyes roaming over their faces. Her fingers traced the angles of his face, over his nose, and around his chin. He wanted to hide from her deep perusal but didn't want to break the spell that traveled between them. After she'd looked her fill, her gaze moved back to his eyes, and her lips curved. "If anyone is beautiful, Terrance, it's you. You are the bravest, most gorgeous, best man I've ever met."

Her words scored through him. He couldn't imagine what she saw, yet he wasn't about to question it. Her expression was real, and all he knew was that he was blessed beyond all men.

He wanted to lose himself in her beautiful body before having to face the ugly reality that surrounded them, but that wasn't fair to her. He wanted sex to be a celebration, not a diversion. Rubbing his fingers over her cheeks, he sighed. "We need to talk about what's happening."

She placed her fingertip over his lips and shook her head. "Later. Not now. All I want to do now is make love. We're alive, Terrance. We're both alive. Let's celebrate that, and then we can deal with everything else."

His smile widened, and then he nodded. Deciding no words were needed, he lowered his head and sealed his lips over hers again. The kiss began like a slow dance—calm and gentle, soft and easy. But soon, it flamed, and the tempo increased. Their tongues danced as their hands rushed to explore and memorize each other's curves and angles.

Ideas of seduction and finesse disappeared as they rolled back and forth, scratching the blanket underneath them. Knowing Edgar had stripped her power when he kidnapped her, Terrance wanted her to feel in control again. Flipping so she was on top, he stared in worship at her rising above him.

With her hands on his shoulders, her hair fell like a curtain around them. Her breasts hung in front of him, the dusty nipples a tantalizing treat that only took the barest lift of his head before he could lick and suck. Her hot core pressed down on his erection as she straddled his hips, rubbing herself on him, careful of his injuries.

Wanting her body satisfied and pliant, he sucked hard on her nipple while his thumb found her clit and pressed as she dragged her swollen nub along his cock. She threw her head back and cried out as her body began to shake. His dick was weeping with need, but Bennett would've been satisfied with just watching her come.

As her release eased, she lowered down on top of his uninjured side, and he wrapped his arms around her back, soothing his hands over her from shoulder to ass and back again. If that was all she needed, he'd be happy.

After a moment, she pushed herself up and stared down at him, a brilliant grin on her face. "Thank you."

"For what, babe?"

"For that orgasm. I didn't realize how much I needed that."

"Proud to serve, sweetheart." He laughed.

She threw her head back and laughed as well, and the sound of their combined mirth filled his heart. She shifted to straddle his cock again, and with her smile still firmly planted on her face, she lifted on her knees before reaching under to grasp his erection and guide it to her entrance.

The anticipation built, and when she lowered herself slowly until he was fully sheathed, he was certain he had entered nirvana. Her movements were tenuous, and he encouraged, "Ride me, Diana."

With her hands on his shoulders again, she rose and lowered on his cock, her hair now wild as it fell over her shoulder, the ends tickling his chest.

He watched as she moved with unrestrained abandon, both giving over to the freedom of the moment while keeping her gaze on his face, giving silent assurance that she knew exactly what she was doing and who she was with. And that *he* was who she wanted to be with.

As her movements slowed, he knew she was exhausted and spanned her waist with his large hands, his fingers gently digging into her ass. With his upper body strength, he held her with ease as he pistoned his hips, burying his cock deep inside her over and over again.

The subtle changes in her breathing gave evidence that she was close. Sliding his thumb down, he circled her clit again, and with a few more strokes of his cock touching deep inside, her body shattered as she cried out his name. Instantly, hearing his name on her lips, his orgasm slammed into him, and ignoring the pain from his stitches, he came deep inside her. Pumping until every last drop was gone, he waited while her body spasmed around him and then slowly eased.

Loosening his grip, he allowed her to bend forward

and settle against his chest, her cheek on his shoulder and her gaze still on his face.

They lay for a long time, catching their breath, letting their heartbeats slow, and allowing the importance of what they'd just done move between them. He didn't wonder what she thought because he knew. Just as she was no fuck for him, every fiber in her being was letting him know that he wasn't just a body for her to fuck either.

He rolled them to the side, kissed her lightly, then stood before bending to scoop her into his arms again. Padding into the bathroom, he set her feet onto the bathmat before leaning over to turn on the shower. Once the water was warm, he led her inside the small, tiled shower, standing her so the water hit her back and not her face.

"Can you get the bandages wet??"

"No worries. It's fine, and I can change them when we finish." Aware of the lack of space, he now wished he'd worked on the bathroom expansion. "Sorry, this is so small."

She plastered her body to his and looked up, grinning. "No worries," she chanted in return. "It just means we have to stay close."

Laughing, he bent to kiss her. "Sounds good to me." In fact, staying close to Diana was exactly what he planned on doing.

25

Diana walked down the hall of Olson GeoTech. Having left Jerry's office, she headed back to her own. She'd spent two nights with Terrance, falling more in love with him. But she existed inside a protective bubble and had to return to work. He'd insisted on driving her to her apartment and checking it out before taking her to work.

The meeting with Jerry, attended by her mom and Phillip, had gone as expected... they'd already been told of the events in Las Vegas, and their reactions had been exactly as she knew they would. Her mom had cried and held her tightly, reacting when she found out that James's death hadn't been an accident. While the FBI had no official comment on that aspect of what Diana reported Edgar had said, she'd wanted her mom and Jerry to know of the possibility.

Phillip had talked to Alex the night before. He'd extended his stay in Las Vegas to hang with his friends, unaware that Diana had been kidnapped. Phillip's news had him flying back today. As always, Phillip provided loving comfort, and Diana was grateful her mom had him in her life now. The grief over her father was hitting them anew, and Phillip would make sure that her mom had the support she needed.

Jerry had reacted with anger after the shock wore off. She'd given him Landon's name and information, saying that she had been told the FBI agent would contact them when they had more information. But he'd also been furious that it appeared someone on the inside of GeoTech might have been working with Edgar. Or, at the very least, susceptible to the idea of selling their industrial research.

As Phillip prepared to take her mom home, he gave Diana a hug. "What do you plan on doing now?"

"I'm heading to my office and downloading all the recent research I have accumulated and tested so far. I'm sending it over to development and having them begin their process for the patents. By the end of the week, my research will be out there for the next level of GeoTech to work on, and there will be no reason for anyone to be after me specifically. Plus, it will also take the bite out of anyone who's hoping to cash in on what we've done. It protects the company."

"Are you sure?" he'd asked. "If you wait, there could be more money for GeoTech down the road."

Her brows had snapped together. "GeoTech isn't hurting for money, and Uncle Jerry should know. I think we're safe, Phillip. And we'll be more protected once I'm finished."

Now, walking into her office, she felt her phone

vibrate in her pocket and looked down at the caller ID. "Hey, Alex."

"Diana! What the hell? I can't believe you didn't let me know what was going on! When dad told me what happened, I couldn't believe that I was so close by when you got shot at, kidnapped, and nearly killed! Jesus, what the hell? Why didn't you tell me?"

"At the time, honestly, I didn't think about anything other than surviving. And when it was over, there were police and FBI, and God knows who else I had to talk to. I was so exhausted that when I got back, I crashed."

"Well, I'm leaving Vegas today and will be home in a little bit."

"I know you wanted to stay extra to have some fun with some of your new friends."

"Fuck that! I think what happened with you takes precedence. Plus, I just got a call from dad that you were jumping forward with your research. You need me there."

"You don't need to come back early for that. I'm fine, and I'm just starting to finalize the preliminary research so it's in the system. Our patents coordinator will start working on it by the end of the week."

"Well, I'm still flying back today. I know what you've been working on, and I can help. Why don't you wait until I come there tomorrow for us to upload your analysis?"

"There'll still be a lot for you to do when you get here, but I want to start the process as soon as possible."

They said goodbye, disconnected, and then she leaned forward and rubbed her aching head. Too much had happened in the past week, especially the past couple of days, for her to process everything fully. But she knew life rarely slowed down just because more time was needed. Sighing heavily, she turned back to her computer, sent out a message to the other members of her team, and began uploading her data.

"I didn't protect her."

Bennett swallowed audibly but didn't give in to the temptation to look away from his fellow Keepers. "I didn't protect her because I was distracted. Distracted by my feelings for her. Distracted by trying to make her trip more enjoyable instead of just keeping my eye out for someone trying to get to her."

"The mission wasn't about someone trying to kill her," Carson said, his words clipped as his brow lowered.

"We're supposed to expect the unexpected," Bennett fired back.

"True, but the mission was to escort her, give her a safe environment with her visual limitation, and make sure no one tried to corner her at the conference. That was what her uncle requested. No one expected a kidnapping."

"You're too hard on yourself," Leo added, taking on the role of Carson's second in command and one of Bennett's mentors when he'd first become a Keeper.

While the others nodded, he grimaced, as though he'd failed her and, by default, LSIWC.

"Since when did you become God?" Natalie quipped, her hands slapping the table in front of her. "All knowing? All powerful? Never failing?"

He blinked, looking over at the diminutive powerhouse, who stared back as though she was bored. But he knew better. Just the glint in her eyes gave evidence that she was as serious as a heart attack.

Leaning forward, she looked around at the other Keepers. "We strive for perfection, but if we aren't human in our efforts, what does that make us? Superman wannabes?"

"You not only protected her, but you made sure she was comfortable," Dolby added. "By taking her to places and being her eyes, you gave her more than just security."

Snorting, Hop nodded. "They're right, Bennett. You took the mission and went above and beyond. You protected Dr. Olson at the conference and when she was shot at. You fought to keep her safe and went into the mine with no backup just to make sure she was rescued as fast as possible. Hell, you took a bullet for her. What else did you need to do to honor the mission?"

Carson placed his forearms on the table in front of him, his gaze boring straight into Bennett's. "If you're looking for someone here to come down on you because your mission went sideways, you won't find one. If you're looking for someone here to tell you that your distraction was wrong, then you're out of luck again."

"Face it, man," Poole said, his brows lifted. "You

found what the others have, so you should be celebrating, not beating yourself up."

"Yeah, but the danger isn't over," he argued in return. "We still don't know who Edgar was working with."

"But," Jeb interjected with a grin, "we've been digging while you were in Nevada and recuperating. And we've come up with some interesting info."

Focus snagged, Bennett gave his attention over to the others.

"You asked me to look into Alex, Diana's stepbrother. I found no connection between him and Edgar. No correspondence, no communication, no money traces. Nothing. Certainly, others at GeoTech could be suspicious, but it would be a narrow group that would be able to get their hands on any research. It's just the members of her team, which is actually very small."

"What about who'd benefit from her father's death?" he asked. "Jerry?"

Nodding, Adam continued. "I investigated Jerry. As James's brother and the financial head of GeoTech, he'd have access to everything, but I can't find any connection to him and Edgar either."

"I told them to look at Phillip," Natalie threw out. "After all, he married James's widow. While that solidified his standing at GeoTech, he is now married to a major stockholder. And as Diana's stepfather, he'd be privy to inside information."

Leaning forward, Bennett held his breath. "And...?"

Sighing heavily, Natalie shook her head. "Nada. Nothing. There's still nothing that ties him with the Australian company of Orica."

"I widened the scope to not just the Australians since that's where Edgar is from, but checked out the Russian locations of NitroSabir also," Adam added. "Nothing."

"We've got a shitload of nothing," he groused, flopping back in his seat.

"No," Jeb said, twisting in his chair to look over his shoulder at Bennett. "We just didn't expand our scope enough. I looked into Alex more since he's Diana's assistant and has direct access to her work, even before official research begins."

"He would have come onto the scene only after becoming her stepbrother, though," Hop said. "He was still in college when her father was killed."

"Yeah, but his dad was already employed with GeoTech. Maybe this was a long-range plan," Leo tossed out.

"What did you find?" Bennett asked, looking at the screen that Jeb had sent his information to be displayed.

"He completed a three-month internship in Korea with the Korean explosives company, NaeGeo, working on a team with Dr. Lin Kang—"

"He was at the conference," Bennett blurted. "Dr. Kang spoke with Diana several times along with another man from there… Hwan Parks."

"I found a lot of information about Dr. Kang, but nothing suspicious. But Hwan Parks is virtually nonexistent. His background before working for the explosives company is nil. No contacts, no information… he's a ghost. Except…"

"What?" Bennett bit out, leaning forward, his fingers curling into fists.

"With help from Cody, I managed to uncover an

encrypted message between Hwan Parks and Edgar during the time they were in Vegas. The message only said, 'Payment has been made. I filled contract.'"

"Hwan Parks is working with Edgar?" Poole asked.

"Can't say for sure, but now there's a definite connection between Hwan, Edgar—"

"And Alex," Bennett said, anger surging to the surface at the thought that she'd given her trust to someone who might be selling her out and profiting on the black market.

"Carson?"

The Keepers looked over as Rachel entered the room.

"Landon Sommers is on the line for you. He says it has to do with Dr. Olson."

Carson nodded, first to Rachel and then to Jeb, who immediately put the FBI agent onto the screen.

Bennett's normal quiet patience wasn't in evidence when he all but growled, "What have you found out about Edgar?"

Landon sighed and shook his head. "No body has been found as of yet. To be honest, I'm not expecting to. He was an explosive engineer like Dr. Olson. He would have known what he was doing. It would have made no sense to have been caught still underground when the explosion occurred."

Bennett observed the lines on Landon's face and the circles under his eyes and figured the FBI agent hadn't slept since he'd arrived in Nevada. While frustrated, he appreciated the agent's diligence.

"But," Landon said, drawing everyone's attention

back to him, "I wanted to let you know that several minor exit points were discovered in the area on the backside of the nearest hill. I have investigators checking them out to see if we can find evidence that Edgar literally slipped out a back door. We've got our eyes on the airport, but we have a feeling that he's on his way back to Australia by private jet already. Cody's team is looking into it."

"Fuckin' hell," Bennett groused. He agreed with Landon's assessment that the man was too smart and too knowledgeable to be caught in his own trap.

Carson had Jeb update Landon on the new information about Hwan Parks and Alex. "Diana said that Alex is still in Las Vegas. He was turning the conference into a week's vacation. He hung out with two younger engineers the whole time I saw him. One from NaeGeo and one from OSHA. They were at a table with Dr. Kang and Hwan Parks one night."

Nodding, Landon said, "I'm still in the area, so I'll check them out."

Once the conference call was disconnected, Bennett sat in silence as he listened to the others discuss the possibilities, all the information rolling over in his mind.

"Edgar Masterson, who works for the largest Australian explosive company, has ties to the Russian company, NitroSabir, and the Korean company is selling intel and actual explosive products on the black market. At least one of his contacts is Hwan Parks from the Korean company, NaeGeo. And there's a connection between Alex Markham and NaeGeo," Dolby recited, ticking off each item with his fingers as he spoke. Leaning back, he shook his head. "What the fuck?"

Bennett looked over at Carson and said, "Where do we fit in with all this mess? 'Cause I need to know how to protect Diana."

Nodding, Carson said, "Good question. The CIA is looking into Edgar's whereabouts, and the FBI is looking into his crimes perpetrated here in the States. LSIWC isn't tasked by the FBI or by Olson GeoTech to investigate the possible industrial espionage occurring. We were only contracted to provide security for Diana. Now, that protection extends beyond the initial contract because she's yours."

At that, Bennett sat up straighter, loving the acknowledgment but wondering how the others would respond. And in typical Keeper fashion, they all clapped with grins on their faces.

"Damn straight," Dolby called out.

Ducking his head, he looked down at his rough hands clasped on the table and chuckled. As Carson continued, he lifted his chin and focused on his boss again.

"We'll still look at the people near her and work to make sure she's safe." Staring at Bennett, Carson added, "And you'll need to let us know what you want or need from us, also."

Nodding slowly, he said, "She's at work today, and while Alex usually drives her home, she's catching a ride with her uncle since he's still in Las Vegas. I know she's busy this week trying to get all her initial theories and research out, but I was going there today after work to see how she's doing. Her place is about an hour from me, but until we know what the hell Alex's game is, I'll stay with her."

With that, the meeting moved on to various mission assignments and reports, but Bennett's mind was firmly on seeing Diana that evening. And a small smile curved his lips.

26

Diana gave her attention to Jerry, who was behind the wheel. He'd offered to drive her home since her usual ride, Alex, was still in Vegas. Jerry was preoccupied, saying little, but then considering the onslaught of news that had hit them recently, she wasn't surprised.

"Are you okay, Uncle Jerry?"

He sighed but plastered a smile as he turned toward her. "Of course. Just… well, just thinking about everything."

"About Dad?"

The lines in his face were deeper, and an air of despondency had settled over him. "Yeah. I just can't believe that his accident wasn't really an accident."

"I know." When Edgar had told her, she'd been too overwhelmed with everything that had happened and too desperate to get out of the mine to truly process what he'd said. And even in the day since then, she hadn't slowed down enough to deal with the assailment of thoughts slamming into her. Blowing out a long breath, she stared at his profile and sighed again. "Of course, we only have Edgar's proclamation that it was deliberate. Maybe he's just crazy and making it all up for attention."

"Maybe. I suppose we'll know more when the FBI investigates, but I can't imagine it would be easy to determine that now. The evidence is long gone."

"I suppose we may never know," she said, her heart heavy. "I hate for our grief to renew so fresh and still not get a resolution. We may always have the question hanging over our heads."

"Well, I can deal with my anger, but your mom will suffer. At least Phillip will help her. He's been there every step of the way for her since James died."

They stopped outside her condo, and she leaned over to kiss his cheek. "Thanks for the ride. Alex will pick me up in the morning, as usual."

She climbed out, then turned to wave goodbye. Walking into the lobby, she greeted Bobby on her way to the elevator.

"Diana!"

Recognizing the voice, she turned with a smile. "Alex!"

He hurried over. "Hey, Diana." Wrapping his arms around her, they hugged. "I got here as soon as I could."

They stepped into the elevator, and he leaned out slightly before ducking back and letting the doors close. Turning to her as the lift carried them upward, she said, "I hate that you cut your Vegas trip short."

He shrugged and snorted. "I was going to come

home tomorrow anyway, so one less day in Vegas is hardly a sacrifice."

"What did you think of the conference?"

His gaze shot to her, and he shook his head. "Really, Diana? Do you want to talk about the conference when you were shot at, kidnapped, and almost buried alive?"

They walked down the hall, and she unlocked her door, looking over her shoulder as she entered. "Come on." The last thing she wanted to do was rehash the past couple of days again when the call of a glass of wine, a hot bath, and an early bedtime when Terrance arrived was all she wanted to focus on. But up close, she could see the haggard expression on Alex's face and felt guilty. She knew he cared about her, and she couldn't repay his kindness by kicking him out.

She walked into her kitchen and took down a wineglass. Opening the refrigerator, she pulled out a bottle and grabbed a beer for Alex. "I hope you don't mind, but if we're going to go over everything again, I need a drink!"

Her phone vibrated from the pocket of her jacket. Wrapping her fingers around it, she lifted it enough to see Terrance's name on the caller ID. Not caring if she and Alex still needed to talk, she pressed the connect button—

"You're not going to need that drink."

She gasped at the Australian accent, and dropping her phone back into her pocket, she turned around. Alex stood at the end of the kitchen counter, his fingers gripping the edge, and she could discern enough of his expression to see his wide eyes. She knew who the voice belonged to, but his features were still blurry as he walked toward her from the living room.

"You! Oh God, Edgar! How did you get in here?"

He didn't appear to have a weapon in his hand, and all she could think was that she and Alex could take him. After all, there were two of them and only one of him. But before she could move, Edgar continued to move closer until he clapped his hand on Alex's shoulder.

"Good job, Alex," Edgar said.

Stunned, she managed to turn her head so that her stepbrother's face was clearly visible with her right eye. She needed to see him. Every nuance. Every flicker of his eyelids. Every quiver in his cheek. And as she stared, the unspoken evidence lay before her. But unlike the scientist she was, she didn't want to accept the obvious conclusion.

"Please tell me no. Please tell me you haven't brought him here. Please tell me you're not selling us out." Her voice was barely a whisper, but Alex's face contorted with each statement as though a whip was lashing across his back.

Alex didn't speak, but from what little she knew of Edgar, staying quiet was not his forte.

"Oh, I'm afraid he can't tell you that." Edgar laughed. "He's been quite the little helper."

She wanted to keep her eye on Edgar, but her gaze shot over to Alex's, and the guilt leeching from his eyes gave her all the proof she needed. "Why? How did you even meet him?"

Alex didn't speak, but Edgar threw his head back

and laughed. "There's a whole world outside your little lab, Dr. Olson. While you're satisfied to work in the family business, looking for newer ways to keep selling to the same clients, millions are to be made by those willing to pay."

"You work for Orica, the biggest explosive industry in your country," she bit out. "Why couldn't you steal from your own people? Or maybe they're the ones who put you up to it?"

"Orica?" Edgar scoffed. "They're no more visionaries than NitroSabir is, but don't think that they're any more pious either. I have no doubt that many at the top make millions off selling on the black market, but none of that trickles down to those of us who create in the labs, build, and grow our businesses. We do all the work, and they reap all the benefits."

She jerked as understanding moved over her. "So that's what this is about? You want to get even with the higher-ups in your own company who are selling on the black market but not sharing the wealth with you. You decided to take your own piece of the pie by going after another company."

Edgar looked at Alex and laughed. "I knew she was smart."

Her gaze darted back and forth between the two, but where Edgar was triumphant, Alex appeared green as though he might throw up.

Ignoring Edgar, she swung her gaze to Alex. "How did he get you to work for him?"

"Let's just say he had a very fortuitous internship several years ago."

Her chin jerked back as her gaze shot over to Alex. "Internship? You weren't in Australia. You were in Korea."

A knock on the door sounded, and Edgar grinned as he clapped and rubbed his hands together. "Right on time. Get the door, Alex."

Alex obeyed and turned to walk to the door, peering out through the security hole first. With a sigh, he opened the door, and she squinted to see who had entered. The man walked straight to her, stopping just on the other side of the counter where she could see him clearly. "Dr. Parks?" Her mind could not process all that was happening but turned her accusing gaze toward Alex. "What have you done? Oh my God, what have you done?"

"Diana, it's not... I didn't... I..." His face crumpled.

"Shut up," Edgar snarled at Alex before turning his attention back to Diana. "Now, *Dr.* Olson, I suggest you start calling up some of the information you've got stored in that brain of yours. I want what you've got on the next phase of contrasting energy or—" He lifted his weapon and pointed it toward her head. "I think you know what I'm capable of."

Bennett was almost to Diana's condo when he decided to call to see if she wanted him to pick up something for dinner before he arrived. He heard her connect, but when he greeted her with, "Hey, babe," she didn't respond. He almost disconnected to try to call again when he heard voices in the background. Wondering who was there with her, his heart jolted when he heard her say, *"You! Oh God, Edgar, how did you get in here?"*

While the sounds were muffled, he could distinctly hear a reply from a man with an Australian accent. Without waiting to hear anything else, he grabbed his phone and hit the emergency dial for LSIWC.

"You've got Adam."

"I'm ten minutes away from Diana's condo. Edgar is in there with her."

He could hear Adam and others speaking before Carson came back on the line.

"We're alerting Landon. He was heading to the area to talk to Diana's mom and uncle. He'll meet you at Diana's. Hop and Poole were at the helicopter pad for maintenance this afternoon and are in the air now. They can be there in about thirteen minutes. We'll coordinate from here."

Pressing down on the accelerator, he gripped the steering wheel until his knuckles turned white. As he continued to listen, his heart jolted again at Alex's name, knowing he was there, too. Making sure to report all he could hear, he radioed, "Alex is there, too."

"Looks like we were right about their tie-in—"

"Shit," he barked. "And Dr. Parks just showed up. All fuckin' three of them are in her condo!" Glancing at his clock, he said, "My ETA is seven minutes. Going around to the back."

"Landon says his ETA is about the same. He'll meet you there. He's calling it in but will get there before any agents."

"Roger that." Steadying his heartbeat and breathing, he listened as he sped down the highway. By the time he parked behind the condo building, barely able to keep the tires from squealing, he looked up just in time to see Landon racing from the other side. Bolting from their vehicles, they met by the back door of the condo building. "Hop and Poole will land at the parking lot one block over in about five minutes."

"I have agents coming, as well as the local police. All coming in soft... no sirens."

Just then, the sound of arriving vehicles met his ears, and he turned to see two unmarked police cars parking nearby. Holding his phone that was still on call with Diana's phone, he said, "I'm still monitoring. She must know I'm on the line and is careful to say whatever she can. I'm recording."

Landon offered a curt nod. "Good."

Fast-approaching boot steps met their ears, and he looked over to see Poole and Hop rounding the corner. Surprised they arrived so quickly, Hop called out, "Decided to see how fast my bird could fly. Turns out... pretty damn fast."

A rush of relief flooded him at the support, and a small grin would suffice as his thanks.

"What have we got?" Poole asked with the others gathered around.

"Her condo is on the front right side. Third floor. Door opens to open living room and dining area. Not a lot of extraneous furniture, so she can maneuver around easily. A counter divides that space and the kitchen. Again, not crowded with items. Hall down the middle. Two bedrooms. Small bathroom at the end of the hall, a guest bedroom on the left, and then her bedroom and en suite bathroom on the right. The best place to get in is her bathroom." He pointed up toward the fire escape. "That small window goes into her bathroom. It's small, but we can make it work."

"Then let's do it," Hop called out, staring upward.

He accepted another weapon from Poole that had been stored in the helicopter. With a nod toward the others, he started up the fire escape stairs. *Hang on, babe. I'm on my way.*

27

"I don't keep my research here," Diana said, throwing her hands up to the side. "Even you should know that. Research does not leave the company." She looked over at Alex. "Surely, you told him that."

"What you have that I want," Edgar said, leaning over the island and tapping the side of her head with the end of his gun, "is up here. Your testing does not matter to me right now. What Dr. Parks is willing to pay for is your theories. Tomorrow, Alex will go to work and be able to download your research for us. But for now, I want your theories."

"This makes no sense," she argued back, sounding braver than she felt, considering her body shook. "I'm just supposed to stand here and spit out what I've worked on? What I've sent in the early testing?"

"I don't see why not," Edgar said, his eyes narrowing on her.

"And how long do you propose this to take? Aren't thieves supposed to want to grab and run?"

Edgar chuckled and looked over at Hwan, who appeared bored with the conversation. "We've got the rest of the evening and night. By that time, you will have given us what we need to know initially, and then Alex will bring us the rest of the data tomorrow while we stay here and keep you company."

She focused her gaze on Hwan. "You're his buyer?" She shook her head in derision. "Can I ask if Dr. Kang is part of this?"

"The very legitimate Dr. Kang does not work with me," Hwan said, his gaze never wavering from her. "But I am just one in a chain, Dr. Olson. And you should know, knowledge is power, and power is worth a great deal in this world."

"And just what do you expect to do with this knowledge?"

"I have contacts that Edgar can't even imagine. By the time it gets into the hands of those who can put it to use, we'll all make a tidy profit."

"Not quite everyone," she bit back.

"Your profit is that you get to live, and your brains aren't blown across your kitchen," Edgar growled, leaning closer.

Once again, she spared her stepbrother a hard stare. "I can't believe you'd betray us like this. Betray me. Betray your dad—" She gasped. "Tell me that Phillip doesn't know about this."

Alex shook his head, his jaw tight. "No. No one else knows."

"Good, because that would break his heart to know

what you've done," she said, sure that she was speaking the truth.

"That reminds me," Edgar said, chuckling. "I can have someone at your parents' house very soon if you need more enticement—"

Alex gasped, his head swinging around to glare at Edgar.

"Stop!" Diana cried out. "I'm sick of your threats!" She hated giving in but was too tired to fight. She walked away and plopped down at her table. "If you want my information, fine. But I'm going to start talking and not stop, so you'd better be ready to take it all down!"

It was almost comical how the three men rushed forward, each quickly sitting as though it was a game of musical chairs, and they didn't want to be the last one standing. Dr. Parks pulled out a tablet, then turned his focus toward her. So far, between he and Edgar, he'd been the quietest, but she had no doubt he could be just as deadly.

Without a preamble, she began spouting chemical equations, savvy enough to know that Dr. Parks and Dr. Masterson would understand that what she was giving them was valid information. But by throwing in small changes that would completely alter the effects of any research, they wouldn't be able to catch her deceptions.

A few minutes into her dissertation, Dr. Parks shifted slightly in his seat, drawing her attention toward him. His expression never changed other than the slight elevation of one eyebrow. From that tiny alteration to his staid demeanor, she wondered if he caught on to what she was doing. But she continued, and he didn't call her out or make any other sound. She didn't dare look at Alex, too fearful that he would give her away or simply distract her.

A small beep came from her bedroom, but she kept talking. Not knowing why the window alarm sounded, she prayed that with her phone still in her pocket with the call from Terrance, he might have caught enough to know he needed to get to her.

"What was that?" Edgar asked, interrupting her spouting equations.

"My laundry. The washing machine beeps when it's finished the cycle," she lied easily.

"Go check it out," Edgar ordered, looking at Alex.

Inhale. Exhale. Inhale. Exhale. Keeping her breathing steady, she hoped the blank expression on her face was convincing as she glanced toward him. Alex scooted his chair back and walked down the hall.

Bennett stopped just inside Diana's bathroom, peering out the door into the bedroom. He'd noticed the alarm but allowed Landon to disarm it before climbing through. After he'd climbed through successfully, the window closed shut behind him, and a small beeping alarm sounded. Landon's face hardened when he realized he hadn't completely shut off the alarm, but Bennett blamed himself for not double-checking. *Fuckin' rookie mistake!*

Voices could be heard in the distance, and he slipped

out of the bathroom, moving to the bedroom door. Landon started to follow until the approaching footsteps caused them both to halt.

Landon moved back into the bathroom silently as Bennett stealthily hid behind the partially opened bedroom door. As it was pushed open wider, he watched as Alex moved into the room, walking toward the bathroom.

Icy cold warred with hot fury in Bennett's veins. Before Alex knew anyone was there, Bennett grabbed the younger, smaller man around the neck and clamped his hand over his mouth. Landon stepped out, his weapon raised. Bennett whispered in Alex's ear, "Give me one fucking reason not to end you right here."

Alex didn't move a muscle.

"Come on. You're making this too easy."

Alex shook his head, and Landon moved forward, his voice slow. "Who's in there besides Masterson and Parks?"

Alex grunted, but Bennett's grip kept him from speaking. Forcing his fingers to relax ever so slightly over Alex's lips, he gave Alex just enough ability to barely whisper.

"Just them. But it's not what you think—"

Bennett tightened his fingers again. "You don't fucking breathe unless we give you permission."

"Where are they sitting?" Landon asked.

With Bennett's fingers eased another millimeter, Alex whispered, "At the table."

Landon's gaze hit Bennett, and he nodded in reply, indicating he knew the condo's layout.

"You're going to walk back in there, and I'll have my gun pointed at your back. Agent Sommers here has to play by the rules, so he won't shoot to kill. But I have no rules," Bennett growled. "You make one wrong move, and I'll end you. Fuckin' nod if you get me."

Alex's body jerked, but his head moved up and down.

Landon stepped back into the bathroom and radioed his agents the status of the situation. Bennett knew that Poole and Hop would be coming in from the front. Steadying his breathing, he prayed Diana would not get caught in the crossfire. Whispering against Alex's ear one more time, he said, "I don't give a fuck what you've done up to now. You protect her with your life."

Again, Alex jerked his head up and down.

With his weapon now shoved against Alex's spine, they turned to walk out of the bedroom. He knew they had about ten feet to walk and would still be hidden from the view of the others. But once they reached the end of the hall, where they were visible by anyone sitting at the table, he and Landon needed to be ready.

They started down the hall, and he stopped as Alex moved into the sight of the others.

"What was it?" Edgar called out.

"Like she said, just the washing machine." Alex continued into the open space and sat back down at the table.

Bennett stared at the window closest to the group, seeing their reflection in the glass. Diana sat at the end with Alex to her left. Hwan Parks was at the other end, and Edgar was sitting just to her right. Pressing his lips together, he felt Landon's presence directly behind him.

"Wait, what the fuck?" Edgar called out.

Bennett stilled, his heart rate kicking up.

"You said aqua ammonia with chloride, sodium, and phosphate but with less than one part per milliliter. Then you added sulfate with the same."

"Yes. So what?"

"All less than one part per milliliter?" Edgar argued.

"I'm giving you what you asked for from memory," Diana bit back. "You'll get the exact research tomorrow when you send Alex in to do your dirty work."

Edgar leaned forward. "Bitch, I blow your brains out, then that'll be my dirty work—"

"Stop," Hwan ordered, his voice hard before turning to face Edgar. "Put the gun down. She's not going anywhere, and it's obvious that you waving it around is making her nervous. We need calm, and we need accuracy."

The tension remained for a long moment before Edgar lowered the gun and placed it on the table before grabbing his tablet and typing. "Okay, okay. Now, go over it again."

Bennett lifted a brow toward Landon. By handling his erratic partner, Hwan had given them the opportunity they needed to take Edgar before he could grab his gun. Landon tapped his earpiece twice, then with a chin lift toward Bennett, they charged forward.

"Hands up! Hands where we can see them!"

Diana screamed, her hands flying up into the air as she jerked around toward the intruders. Alex leaped from his chair in a flying tackle, taking her down to the floor as he covered her body with his as she continued to scream.

Edgar snatched his gun, managing to fire a random shot wildly as Landon returned fire, hitting him in the shoulder. He screamed in pain and dropped his weapon while grabbing his shoulder, blood seeping through his fingers.

The front door slammed open, and two agents darted in, weapons aimed, followed by Hop and Poole. Bennett wanted to get to Diana but didn't trust Hwan not to have a hidden weapon, so he kept his gun aimed at him as he moved closer to ensure she was safe. "Cover him!" he ordered, not taking his eyes off Hwan until the agents had their weapons trained on him. Bending, he shoved Alex while calling out, "Diana. Diana. It's me."

She gasped, then turned her pale, wide-eyed face toward him. "Terrance?" He barely had time to holster his gun before she launched into his arms. Wrapping her in his embrace, he held her so tight he wasn't sure she could breathe. Her heart pounded against his chest, but he'd swear his matched hers beat for racing beat.

"Get down! Get down!" Landon shouted as one of the other agents called for an ambulance.

When a hand landed on his shoulder, Bennett glanced up to see Hop just behind him. Standing, he pulled Diana up with him, keeping her protected by his body while Landon moved to Alex, hauling him up. She slumped against Bennett, and he bent to kiss the top of her head, murmuring, "I have you, babe."

Hwan stood, his hands still held up, but a smile played about his lips as he nodded toward Alex. "Good work, Mr. Markham. You played your part excellently."

The voices came to a halt as all eyes turned toward Hwan. He looked at Landon and said, "I'm sure you have questions. Let me introduce myself. I'm Kwan Chung. Undercover for Interpol. My identification is in my right pocket."

Diana gasped, her head moving between the various characters in the room, and Bennett knew she was trying to discern who was who and what the fuck was going on. For that matter, so was he, and his vision was perfect. Twisting around, she peered up at him. "Terrance? What's happening?"

Shaking his head, he watched as Landon approached Hwan. Pulling out the leather identification badge holder, he studied it and then flipped it around to show Bennett. It was an Interpol badge for Kwan Chung. *Holy shit.*

"What the fuck?" Edgar yelled.

"EMT is in the hall. Get him out of here," Landon ordered. "Armed guards on him all the way. Those handcuffs don't come off."

One of the agents and two police officers who'd arrived escorted Edgar out of Diana's condo. His curses were still heard until the elevator doors finally closed.

Bennett's arms stayed tightly around Diana, but his gaze swung to Alex. Before he could ask, she blurted, "Alex? You're working for Interpol?"

"Hell, Diana, it's a long story. But yeah…"

Her hands landed on her hips as she bit out, "Well,

good thing we've got time!" She twisted her neck to look up at Bennett again and asked, "Right?"

Chuckling, he looked over at Hop and Poole as they met his grin with one of their own. Kissing her head again, he nodded. "That's right, babe. We've got time. We've got all the time we need."

28

It was after midnight by the time everyone left Diana's condo. Jerry, as well as Philip and her mom, had arrived as soon as Diana had called them to come over, letting them know what was happening.

The CIA agent she'd met previously, Cody Mansford, also arrived. Her living room soon became crowded with family, Landon and Cody, another FBI agent, Hop and Poole, Kwan, Alex, and of course, she and Terrance. Hop had called for her door to be fixed, and a few men showed up to replace her broken locks.

Kwan explained that the Pacific offices of Interpol had been looking into the explosives black market for years, and they'd focused on Edgar Masterson of Orica when he'd approached someone at NaeGeo. Edgar was visiting at the same time that Alex was interning at NaeGeo. Alex had inadvertently come into Edgar's crosshairs when he learned that Alex worked at GeoTech. Alex reported the overture to Dr. Kang, who, in turn, reported it to Interpol. Kwan thought to recruit

Alex for assistance, and it was easy to *allow* Edgar to think that Alex was amenable to working for him.

It was soon after he'd returned to work at GeoTech that Diana's accident occurred, giving Alex even more reason to work closely with her, making him the perfect ace for Edgar to obtain information. When Diana was going to be at the conference, Edgar saw it as the most opportune chance to gain information from her before it became locked into GeoTech's proprietary research.

"I'm really sorry," Alex said, tension lining his face. "I never meant for you to come to harm. When Edgar suggested he talk to you at the conference, I told Kwan he would be there, too."

"I'm afraid we anticipated much, Dr. Olson," Kwan said, "but Edgar deciding to kidnap you exceeded expectations. I think because you came with a bodyguard, he grew desperate."

Alex sighed. "That's why I was so keyed up about your security." He glanced toward Bennett. "Edgar didn't like not being able to get close to her, and I was afraid he might become more forceful to get the information. But, Jesus, I never expected him to go crazy."

"Then why did he shoot at me? Why try to kill me?" she asked, not understanding.

Kwan's gaze moved to Bennett before answering, "He indicated it was Mr. Bennett he was trying to kill."

"What?" she barked, jumping to her feet in rage.

"Down, babe," Terrance said, pulling her back to the sofa beside him.

"How dare he!"

"I like her fire." Hop chuckled, and Poole nodded.

From the looks the three Keepers shared, she wondered if that statement was a compliment. *I'll ask Terrance later.* For now, her brain was on overload.

Kwan took over the explanations for the law enforcement present before they all stood. He walked over and took her hands in his. "Dr. Olson, I'm sorry for what you've had to endure at the hands of Edgar Masterson. But I thank you on behalf of those of us who fight the battle of international explosives black markets for your continued professionalism and diligence." Turning to Alex, he nodded, saying, "That goes for you as well, Alex. We couldn't have gained the necessary evidence against him without you."

Cody and Landon shook everyone's hands before the law enforcers and Kwan walked out of her condo. Hop and Poole clapped Terrance on the shoulder, saying, "Take a few days off. We'll report to Carson." They both kissed her cheeks before they walked out as well.

Now, with just Terrance and family, Diana slumped against him as all the energy from her body leaked out.

"Son, I'm proud of you," Phillip said, hugging a blushing Alex.

"You're a true hero," Ellen added. "All of you are." She hugged Alex before pulling Diana into her embrace.

"Oh, I didn't start this to be a hero," Alex protested. "I was just curious and wanted to do the right thing. When Kwan recruited me, I honestly thought I'd never really have to do anything but report whatever correspondence I might have with Edgar. But damn, Diana," he said, turning to her, "I never wanted you to be in danger."

"I hated to think you'd turned on us. I'm so sorry, Alex. I should have known better."

"Well, thank God you had Bennett!"

Jerry walked over and shook Terrance's hand. "Mr. Bennett, you have our gratitude." Looking back and forth between Diana and Terrance, he winked. "And our blessing... if you need it."

More embraces ensued, then Jerry ushered Ellen, Phillip, and Alex out. Terrance closed the door and locked it. Turning, he walked straight to her, and she leaned back to keep her gaze on him. Their arms encircled each other, and no words were spoken as they simply embraced, her cheek resting against his heartbeat.

"I know you've got to be exhausted, babe."

She nodded and sighed. "I can't believe everything that's happened in the past week. Honest to God, my brain is on overload."

"Then let's get you into a hot bath. I'll pour a glass of wine, and then you can crawl into bed. Right now, you need to shut your mind down and rest."

With her arms still around him, she leaned back again and smiled as he dipped his chin and held her gaze. "I'm not sure a hot bath and a glass of wine will be enough to shut my mind down. I might need something else."

A slow smile curved his lips, and her heart beat with the emotions swirling inside every time she looked at this man.

"Oh yeah? What do you think you might need to help you relax?"

"How about we shower together, skip the wine, and go straight to bed? Once there, I have no doubt we'll find something to keep us occupied so we're not thinking about explosions, mines, the black market, and who the hell we're supposed to trust."

He threw his head back and laughed. "Let's do it." With that, he scooped her up, and she wrapped her arms around his neck, tucking her face under his chin. As he carried her through her condo to the bedroom, she smiled.

29

TWO MONTHS LATER

"Are you sure this is all?"

Bennett looked over at Poole. "Yeah, she didn't bring much. She's leasing her condo as furnished, saying she preferred not to bring more furniture into my place. It's actually better for her to have more room to walk around and fewer things to trip over."

"That makes sense. But I know this pushes up your work on the house. You wanted to do a lot of it yourself, but the rest of us want to help you."

Bennett nodded, knowing that in the past, he would have resisted accepting the help from the other Keepers. Both because he wanted to work on his house and always relished the time alone. But now, being with Diana and having her move in was more important than his self-imposed solitude.

For two months, they'd dated and traveled back and forth, spending nights at his place and at hers. She was still going to work at GeoTech, but two days a week, she'd work remotely, and three days a week, she'd go in.

Living with him, she had a much longer commute, but he'd drive her halfway to Alex's new apartment, where she'd catch a ride with her stepbrother. At the end of the day, they'd reverse the process. And if Bennett was on a mission, it had proved easy for either Alex to bring her all the way or for one of their friends to pick her up.

Just as Diana hated to be a burden to anyone, she was learning to accept more help. *I suppose in any good relationship, we all change for the better, finding we don't lose ourselves in the process.*

In the past three weeks, he and the other Keepers had expanded the bathroom and kitchen at the back of the house. They still had much to do, but both rooms were functional and safe for Diana. And her safety was all he cared about.

He walked to the window and peered out. He, Poole, and Dolby had been able to bring her belongings to his place, and while she put her clothes in the closet and dresser, the women kept her company. They soon adapted to her needs, making sure not to take over, understanding that Diana needed to know where her clothes, toiletries, and kitchen items were placed.

But now, they were all in the backyard around the porch firepit Leo and Natalie had brought over. They ate and drank while Diana laughed with the rest as they regaled them with their own tales of meeting their Keepers.

That night, once they were alone and the embers glowed and sparks lifted into the night sky, she sat in his lap as he held her tightly. "This means the world to me, babe," he confessed, still learning to give voice to his emotions.

She twisted around and clutched his jaw, kissing him lightly. "I'm glad because moving in with you means a lot to me, too."

"Does it scare you if I say I want it all? I want it all with you?"

She held his gaze, her eyes searching his face. He never minded when she did that, knowing it was her way to really see what someone was thinking. And he didn't want to hide anything from her, so she was free to get close and look all she wanted. He now craved the close perusal he used to hate.

"It doesn't scare me at all, Terrance. Maybe we've only been together a few months, but I want it all with you, too."

Her brow then furrowed, and he lifted a finger and soothed the line between her eyes. He didn't demand her to tell him what was on her mind, knowing it would come out when she was ready.

Finally, she said, "It's easy for us to say we want it *all*, but…"

"You're wondering what defines *all*, right?"

She nodded, and he pulled her closer.

He kissed her lightly, then said, "I want to be with you all the time. I want to share my life with you. The good times. The bad times. Your moving in today is the first step, Diana. And one day, I hope you'll accept my ring and become my wife."

Her breath hitched, and she clutched him tighter.

"What about children? Do you worry about my visual limitations in becoming a mom?"

"Sweetheart, I've known women who could see perfectly with their eyes but never with their hearts. I've known people with no physical limitations but have emotional limitations that choked all the love out of them. But you? With all the love you have to give, you'll be an amazing mom."

A tear escaped, but he captured it with another kiss. Then she smiled, and he knew that even a man like him could be graced with beauty. Nuzzling her hair, he breathed her in.

Inhale. Exhale. Inhale. Exhale.

Standing, he carried her inside their home.

For the next Lighthouse Security Investigations West Coast Keeper
Poole
Make sure to join my reader group!
Maryann Jordan's Protector Fans

ALSO BY MARYANN JORDAN

Don't miss other Maryann Jordan books!

Baytown Boys (small town, military romantic suspense)

Coming Home

Just One More Chance

Clues of the Heart

Finding Peace

Picking Up the Pieces

Sunset Flames

Waiting for Sunrise

Hear My Heart

Guarding Your Heart

Sweet Rose

Our Time

Count On Me

Shielding You

To Love Someone

Sea Glass Hearts

Protecting Her Heart

Sunset Kiss

Baytown Heroes - A Baytown Boys subseries

A Hero's Chance

Finding a Hero

A Hero for Her

Needing A Hero

For all of Miss Ethel's boys:

Heroes at Heart (Military Romance)

Zander

Rafe

Cael

Jaxon

Jayden

Asher

Zeke

Cas

Lighthouse Security Investigations

Mace

Rank

Walker

Drew

Blake

Tate

Levi

Clay

Cobb

Bray

Josh

Knox

Lighthouse Security Investigations West Coast

Carson

Leo

Rick

Hop

Dolby

Bennett

Poole

Hope City (romantic suspense series co-developed with Kris Michaels

Brock book 1

Sean book 2

Carter book 3

Brody book 4

Kyle book 5

Ryker book 6

Rory book 7

Killian book 8

Torin book 9

Blayze book 10

Griffin book 11

Saints Protection & Investigations

(an elite group, assigned to the cases no one else wants…or can solve)

Serial Love

Healing Love

Revealing Love

Seeing Love

Honor Love

Sacrifice Love

Protecting Love

Remember Love

Discover Love

Surviving Love

Celebrating Love

Searching Love

Follow the exciting spin-off series:

Alvarez Security (military romantic suspense)

Gabe

Tony

Vinny

Jobe

SEALs

Thin Ice (Sleeper SEAL)

SEAL Together (Silver SEAL)

Undercover Groom (Hot SEAL)

Also for a Hope City Crossover Novel / Hot SEAL…

A Forever Dad

Long Road Home

Military Romantic Suspense

Home to Stay (a Lighthouse Security Investigation crossover novel)

Home Port (an LSI West Coast crossover novel)

Letters From Home (military romance)

Class of Love

Freedom of Love

Bond of Love

The Love's Series (detectives)

Love's Taming

Love's Tempting

Love's Trusting

The Fairfield Series (small town detectives)

Emma's Home

Laurie's Time

Carol's Image

Fireworks Over Fairfield

Please take the time to leave a review of this book. Feel free to contact me, especially if you enjoyed my book. I love to hear from readers!

Facebook

Email

Website

ABOUT THE AUTHOR

I am an avid reader of romance novels, often joking that I cut my teeth on the historical romances. I have been reading and reviewing for years. In 2013, I finally gave into the characters in my head, screaming for their story to be told. From these musings, my first novel, Emma's Home, The Fairfield Series was born.

I was a high school counselor having worked in education for thirty years. I live in Virginia, having also lived in four states and two foreign countries. I have been married to a wonderfully patient man for forty-one years. When writing, my dog or one of my four cats can generally be found in the same room if not on my lap.

Please take the time to leave a review of this book. Feel free to contact me, especially if you enjoyed my book. I love to hear from readers!

Facebook
Email
Website

Made in the USA
Middletown, DE
29 June 2023